Nine Inches

Nine
Inches

STORIES

TOM PERROTTA

ST. MARTIN'S PRESS *New York*

NINE INCHES. Copyright © 2013 by Tom Perrotta. All rights reserved. Printed in the United States of America. For information, address St. Martin's Press, 175 Fifth Avenue, New York, N.Y. 10010.

www.stmartins.com

Some of the stories in this book appeared in the following publications:

"The Smile on Happy Chang's Face" and "Nine Inches" in *Post Road;* "The Chosen Girl" in *The Gettysburg Review;* "Kiddie Pool" in *Best Life;* "Grade My Teacher" in *Five Points.*

Library of Congress Cataloging-in-Publication Data

Perrotta, Tom, 1961–
   [Short stories. Selections]
   Nine inches : stories / by Tom Perrotta. — First U.S. edition.
      pages ; cm
   ISBN 978-1-250-03470-0 (hardcover)
   ISBN 978-1-250-03469-4 (e-book)
   I. Perrotta, Tom, 1961– Backrub.   II. Title.
   PS3566.E6948N56 2013
   813'.54—dc23

                                                2013013488

St. Martin's Press books may be purchased for educational, business, or promotional use. For information on bulk purchases, please contact Macmillan Corporate and Premium Sales Department at 1-800-221-7945, extension 5442, or write specialmarkets@macmillan.com.

First Edition: September 2013

10 9 8 7 6 5 4 3 2 1

ACKNOWLEDGMENTS ....➤

I'd like to thank Maria Massie, Elizabeth Beier, Dori Weintraub, and Sylvie Rabineau for their enthusiasm and support, not just for this book, but over the many years in which it was written. Navjeet Bal, Nina Perrotta, and Luke Perrotta told me anecdotes that later blossomed into stories. And I'm grateful to Mary Granfield for too much to enumerate here.

CONTENTS ·········➤

Nine Inches

BACKRUB ········►

THE FIRST TIME LT. FINNEGAN PULLED ME OVER, I ACTU-
ally thought he was a pretty decent guy. I mean, there's no
question I was going over the limit, maybe thirty-five in a residential zone, so I can't say I was surprised to see the lights
flashing in my rearview mirror. I was mostly just frustrated—
disappointed in myself and worried about what Eddie would
say when he found out I'd gotten a speeding ticket in the
company Prius after just a few weeks on the job.

The cop who tapped on my window was older than I expected, a big, white-haired guy with a white mustache, probably not too far from retirement. He looked a little bored, like
he'd asked a few too many people for their license and registration over the years.

"What's the hurry, son?"

"Just running a little late." I glanced at the insulated pouches
stacked on the passenger seat, in case he'd missed the mag-
netic decal on my door: SUSTAINABLE PIZZA . . . FOR THE

PLANET WE LOVE. "I got stuck at the railroad crossing. I was trying to make up for lost time."

That was the wrong answer.

"You need to be more careful, son. There's a lotta kids in this neighborhood."

"I know." I could feel my face getting warm. "It's just . . . I'm supposed to make the deliveries in thirty minutes or less."

"Try telling that to a dead kid's parents," he suggested. "Let me know how it goes over."

He was just messing with me, but for some reason I found it all too easy to picture the scene in my head—the child's fresh grave, the weeping mother and the broken father, the pathetic delivery driver explaining that the tips are better when the pizza's still hot. It seemed like a plausible version of my future.

"I'm really sorry, Officer. It won't happen again."

"Not *officer,*" he corrected me. *"Lieutenant."*

"Sorry, Lieutenant."

He squinted at me for a few seconds, as if coming to a decision, then brought his hand down hard on the roof of the Prius. The thump made me flinch.

"All right," he said. "Get the hell outta here."

"Really?" I was embarrassed by the relief and gratitude in my voice, as if I'd just dodged a murder charge rather than a speeding ticket. "I can go?"

"It's your lucky day," he told me.

I WAS eighteen that fall and all my friends were in college— Evan at Harvard, Lauren at Stanford (we were still scratching our heads about that one), Josh at Bowdoin, Lily at Northwestern, Carlos at Cornell. My best friend, Jake, was having the time of his life at Wesleyan—he kept inviting me down to hang with his new roommates, but my heart wasn't in it—and my ex-girlfriend, Heather, was chilling at Pomona, raving about sunny California in her status updates. That was my high school posse in a nutshell. We were the AP kids, the National Merit Scholars, the summer interns, the future leaders, the good examples. We enrolled in SAT prep classes even when we didn't need to, shared study tips and mnemonic devices, taunted one another with Shakespearean epithets, and made witty comments about the periodic table. We stayed up late going over our notes one last time, threw parties where we studied together for history finals. On Saturday nights, instead of getting drunk and hooking up, we popped popcorn and watched Pixar movies. It wasn't that we were anti-fun; we'd just made a group decision to save ourselves for college.

The only problem was, I didn't get into college.

I'd applied to twelve institutions of higher learning and got rejected outright by ten of them, including my safeties. I got wait-listed by two of my likelies, but neither one came through in the end. I got shut out, just like the kid in *Accepted,* except it was nothing like that because he was a slacker and didn't deserve to get in.

I totally deserved it. I mean, I got a combined 2230 on the SATs (superscored, but still), and had a GPA of 3.8, all Honors and APs, top ten percent of my graduating class in one of the premier public high schools in the state. Student Council rep, stagehand for the musicals, helped start a recycling program in the cafeteria. I ran cross-country all four years, even though I hated every tedious mile. But I did it, just so I could list a varsity sport on my transcript. Every goddam miserable thing I ever did, every shortcut I avoided, every scrap of fun I missed out on, I did it just so I could get into a decent college. And none of it mattered.

My guidance counselor insisted that it was just a freak occurrence, a perfect storm of bad luck and rotten demographics. A record year for applications, too many international students, preferences for minorities and athletes, a need for geographic diversity, blah blah blah. But come on, not to get in *anywhere*? Even when kids from my own high school with lower grades and test scores got into colleges where I was rejected? Where's the fairness in that?

There was no logical way to explain it, but that didn't stop people from trying. Maybe I was too well-rounded for my own good, or my recs were underwhelming; maybe my essay was pompous, or maybe it was pedestrian. Maybe I hadn't done enough to set myself apart from the crowd, should have written about my lifelong passion for shoemaking, or my desire to someday design prosthetic limbs for transsexuals who'd stepped on landmines. Or maybe I'd just aimed a little too high, which was possibly true for Dartmouth and Brown, but those were my reaches, so that's the whole point. But what about Connecticut College or George Washington? Was that really too much to ask?

April of senior year was such a nightmare. Everybody else was all excited, hugging one another and squealing with delight, the future unfolding before their eyes—*Colgate! Hampshire! UVM!* And then they'd notice me, and everything would get all awkward and quiet, almost like somebody in my family had died. People just kept moaning and shaking their heads, telling me how sorry they were, how unfair it was, a complete injustice that shook their faith in the entire system, and I kept telling them not to worry.

I'm on the wait list at Duke and Grinnell, I'd say. *I'm sure something will pan out.*

THE SECOND time Lt. Finnegan pulled me over—just a week after the first incident—he was all business. He took my license and registration, went back to his car, and wrote me a ticket for failure to obey a traffic sign, a moving violation punishable by a hundred-dollar fine.

"Oh, come on," I said. "A hundred bucks? That's crazy."

"You have the right to contest this citation in the district court," he informed me in a robotic voice. The lights on the police cruiser were flashing lazily, the whole neighborhood pulsing with red. "Should you choose to do so, you must notify the court of your intention within twenty days."

I didn't reply, because there was no point in going to court. I'd definitely rolled through the stop sign—I wasn't about to deny it—but I thought he could cut me a little slack. It was ten-thirty at night, and I was driving on a quiet side street out by the conservation land. I'd just made my final delivery—a lousy one-dollar tip, thank you very much—and there was no one else around, no one except for Lt. Finnegan, hiding on the dark street with his lights turned off.

"Shit," I muttered. "I can't believe this."

"Excuse me?" Lt. Finnegan shined his humongous flashlight in my face. "What did you say?"

I raised my hand to block the glare. "Nothing. I was just talking to myself."

He clicked off the light and leaned in. His broad face filled my window frame, just a few inches from my own. He wasn't smiling, but I had the feeling he was enjoying himself.

"Do we have some kind of problem, Donald?"

"No, sir. There's no problem."

"Good. 'Cause I don't see any reason why we can't be friends." He straightened up, tugged on his gun belt, and turned in the direction of his car. But then he swiveled right back.

"Tell me something." His voice was casual now, almost friendly. "What's that mean? *Sustainable Pizza?*"

"It's just a name. They use lots of organic ingredients and recyclable boxes. Some of the produce comes from local farms."

"People like that, huh?"

"Some of 'em."

"Is it better than regular pizza?"

"It's okay. Kind of expensive. But the customers keep coming back."

"Huh." He nodded, as if that was good enough for him. "I'll have to give it a try."

I HAD two bosses at Sustainable—Entrepreneurial Eddie and Stoner Eddie. Entrepreneurial Eddie was an impressive guy, a twenty-four-year-old Middlebury grad who'd returned to his hometown to start an eco-friendly pizza restaurant that he hoped someday to grow into a regional, and possibly even national, chain. He was organized, ambitious, and charismatic, a crunchy-granola preppy with shaggy blond hair and the strapping physique of the rugby player he'd been in college. He happened to be Jake's cousin, which was the reason I'd gotten the delivery job, despite my complete lack of work experience, and the fact that I'd only had my license for a couple of months.

I'm taking a chance on you, Donald. Don't let me down.

Entrepreneurial Eddie was always in charge when I started my shift, but he got replaced by Stoner Eddie at the end of the night, after the restaurant section had closed, and Malina and Jadwiga, the two Polish waitresses, had gone home. At that point, it was just me and Eddie and Ignacio, the Salvadoran pizza maker, who stuck around to fill any late-night delivery orders and help out with the cleanup.

Entrepreneurial Eddie could be tense and short-tempered, but Stoner Eddie absorbed the news of my moving violation with a philosophical shrug.

"That's the way it goes, bro. The cops in this town are ballbusters. There's no crime, so they have to make shit up to keep themselves from dying of boredom."

"But a hundred bucks?" I whined. "I work for tips."

"That's how the government rolls, my friend." The two Eddies were different in many ways, but they were both big Ron Paul supporters. "It's all just taxes in disguise. Right, Ignacio?"

Ignacio looked up from the floor he was mopping and said something in Spanish. Eddie nodded and said something back. His accent was atrocious, but his meaning must have been clear enough, because Ignacio grinned and added another rapid-fire burst of commentary, to which Eddie replied, *"Verdad,* bro, *verdad."* I wished I'd taken Spanish in high school instead of four years of Latin, which was utterly useless in the real world. It was my guidance counselor's fault: he'd insisted that colleges liked students with "a classical background," and who was I to doubt him? At that point in my life, I would've cut my arm off if *U.S. News & World Report* had mentioned that selective colleges were looking for amputees.

After we settled up, Eddie walked me to the front door. We were almost there when he put his hand on my shoulder.

"Yo, Donald," he said. "You're friends with Adam Willis, right?"

"Kind of."

"Could you do me a favor?" He reached into his pocket, pulled out a serious wad of bills, and counted off five twenties. For a second, I thought he was reimbursing me for the ticket. "See if you can hook me up with some of that superior weed of his."

I didn't take the money. "Can't you ask him yourself?"

"He never answers my texts."

"He's probably just busy. I'm sure he'll get back to you."

"Come on, bro. Help me out here. I got a big date this weekend." His voice got soft and confidential. "I'm telling you, that stuff's some kind of aphrodisiac. I smoked half a joint with Malina last week, and that was all it took."

"Malina?"

"I know, bro." He grinned at the miracle. "I've been working on her for weeks, and she wouldn't give me the time of day. Couple hits of that magic bud, and the panties just slid right off."

It was hard to imagine Malina's panties sliding off for Eddie, or any guy around here. She was pale and chillingly beautiful, with sad eyes and a husky, disdainful voice. She always seemed vaguely offended in the restaurant, as if waitressing was beneath her dignity, and life a bitter disappointment.

"Wow."

"I know." Eddie tucked the money into my jacket pocket and patted me on the shoulder. "I'm counting on you, bro."

THE NEXT afternoon, I joined Adam Willis and his chocolate Lab for their daily hike through the woods behind the abandoned state mental hospital. It was creepy back there—lots of rusty appliances and old tires lying around, not to mention a tiny cemetery with maybe twenty unmarked headstones and a sign explaining that the graves belonged to former mental patients who'd died in the hospital: THOUGH YOUR NAMES ARE UNKNOWN, WE HOLD YOU CLOSE IN OUR HEARTS. I waited until we'd been walking awhile before I told Adam that my boss wanted to buy some of his weed.

"No way," he said. "I don't sell to strangers."

"I could introduce you. Eddie's a pretty good guy."

Adam stopped and scanned the woods, shielding his eyes from the golden light streaming down through the red and gold treetops. It was mid-October, and the leaves had just begun to drop.

"Yo, Hapster?" he called out. "Where are you, dude?"

The question was barely out of his mouth when Happy burst out of the woods and onto the trail, his ears flapping as he galloped toward us, the usual look of crazed anticipation on his face.

"Dassagoodboy." Adam crouched down, scratching Happy's ears and slipping him one of the little bone-shaped treats he carried in his pocket. "Dassaverygoodboy."

He gave the dog a booming thump on the ribs, and we started walking again.

"I don't get it," Adam said. "Why are you even involved with this? If your boss wants some weed, why doesn't he just ask me himself?"

"He did. He said he texted you a bunch of times and you never got back to him."

"Damn right. I'm not gonna text some guy I don't know. What if he's a cop?"

"Eddie's not a cop. He's Jake Hauser's cousin."

"Jake Hauser," Adam scoffed. "Dude never said shit to me."

Adam and I had been high school classmates, but our social circles didn't really overlap. We'd been close as kids—pretty much best friends—until his mom died of cancer when we were in seventh grade. He turned angry and distant after that, started listening to this dark metal, Slipknot and stuff like that, and hanging out with a druggy crowd. His dad wasn't around a lot of the time—I heard he had a girlfriend in another town—and Adam did pretty much whatever he wanted, which was mainly just playing video games and getting high and skipping school. Whenever his name came up, my mother called him *poor Adam* and referred to him as *a lost soul*. I'm pretty sure he didn't graduate.

I ran into him outside of CVS one day in September, after everybody else had left for college, and we got to reminiscing about the old days and the fun we used to have. He had his dog with him, and I had nothing else to do, so I tagged along on their afternoon walk. He texted me the next day, asking if I wanted to do it again.

Any time, he said. *Happy enjoyed the company.*

If you'd told me six months ago that I'd be spending my fall living at home and hanging out with Adam Willis, it would've sounded like a nightmare to me. But it was weird how normal it was starting to feel, like *this* was my life now, and Adam was way more a part of it than Jake or Josh or even Heather, who'd broken up with me a couple of weeks after she got to Pomona, sparing me the nightly Skype updates about her awesome roommates and amazing professors.

At the top of the hill, we sat down on a fallen log in the shade of the water tower. Adam took out his little one-hit pipe and packed it with weed. He offered it to me, and I shook my head, the way I always did, though I wasn't sure what was stopping me. In high school, I'd stayed away from weed because I thought it might interfere with my studies and sap my motivation, but what did that matter now?

"The thing I don't get," he said, in that squeaky, holding-it-in voice, "is how your boss even knows my number."

"Don't look at me. I didn't give it to him."

"And how'd he know I was selling?" Adam released a cloud of smoke so big I couldn't believe it had all been stored inside his lungs. "It's not like I'm advertising."

I shrugged, not wanting to tell him that it was common knowledge that he sold some kind of killer weed, the source of which no one could pinpoint. We lived in a small town, and you couldn't keep something like that a secret for long.

"You know what?" I said. "Don't even worry about it. I'll just give Eddie his money back. It's no big deal."

Happy was sitting at our feet, panting cheerfully, thick body heaving, tongue lolling sideways from his mouth. Adam leaned forward and kissed him on top of his big square head. When Adam looked up, I could see that the weed had kicked in. His eyes were cloudy, his face dreamy and trouble-free.

"Chill out," he told me. "I'll take care of you. I don't want to jam you up with your boss."

I DIDN'T realize I had a problem until my next run-in with Lt. Finnegan. This time I wasn't speeding and hadn't violated any traffic laws. I was just minding my business, heading back to Sustainable around nine-thirty on a Wednesday night, when an unmarked.Crown Victoria popped up in my rearview mirror, that familiar white-haired douchebag at the wheel. There were no flashing lights, but he tailgated me for a couple of blocks before finally hitting the siren, a quick *bloop-bloop* to get my attention.

We were right by Edmunds Elementary School, the quiet stretch of Warren Road that runs alongside the playing fields. I pulled over, his car still glued to my bumper, and cut the engine. It felt like a bad dream, the same cop stopping me for the third time in less than two weeks.

I was fishing around in the glove box for the registration when he startled me by tapping on the passenger window—he usually approached from the other side—and yanking the door open. Before I could react, he had ducked inside my car and shut the door behind him.

The Prius was pretty roomy, but Lt. Finnegan seemed to

fill all the available space. He reached down, groping for the adjuster bar, then grunted with relief as the seat slid back.

"That's better." He rotated his bulk in my direction. He was wearing civilian clothes, khakis and a sport coat, but he still looked like a cop. "How are you, Donald?"

"Did I do something wrong?"

"I don't think so," he said. "Not that I know of."

"Then why'd you pull me over?"

"I didn't pull you over."

"Yes, you did. You hit the siren."

"Oh, that." He chuckled at the misunderstanding. "I just wanted to say hi. Haven't seen you for a couple of days."

"Oh. Okay." I nodded as if this made perfect sense. "I just assumed—"

"I get it." He laid his hand on my knee. "I'm sorry if I scared you."

I waited for him to remove his hand, but he kept it where it was. I could feel the warmth of his palm through the fabric of my jeans.

"Umm," I said. "You know what? I really have to get back to work."

"You're dedicated," he observed. "I like that."

"I just got hired. I'm trying to make a good impression."

He tilted his head, giving me a thorough once-over. I was uncomfortably aware of his aftershave, a sharp lime scent that mingled badly with the stale pizza funk inside the car.

"You seem a little tense, Donald." He lifted his hand off my knee and placed it on my shoulder. "I bet you could use a backrub."

I shook my head, but he didn't seem to notice. His left hand was already cupping the back of my neck, squeezing and releasing, exerting a gentle, disturbing pressure.

Oh, God, I thought. *This isn't happening.*

"Just relax, Donald. I'm really good at this."

He slipped his hand under my collar, his fingers rough against my skin, tracing the knobs on my spine.

"Please don't do that," I told him.

He pretended not to hear me, shifting in the seat so he could get his other hand into the act. He went to work on my right arm, stroking and kneading my shoulder. I could hear him breathing raggedly through his nose, as if he were climbing a hill.

"Wow," he said in this faraway voice. "Your deltoid's really tight."

"Stop it!" I twisted out of his grasp, scooting away from him until my back was pressed against the door. The violence of my reaction startled us both.

"Whoa!" he said, raising both hands in a gesture of surrender. "Jesus."

"I don't want a backrub," I told him.

"Okay, fine." He sounded a little hurt. "Take it easy, Donald. I was just trying to be nice."

"Could you please get out of my car?"

He turned away, scowling at the empty street in front of us. There was something sulky and stubborn in his posture.

"I really don't get you, Donald." He said this with weird conviction in his voice, like we'd had some kind of long history together. "I just don't understand what you're doing with your life."

"What's that supposed to mean?"

"I've been asking around. People say you're a pretty smart kid."

"Yeah?" I was flattered in spite of myself, glad to know that people still thought well of me. "So?"

"So what's the deal? How come you're not in college?"

"I'm taking a gap year."

This was the explanation my parents and I had agreed on, but I could hear how lame it sounded.

He heard it, too, and snorted with contempt. "A gap year to deliver pizza? What was that, your lifelong dream?"

I should have just kept my mouth shut. But I didn't like the way he was looking at me, like he had the right to judge me.

"I'm trying to save some money," I said. "I'm going to Africa in the spring to work in an orphanage. Is that okay with you?"

He didn't answer right away, and I could see that I'd caught him off guard.

"Africa, huh? What country?"

"Uganda."

"Wow." He sounded skeptical, but I could tell he was impressed. "Good for you."

Just then my phone started buzzing. It was Eddie. I held it up so he could see the display.

"You mind if I take this, Lieutenant? My boss is wondering where I am."

MY STORY about the orphanage wasn't exactly true, but it wasn't just a load of random bullshit, either. For most of the spring and all of the summer, it had been an actual plan, the answer I gave whenever anyone asked about my future. It was a pretty good answer, too, which is probably why I dusted it off for Lt. Finnegan.

According to my mother's Monday-morning analysis, the fatal flaw in my otherwise excellent college application had been a lack of genuine humanitarian service. She was pretty sure the admissions officers had seen right through my meager list of good deeds—a Walk for Hunger here, some Toys for Tots there, a weekend with Habitat for Humanity, a handful of cans for the Food Drive.

"There was no follow-through," she pointed out. "It was all for show, like you were just checking some boxes."

"I was," I said. "I thought that was the whole point."

Unbeknownst to me, she started doing some research on the Web, scouting out programs that offered young volunteers an opportunity to demonstrate their commitment to the less fortunate, putting their skills and ideals to the test in challenging third-world environments. She was especially impressed by an organization called Big Hearts International, whose mission was to connect college-age Americans with "the struggling but resilient children of sub-Saharan Africa."

"Just think about it," she told me. "This could be a real game-changer."

"Africa's pretty far away," I reminded her. "And kinda dangerous."

"It's just for a few months, Donald. I really think you should consider it."

I'd filled out the application in mid-May, when it became clear that I wasn't going to be saved by the wait list at Duke or Grinnell. The way I figured it, my options were either Africa or community college, and I really couldn't see myself at community college. By the time graduation rolled around, Big Hearts had already assigned me to an orphanage in Mityana, Uganda, not too far from the capital city, whose name I kept forgetting. Heather was almost as excited as my mom, clutching my arm, beaming at me like I was some kind of saint.

"This is my boyfriend, Donald," she kept telling her relatives. "He's going to Africa in September."

That's who I was for the rest of the summer, the Great Humanitarian and Intrepid World Explorer, Friend to the Struggling but Resilient Orphans. If nothing else, this identity got me through a lot of awkward situations, gave me something to contribute to what would otherwise have been extremely painful conversations about distribution requirements, course schedules, Greek Life, and Facebook groups for admitted students. Jake bought me a pith helmet at a secondhand store, and I used to wear it when we went to the beach or the movies, sort of as a joke, but also as a badge of honor, a token of my good intentions.

I swear, I was all set to go. I updated my passport, got my shots, read a whole bunch of books about AIDS and genocide and colonialism, even drove to Connecticut to meet with a volunteer who'd just finished the program, this skinny, haunted-looking dude whose arms and legs were mottled with bug bites.

"It's pretty freaky," he said, scratching himself like a monkey. "You wouldn't believe the poverty over there. But it's like the most rewarding thing I've done in my entire life."

The last two weeks of August were like one big going-away party, the population of well-wishers dwindling nightly until

I was the only one left. I had a few days to finalize my packing and spend some quality time with my parents and little sister, who was starting her freshman year in high school. My mom baked a cake on my last night, and we sat around talking about what a great adventure I was embarking on, how I was going to learn some real-life lessons that couldn't be taught in any ivory tower. Then I skyped with a bunch of my friends and had a long goodbye talk with Heather, during which we both promised to be faithful during our separation. We'd had sex for the first time the night before she left, and we reminded each other how amazing it had been, and how we couldn't wait to do it again over Christmas vacation.

"I love you," she sniffled. "You take care of yourself, okay?"

"I'll be fine," I told her. "I'll see you soon."

That was it. I went to bed feeling brave and melancholy, ready for my big journey into the unknown. But when I woke up the next morning, I couldn't move. I wasn't sick; it just felt like my body had been sliced open and pumped full of wet cement.

"Come on, sweetheart," my mother said from the doorway. "You don't want to miss your plane."

"I'm not going," I said. "It's not fair."

She withdrew and my father appeared a few minutes later. He told me that I needed to get my ass moving, that I'd made a commitment and damn well better stick to it. He said there were orphans in Uganda who were counting on me.

"Fuck the orphans," I said.

"What?" I could see how shocked he was. "What did you say?"

But by then I was crying too hard to repeat myself.

• • •

I REALLY didn't know what to do about Lt. Finnegan. I thought about talking to Eddie, or maybe to my parents, possibly even writing an anonymous letter to *The Clarion,* our terrible local paper, just to let *someone* know what had happened, but I wasn't sure what good it would do. In the absence of any proof, it would just be my word against his, and I had a feeling my word wasn't worth all that much at the moment. The only thing I knew for sure was that I didn't want to quit my job. I liked working at Sustainable and liked having a good reason to get out of the house at night. My parents were still pissed about Uganda and never missed a chance to remind me of how badly I'd let them down.

In the end, I decided to keep my mouth shut and my fingers crossed, and to drive as carefully as possible. I stuck religiously to the speed limit, checking my rearview mirror like a murderer with a corpse in the trunk, never failed to use my turn signal, and came to a complete and lingering halt at every stop sign, even though I knew it didn't matter. If Lt. Finnegan wanted to pull me over, he could do it whenever he felt like it, regardless of whether I'd broken the law.

To my surprise and immense relief, the safe-driver strategy seemed to work. Two weeks passed without incident, and I started to wonder if maybe I'd overreacted, letting a minor problem mushroom in my imagination into something more important than it really was. Very slowly, I began to let my guard down, to relax and enjoy the job again.

I was in an especially good mood on the Saturday after Halloween, which happened to be crazy busy. It was like half the town had suddenly come down with an uncontrollable urge for gourmet pizza and had all called in their orders at the same time. Amazingly, Eddie and Ignacio handled it without a single glitch—not even a botched topping or a transposed address—and the customers were unusually patient and forgiving. No one yelled at me for being late or forgot to tip. By the time the rush was over—it was a little after eight—I had a big wad of bills in my pocket and one last pie to deliver, to a guy named Roy in Starlite Court, an ugly brick apartment complex over by the train station, where a lot of senior citizens lived. I'd only been there once or twice before.

I found Unit 5 and pressed the buzzer for Apartment B. While I was waiting, a text arrived from Eddie asking if I wanted to party with him and the Polish girls after we closed up. He was a lot friendlier now that I was acting as his go-between with Adam, ensuring him a regular supply of what he liked to call the Magic Love Bud. The door opened and I looked up.

"Donald." Lt. Finnegan's smile was warm and welcoming. "I was hoping it would be you."

For a second or two, words failed me. I couldn't understand what he was doing here, standing in the doorway in a shimmery blue bathrobe with white piping. It looked like something a boxer would wear before a fight, except shorter, exposing a lot more thigh than anyone wanted to see on a guy his age. I must have been staring too hard because he reached down and tightened the belt. The robe was still pretty loose on top, displaying a triangle of tufty white chest hair.

"Pizza for Roy?" I finally managed to say.

"That's me. Large sausage, right?"

"That'll be sixteen dollars."

"Could you bring it into the kitchen?" He took a step back and beckoned me inside. "I left my wallet in the bedroom."

I was about to tell him that it was our policy never to enter the customer's home when it occurred to me that this might be a good time to make an exception. I stepped into the cramped foyer and followed him into the hallway.

"You go ahead," he said, stopping outside the bedroom. "I'll be right with you."

I continued into the kitchen, set the insulated pouch on the countertop, and pulled out my iPhone. It only took a couple of swipes to find the Voice Memo app and touch the red button to record. By the time he emerged, the phone was back in my pocket, and the pizza was out of the pouch.

"Smells good," he said.

If I'd been him, I might've taken an extra minute or two to put on some clothes, but he was still just wearing that pervy robe. It was looser than before, providing an unobstructed view of his broad chest and bulging belly.

"I think you'll like the sausage," I told him. "It supposedly won some awards."

Lt. Finnegan slipped one hand inside the robe and began absentmindedly massaging his left pec. It was bright in the kitchen, and I noticed a pale scar on his knee, one of those old-time Frankenstein sutures, like the stitching on a softball.

"You hungry?" he asked. "I can't eat that whole pizza by myself."

"I'm on the clock."

"How about a drink then? I got soda and OJ. Beer, too, but that's probably not a good idea."

"Maybe just some water."

He took two glasses from the dishwasher and filled them straight from the tap. We never did that at home, only drank from the Brita pitcher. We sat down at the table and touched our glasses.

"Cheers," he said. "It's nice to have some company."

I let that pass, even though *company* hardly seemed like the right term for the guy who delivered your pizza. He smiled at me. His expression was shy, strangely boyish.

"I like you, Donald. You're really easy to talk to."

I took a sip to calm my nerves. The water was tepid, with a sweet, chemical aftertaste.

"We hardly know each other," I said, speaking slowly and clearly for the benefit of the recorder. I didn't feel great about what I was doing, but I knew it had to be done. "We only ever talk when you pull me over."

"I know." He laughed, like this was a cute story we would someday share with our friends. "It's crazy, right?"

"You pulled me over three times last month. And the third time, the night you were in the unmarked car, you tried to give me a backrub. It kinda scared me, Lieutenant Finnegan."

He stiffened a little, and I could see I'd hit a nerve.

"Look, Donald, I'm really sorry about that. I got carried away, you know? I do that sometimes. But I hope you'll give me another chance."

"What do you mean?"

He gave me a sly look, like he thought I knew exactly what he meant.

"I mean, you can't get a good backrub in a car. You need to be able to take your shirt off, stretch out on a bed, and relax."

He reached across the table and laid his hand on mine. "Why don't you come by after your shift tonight. That way we can take our time."

I slid my hand out from under his and stood up.

"Please listen to me, Lieutenant Finnegan." My voice was shaky, and I was surprised to realize I was on the verge of tears. "I don't want a backrub. I didn't want one when you pulled me over, and I don't want one now. I think you have a problem, and you should probably get some help."

"Whoa, hey." He held up one hand, as if he were stopping traffic. "I'm just trying to be nice here."

"And just so you know"—I held up the phone—"I've been recording this entire conversation."

It took him a few seconds to process what I was telling him. I could see it in his face, that awful moment of clarity.

"Jesus, Donald. Why would you do that?"

"Look, I don't want to get you in trouble. I'm just asking you to leave me alone. Is that so hard to understand?"

I waited awhile, but I never got an answer. I wasn't even sure he'd heard the question. He just lowered his head into his hand and started cursing softly, telling himself how fucking stupid he was, how he knew this was gonna happen, how he'd told himself to stop and had kept on doing it anyway, and now he was totally fucked, wasn't he, muttering this pitiful monologue that followed me all the way down the hallway and out the door.

A YEAR and a half went by before the next time I got pulled over. Lt. Finnegan was retired by then, forced to leave the department after a bunch of people had complained about his strange behavior. Apparently, I wasn't the only young guy in town who'd gotten a backrub along with his traffic ticket. It was a minor scandal for a week or two, but they hushed it up somehow, and he managed to leave the force without facing any charges or losing his pension. Last I heard, he was living in Florida.

Lots of other things had changed, too. I'd become Eddie's right-hand man at Sustainable, managing the original restaurant while he opened a new one in Rosedale. We were working hard, making good money, and I wasn't sure I'd ever have the time or the patience to go back to school. Shortly after my nineteenth birthday, I'd moved out of my parents' house, into a studio apartment across the street from the bike shop. The rent wasn't too steep, and I needed the privacy now that I'd gotten together with Karen, one of the new waitresses we'd hired after Malina and Jadwiga had gone back to Poland. We got along okay, though she could be kind of moody and relied on me for pretty much her entire social life, not that I had a whole lot to offer in that department. Mostly we just got high and watched TV.

I'd lost touch with most of my high school friends, but hadn't made any new ones except for Adam and Eddie. The three of us had gotten pretty tight over the past year, ever since we'd started our weed business. Using Eddie's money and Adam's connection, we'd developed quite a sideline, buying in bulk and selling to a handful of carefully selected clients, moving a pound here and a kilo there, lots of profit with what seemed like minimal risk. We transported our product in Sustainable's delivery cars, hidden in pizza boxes tucked inside insulated pouches. It was my idea, and I was pretty proud of it. You could drive right up to the front door of a dealer's house, make a cash transaction, and no one would suspect a thing.

So I wasn't nervous that night in April, heading over to Rick Yang's house—he was one of our best customers—with a large onion-and-pepper in one box and a pound of weed in another. I'd done it a dozen times before, never a problem.

It all went down so fast. I barely had time to register the lights in my rearview mirror when I saw two more cop cars right in front of me, blocking the intersection. I got out with my hands on my head, like they told me to, and the next thing I knew I was lying facedown in the street, with my hands cuffed behind my back.

It's funny what goes through your head at a time like that. I didn't think about my parents, or about Eddie and Adam, or even about Karen. I didn't wonder about what kind of trouble I was in or consider how my life might have been different if I'd gone to Uganda. What I thought about while they searched the Prius was something I'd almost forgotten, a stupid thing I'd done while applying to college.

The applications were due on December 31, and I'd left my safeties to the last minute. I was just so sick of the whole process by then—it had consumed almost a year of my life—fed up with answering the same useless questions over and over, tailoring my responses to whoever was doing the asking. It was ten o'clock on New Year's Eve, and there I was, sitting at my desk, staring at the question *Why Fairfield?* and I guess I just lost it. Instead of repeating my usual bullshit about a liberal arts education, I went ahead and told the truth: *You're my Safety School, motherfucker!* And then I pressed SEND before

I had a chance to stop myself. It felt so good I did the same thing for Roger Williams and Temple. I'd never told anyone about it, not even when people were scratching their heads, wondering how it was possible that an honor student like me had been rejected by all three of his safeties.

That's what I was thinking about when they found the weed. I was thinking about the kid who'd filled out those applications, remembering how cocky and obnoxious he'd been, so sure of his own worth, and the world's ability to recognize it. I was lying on the street with my cheek pressed against the blacktop, thinking about what an asshole he was, and how much I missed him.

GRADE MY TEACHER ·········▶

SIXTH PERIOD WAS ENDLESS. VICKI STOOD BY THE
Smart Board, listening to herself drone on about the formula
for calculating the volume of a cylinder, but all she could
think about was Jessica Grasso, the heavy girl sitting near the
back right corner of the room, watching her with a polite,
seemingly neutral expression. It was almost as if Jessica grew
larger with each passing moment, as if she were being inflated
by some invisible pump, expanding like a parade float until
she filled the entire room.

She hates me, Vicki thought, and this knowledge was somehow both sickening and exciting at the same time. *But you
wouldn't know it from looking at her.*

Vicki hadn't known it herself until last night, when she
read what the girl had written about her on grademyteacher
.com. She had stumbled upon the post while conducting a routine self-google, exercising a little due diligence so she didn't
get blindsided like her old friend and former colleague Anna

Shamsky, a happily married mother of three who'd lost her job over some twenty-year-old topless photos that had appeared without her knowledge on a website called Memoirs-of-a-Stud.com. The site was the brainchild of an ex-boyfriend of hers—a guy she hadn't thought about since college—who had decided in a fit of midlife bravado that the world needed to know a little bit about every woman he'd ever slept with ("Anna S. was a sweet innocent sophomore with boobs to die for," he wrote. "When I was done with her, she could give head like nobody's beeswax"). The surprisingly steamy photos—Anna's youthful breasts totally lived up to the hype—had spread like a virus through the entire Gifford High School community before the subject herself even remembered they existed, and by then there was nothing to do but submit her resignation.

Vicki didn't have to worry about nude photos—she'd never posed for any, not even when her ex-husband had asked her nicely—but that was just one risk among many in a dangerous world. She told herself she was simply being prudent—in this day and age, googling yourself was just common sense, like using sunscreen or buckling your seatbelt—but she was sometimes aware of a tiny flutter of anticipation as she typed her name into the dialog box, as if the search engine might reveal a new self to her, someone a little more interesting, or at least a little less forgettable, than the rest of the world suspected. She remembered feeling oddly hopeful last night, just seconds before she found herself staring at *this:*

OMG my math teacher Vicki Wiggins is an INSANE B*#@&! One day she called me a FAT PIG for eating candy in class. I know I'm no supermodel but guess what she's even worse! Hav u seen the panty lines when she packs her HUGE BUTT into those ugly beige pants? Hellooo? Ever hear of a thong? Everyone cracks up about it behind her back. She might as well be wearing her extralarge granny pants on the outside. Vicki Wiggins, you are the pig!

Vicki's first reaction to this was bewilderment—she honestly had no idea what the writer was talking about—followed by a combination of searing embarrassment (she'd had her doubts about those beige pants) and righteous indignation. In her entire career—her entire adult life!—she'd never called anyone a fat pig. She wouldn't dream of it. As a woman who'd struggled with her own weight, she knew just how hurtful such epithets could be.

What made it even worse was that she realized she was making a mistake even as she clicked on the link, violating her long-standing policy to stay as far away from grademy teacher.com as possible. It was just too depressing, and she wasn't even one of the truly unpopular teachers, the unfortunates whose names were flagged with a big red thumbs-down icon—people like Fred Kane, the marble-mouthed biology instructor whose average score was 2.4 out of 10, or Martha Rigby (a mind-boggling 1.8), the ancient English teacher who regularly referred to the author of *Great Expectations* as Thomas Dickinson. Vicki herself was stuck in the middle of the pack (5.5, to be exact), with fewer than a dozen comments to her name, most of which contained a variant on the phrase "Boring but okay." By contrast, Lily Frankel, the lively and hip young drama teacher, had received a whopping sixty-two reviews for an overall rating of 9.3, highest on the entire faculty, thereby earning herself a coveted smiley face with sunglasses and a crown.

Vicki read the post over and over—the author was identified only as "Greensleeves," a pseudonym that meant nothing to her—wondering what she could have done to provoke such a hateful and dishonest attack. You'd think that if someone despised you enough to call you an insane bitch, you'd have a pretty good idea of who it was, but Vicki's mind was blank, unable to produce a suspect. It wasn't until she gave up and went to bed that the answer came to her, almost as if it had been jarred loose by the impact of her head against the pillow.

SHE'D BEEN circulating through her classroom during a quiz—this was back in February, either right before or right after winter vacation—when she spotted Jessica Grasso munching on a Snickers bar. Some teachers allowed snacks in class, but Vicki wasn't one of them, and she'd been teaching long enough to know that you had to stick to your guns on stuff like that. Not wanting to embarrass the girl, who'd never given her any trouble, Vicki tapped her on the shoulder and spoke in a barely audible whisper as she held out her hand.

"Please give me that."

Instead of surrendering the contraband, Jessica took another bite. She was a big girl with a pretty face—except for the ridiculous raccoon eyeliner—and sleek dark hair that swept down across her forehead, partially obscuring one eye. She chewed slowly, taking a languorous pleasure in the activity, staring straight at Vicki the whole time.

"Did you hear me?" Vicki demanded, this time in a normal voice.

Jessica's expression remained blank, but Vicki detected a challenge in it nonetheless. She began to feel foolish, standing there with her hand out while the girl gazed right through her. It was possible—she wasn't clear on this point in retrospect—that Vicki lowered her gaze, taking a moment or two to perform a less-than-charitable assessment of Jessica's figure.

"It's not like you need it," she said.

Jessica blinked and shook her head, as if maybe she hadn't heard right, and Vicki took advantage of her confusion to snatch the candy bar right out of her hand.

"Hey!" Jessica cried out, loudly enough that several heads snapped in their direction.

Now it was Vicki's turn to do the ignoring. She marched back to her desk and dropped the stub of the Snickers into her empty wastebasket, where it landed with an unexpectedly resonant thud. By now, everyone in the room was looking at her.

"I've said it before and I'll say it again," she told them. "Food is not allowed in this room."

That was it, the whole ridiculous, deeply forgettable incident. Vicki was more than willing to admit that it wasn't her finest hour as an educator, but she hadn't called anyone a fat pig and didn't think she had anything to apologize for. If anyone was at fault it was Jessica, who'd knowingly broken a rule and then treated a teacher with blatant disrespect. So it was frustrating for Vicki—humiliating, even—to see herself portrayed in a public forum as a nasty woman in unflattering pants, nothing more than a joke to the kids she was trying to help.

Like a lot of people her age, Vicki had grown accustomed

to taking the punishment life dished out. Most of the time she didn't even bother to complain. But every once in a while she found it necessary to stand up and defend her dignity—her worth as a human being—and this was apparently one of those occasions, because after the bell rang, instead of sitting quietly at her desk and organizing her papers as the students filed out, she found herself moving toward the door with an unusual sense of purpose, arriving just in time to form a barrier between Jessica Grasso and the hallway. She couldn't deny that she derived some pleasure from the look of confusion on the girl's face, the slow-dawning knowledge that she'd been busted.

"Greensleeves," Vicki told her. "You and I need to talk."

THEY SHOULD have had it out there and then, when Vicki had a head of steam and the element of surprise working in her favor, but Jessica was rushing off to a big chem test; apparently Mr. Holquist took points off if you were late, even if you had a pass. She offered to come back right after school let out, but Vicki had to nix that due to a faculty meeting. Not keen on hanging around for an extra hour, Jessica suggested postponing their talk till the morning. Vicki was adamant that it couldn't wait that long, and after a brief, somewhat hectic negotiation, they settled on Starbucks at four-thirty in the afternoon.

As soon as she sat down with her cup of green tea, Vicki began to suspect she'd made a mistake in agreeing to meet in the coffee shop, the atmosphere too mellow and unofficial—Joni Mitchell on the sound system, retired men playing chess, young hipsters tapping on their laptops—for the kind of chilly confrontation she'd been rehearsing in her mind. This conviction only deepened when Jessica arrived a few minutes later, waving to Vicki and miming the act of drinking as she took her place on the coffee line. The girl seemed perfectly happy to be there, as if the two of them were regular coffee buddies, and Vicki found herself momentarily disarmed, unable to muster any of the feelings of anger or shame that had made this rendezvous seem so urgent in the first place.

"Sorry I'm late." Jessica smiled as she took her seat, her cheeks rosy from the damp April breeze. "My mom made me fold the laundry."

"That's okay. I just got here myself."

"Mmmm." Jessica sipped from her enormous drink, a clear, domed cup full of what looked like a milk shake with whipped cream on top. "This is awesome."

"What is it?"

"Venti caramel Frappuccino." She held out the cup. "Want some?"

Vicki was horrified—there must have been a thousand calories in there—but she just smiled politely and shook her head. What Jessica ate and drank outside of class was none of her business.

"I'm fine with my tea," Vicki said. "How'd you do on your chemistry test?"

"Terrible." Jessica gave a cheerful shrug, as if *terrible* were a synonym for *pretty good*. "I suck at science even worse than I suck at math, if you can believe that."

"You don't suck at math. I just don't think you apply yourself."

"That's exactly what my dad says."

"You should listen to him."

Jessica rolled her eyes. They were honey-colored, and there was an appealing cluster of freckles spattered across the bridge of her nose that Vicki had never noticed before. *It's the makeup,* Vicki thought. *She's not wearing that awful makeup.* She wished she knew the girl well enough to tell her she was better off without it.

Something caught Jessica's eye and she leaned to the left, a look of such longing on her face that Vicki couldn't help turning to see what had caused it. At a table near the front window, a slender blond woman in a boldly patterned wrap-around dress was flirting with a cop, a big-bellied, broad-shouldered man holding a coffee cup in each hand. He said something that made her laugh, then reluctantly took his leave, shuffling backward out the door so he could keep his eyes on her for as long as possible. When he was gone, the woman smiled to herself and reflexively checked the messages on her cell phone. Vicki felt a sharp stab of envy—something that happened to her several times a day—irrational hatred for the smug woman coupled with an intense desire to *be* her, or at least to be looked at the way the cop had looked at her.

"So you read it, huh?"

Vicki turned around, her mind a beat behind the question. She felt flustered, as if Jessica had caught her in a private moment.

"Excuse me?"

"That thing I wrote? That's why you wanted to talk to me, right?"

"Yes." Vicki straightened up, hoping to regain some of her teacherly authority. "I was hurt by it. You said some really awful things about me."

Jessica nodded contritely. "I know."

"You really need to be more considerate of other people's feelings."

"I didn't think you'd read it."

"Well, I did." Vicki's eyes locked on Jessica's. "I cried myself to sleep last night."

"Wow." Jessica didn't seem to know what to do with this information, and Vicki wondered if she'd made a mistake in revealing it. "I'm really sorry."

"I'm only human," Vicki continued, a slight tremor entering her voice. "You think I like reading about my big backside on the Internet? You think that makes me feel good about myself?"

"Well, how do you think I felt?" Jessica shot back. "You called me a fat pig."

She said this with such conviction that Vicki couldn't help wondering if it might actually be true, if she really could have said something so mean and then repressed the memory. But it didn't make sense. If she'd called Jessica a horrible name like that, she would have remembered. She would have gotten down on her knees and begged for forgiveness.

"I never said that." Vicki's voice was calm but insistent. "You know I didn't."

"But you thought it." Jessica was blushing fiercely. "I remember the way you were looking at me. Judging me. *You don't need that candy bar.*"

"No," Vicki murmured, but the certainty had drained from her voice. "I wasn't judging you."

Jessica took a long pull on her Frappuccino, squinting at Vicki the whole time.

"I didn't ask to be fat, you know."

"You're a lovely girl," Vicki told her. "You have a very pretty face."

"My mother tells me that five times a day."

"It's true."

"I used to be really cute." Jessica laughed, but all Vicki heard was pain. "People used to tell me I looked just like my big sister."

"How old's your sister?"

"She's a senior. Jenny Grasso? Cheerleader? Like the hottest girl in the whole school?"

"Oh." Vicki knew Jenny Grasso. You couldn't spend a day in Gifford High School and not be aware of her. It was like living in America and not knowing about Britney Spears. "I didn't realize that the two of you—"

"Why would you? It's not like we have the same last name or anything."

"It's a big school," Vicki replied lamely. "You could be cousins."

Jessica shook her head. She didn't seem upset, just defeated. "Her clothes are so tiny. You can't believe she fits in them."

Vicki had never taught Jessica's sister, never even spoken to her, but she had an oddly vivid image in her mind of Jenny Grasso walking slowly past her classroom in tight jeans and a pink tank top, clutching a single red rose.

"Do you get along?"

"Sometimes. I mean, she's pretty nice most of the time. But it kinda sucks living in the same house with her. Boys are always texting her and she's always going to the mall with her friends and coming home with these really cute outfits. It's

NINE INCHES | 37

just—her life's so great and mine…" Jessica's eyes pleaded with Vicki. "Sometimes I want to kill her."

"I don't blame you."

"I don't see why she gets to have all that and I don't. It's like I'm being punished and I didn't do anything wrong."

"There's no justice."

Jessica nodded grimly, as if she'd figured that out a long time ago. "You want to see something?" She picked up her phone, took a couple of swipes at the screen, then handed it to Vicki. "I mean, look at this."

Even on the small screen, the photograph was heartbreaking. It had been taken on prom night, the two Grasso sisters—the fat one and the pretty one—standing side by side on the stoop of a pale blue house, the camera far enough away that their bodies were visible from the knees up: Jenny in a slinky, low-cut yellow dress, not smiling but looking deeply pleased with the world, Jessica in a tentlike hoodie, grinning till it hurt, her face at once large and indistinct, one beefy arm draped over her sister's delicate shoulder.

Poor thing, Vicki thought as she handed back the phone.

"I know," Jessica said, as if Vicki had spoken the words aloud. "Story of my life."

"Believe me," Vicki told her, "I know just how you feel. I mean, I was never petite or anything, just normal-sized. But then I put on fifty pounds when I was pregnant with my son. Fifty pounds, can you believe that? And I couldn't take it off. I did Weight Watchers, I fasted, I exercised, I tried every diet in the world, but I just got bigger and bigger. It was like my body was saying, *Guess what, this is how it's gonna be from now on. Better get used to it.* My husband told me he didn't care, said he loved me no matter what, but a few years later he left me for a Chinese woman, I don't think she weighed a hundred pounds. They have three kids now."

"He sounds like a jerk."

"I loved him." Vicki flicked her hand in front of her face as if it wasn't worth talking about. "That was almost twenty years ago."

"You ever get married again?"

"Nope."

"Any boyfriends?"

"Nothing serious. I was a divorced working mother. Not young and not thin. My phone wasn't ringing off the hook." Vicki hesitated long enough to realize she was making a mistake, then kept going. "For a lot of that time, I had a crush on another teacher."

Jessica's eyes widened. "At Gifford?"

"I was crazy about this guy. He was divorced, too. We ate lunch together every day, went to the movies with a group of other single teachers, even played on a coed softball team. It was a lot of fun."

"Was it Mr. Oberman?"

"*Mr. Oberman?*" Vicki couldn't help laughing. Dan Oberman was a slovenly history teacher, a sadsack who lived with his mother and had been wearing the same three sweater vests for the past ten years. "You think I'd have a crush on Mr. Oberman?"

"He's not so bad."

"Anyway, I got really motivated about walking every day and watching what I ate, and I lost about twenty pounds. I could see he was looking at me in a different way, complimenting my outfits, and you know, just paying attention, and I finally decided to go for it. At the faculty Christmas party, I took him aside and told him how I felt. He said he had feelings for me, too. He drove me home that night and we . . ." A bit late, Vicki's sense of decorum kicked in.

"You hooked up?" Jessica pretended to be scandalized. "Was it Mr. McAdams?"

"He's a married man."

"Come on, just tell me."

"It doesn't matter. What matters is that we had that one night together and I was so happy. I could see my whole life laid out in front of me." Vicki laughed at herself, a short, scornful bark. "But he didn't call the next day, or the day after that . . ."

"Or the day after that," Jessica continued. "Been there."

"Finally, I couldn't take it anymore and I called him. He got all serious on me. You know that voice, like a doctor telling you you're gonna die. *You have to understand, Vicki, I like you a lot but what happened the other night was a mistake. I had too much to drink, blah, blah, blah . . .*"

"Let's be friends," Jessica added knowingly. "That totally sucks."

"I'll tell you what sucks. Three months later he got engaged to a pretty, young gym teacher. And guess who got invited to their wedding? Good old Vicki."

"Mr. Turley?" Jessica gasped. "You hooked up with Mr. Turley?"

"It was just that once."

"He's cute for an old guy," Jessica said. "Didn't Ms. Leoni just have a baby?"

"Yeah. Sweet little boy."

"Ouch."

Vicki nodded. *Ouch* was right. She didn't tell Jessica about how drunk she'd gotten at the wedding, how the bride's mother found her crying in the bathroom and listened to Vicki's confession of her love for the groom with surprising compassion, telling Vicki that she understood how hard it must be, that she'd gone through something similar back when she was single. *You have to forget him,* she said. *You have to move on with your life.*

Jessica slurped the last of her Frappuccino and studied Vicki with a look of anxious sympathy. "You think you're ever gonna meet someone else?"

Vicki wasn't surprised by the question. It was something she'd asked herself frequently in recent years. If she'd been honest, she would've said that she'd come to the conclusion that Mr. Turley had been her last shot, and that she'd pretty much resigned herself to spending the remainder of her life alone. But it was clear from the way Jessica was looking at her—hungrily, with the kind of focus Vicki rarely inspired in the classroom—that she was asking an entirely different question.

"Of course," Vicki told her. "Of course I'll meet someone. I just have to be patient."

THAT NIGHT she ate dinner alone, graded some homework assignments she should've handed back a week ago, and called her son, who was a junior at Rutgers. As usual, Ben didn't pick up, so she just left a brief message: *Hey, honey, it's your mom. Give me a call when you get a chance. Love you.* Then she watched an episode of *CSI: Miami* and the first part of the news before finally working up the nerve to turn on her computer.

She wasn't sure why she was so nervous. She and Jessica had parted on good terms, joking in the Starbucks parking lot about heading across the street to Bruno's for a large sausage-and-pepperoni pizza with extra cheese. It was early evening, and the light had seemed unusually soft and forgiving as they said goodbye. Left to her own devices, Vicki wasn't much of a hugger—she saw how people hesitated sometimes, and it took a lot of the pleasure out of it—but Jessica didn't share her qualms. Before Vicki understood what was happening, the girl was moving toward her with her arms out, their two bodies bumping together, the sensation so familiar it was almost as if she were embracing herself.

"So," Jessica said. "I guess I'll see you tomorrow."

"Okay." Vicki felt a sudden odd emptiness as the girl let go. She was surprised to realize that she was close to tears "You have a nice night."

Jessica had promised to delete the offensive post on grademyteacher.com, and Vicki was pretty sure she trusted her to keep her word. Still, she felt a vague sense of foreboding as she scrolled down the alphabetical list of Gifford teachers—there was Becky Leoni (6.7) and good old Sam Turley (7.2)—a queasy suspicion that something unpleasant was about to unfold.

But it was okay. The post was gone, wiped away as if it had never even existed. Vicki felt a moment of pure satisfaction—justice had been done, a crooked thing made straight—as well as a rush of affection for the girl, who really was a lovely person despite the awful things she'd written. Her attack was just a projection, an attempt to displace negative feelings for herself onto someone else. Vicki understood all too well how that sort of thing worked.

Her relief didn't last for long, though. Without meaning to, she found herself reading the review that had taken the place of Jessica's at the top of the Vicki Wiggins's page on grade myteacher.com. It was several months old, written by a student who called himself "Mr. Amazing":

All in all Ms. Wiggins is a pretty good math teacher, except she's pretty strict about stupid little things. Like she gave this one kid detention cause his cellphone rang in class. Ok he should have turned it off, but was it his fault that someone called him? But like I said she's not that bad. I don't care what anybody says there is no way she's more boring than Mr. Ferrone.

Vicki had read this post when it first appeared and had barely given it a second thought. It was actually pretty good as far as these things went—Mr. Amazing had given her a higher-than-average overall rating of 6.0—but right now it just seemed heartbreaking. Was this what she would be remembered for when all was said and done? That she gave some kid detention for a minor offense? That maybe—just maybe—she wasn't as mind-numbingly dull as Dennis Ferrone?

I have so much to offer. And no one even notices.

For a few seconds, she thought about approaching Jessica after class tomorrow, suggesting that she post a new, more generous review on the site just to set the record straight. But it was a lot to ask. And the thought of making such a request was embarrassing beyond words.

She wasn't sure why it mattered so much, but it did. It just did. Why wouldn't it? She was a good person, she worked hard, and it seemed crazy—crazy and wrong—that these things went unacknowledged.

It turned out to be easier than she expected to register on grademyteacher.com. You just typed in an e-mail address and checked a box that said I AM A STUDENT AT GIFFORD HIGH SCHOOL. She chose the username Frappuccinogrrrl and wrote the following in the comments box:

> My math teacher Vicki Wiggins is really nice. She's pretty and really cares about us kids. Like if you were having a problem she'd meet you after school and try to make you feel better because she just wants everybody to be happy. And she knows a lot about math too.

There was more to say—much more—but space was limited and she decided to stop there. She checked her work, pressed SEND, and turned off her computer. There would be time enough in the morning to wake up and drink a cup of coffee, then maybe google herself before heading off to work. It would be nice, she thought, clicking on her own name and, just for once, finding something that felt like the truth.

THE SMILE ON
HAPPY CHANG'S FACE ·········➤

THE SUPERIOR WALLCOVERINGS WILDCATS WERE PLAY-
ing in the Little League championship game, and I wanted
them to lose. I wanted the Town Pizza Ravens and their star
pitcher, Lori Chang, to humiliate them, to run up the score
and taunt them mercilessly from the first-base dugout. I know
this isn't an admirable thing for a grown man to admit—
especially a grown man who has agreed to serve as home-plate
umpire—but there are feelings you can't hide from yourself,
even if you'd just as soon chop off your hand as admit them to
anyone else.

I had nothing against the Wildcat players. It was their
coach I didn't like, my next-door neighbor, Carl DiSalvo, the
Kitchen Kabinet King of northern New Jersey. I stood behind the backstop, feeling huge and bloated in my cushiony
chest protector, and watched him hit infield practice. A shame-
lessly vain man, Carl had ripped the sleeves off his sweatshirt,
the better to display the rippling muscles he worked for like a

dog down at Bally's. I knew all about his rippling muscles. Our driveways were adjacent, and Carl always seemed to be returning from an exhilarating session at the gym just as I was trudging off to work in the morning, my head still foggy from another rotten night's sleep.

"I'm getting pretty buff," he would tell me, proudly rubbing his pecs or biceps. "Wish I'd been built like this when I was younger."

Fuck you, I invariably thought, but I always said something polite like "Keep it up" or "I gotta start working out myself."

Carl and I had known each other forever. In high school we played football together—I was a starter, a second-team all-county linebacker, while Carl barely dirtied his uniform—and hung out in the same athletic crowd. When he and Marie bought the Detmeyers' house nine years ago, it had seemed like a lucky break for both of us, a chance to renew a friendship that had died of natural causes when we graduated and went our separate ways—me to college and into the management sector, Carl into his father's remodeling business. I helped him with the move, and when we finished, we sat on my patio with our wives, drinking beer and laughing as the summer light faded and our kids played tag on the grass. We called each other "neighbor" and imagined barbecues and block parties stretching far into the future.

"Nice pickup, Trevor," he called to his third baseman. "But let's keep working on that throw, okay, pal?"

Go fuck yourself, I thought. *Okay, pal?*

• • •

"JACKIE *BOY.*" Tim Tolbert, the first-base umpire and president of the Little League, pummeled my chest protector as though it were a punching bag. "Championship *game.*" He looked happier than a grown man has a right to be. "*Very* exciting."

As usual, I wanted to grab him by the collar and ask what the hell he had to be so cheerful about. He was a baby-faced, prematurely bald man who sold satellite dishes all day, then came home to his wife, a scrawny exercise freak obsessed with her son's peanut allergy. She'd made a big stink about it when the kid entered kindergarten, and now the school cafeteria wasn't allowed to serve PB&J sandwiches anymore.

"Very exciting," I agreed. "Two best teams in the league."

"Not to mention the two best umps," he said, giving me a brotherly squeeze on the shoulder.

This much I owed to Tim—he was the guy who convinced me to volunteer as an umpire. He must have known how isolated I was feeling, alone in my house, my wife and kids living with my mother-in-law, nothing to do at night but stare at the TV and stuff my face with sandwich cream cookies. I resisted at first, not wanting to give people a new opportunity to whisper about me, but he kept at it until I finally gave in.

And I loved it. Crouching behind the plate, peering through the bars of my mask, my whole being focused on the crucial, necessary difference between a ball and a strike, I felt clearheaded and almost serene, free of the bitterness and shame that were my constant companions during the rest of my life.

"Two best umps?" I glanced around in mock confusion. "Me and who else?"

An errant throw rolled against the backstop, and Carl jogged over to retrieve it. He grabbed the ball and straightened up, turning to Tim and me as if we'd asked for his opinion.

"Kids are wound tight," he said. "I keep telling them it doesn't matter if you win or lose, but I don't think they believe me."

Carl grinned, letting us know he didn't believe it, either. Like me, he was in his midforties, but he was carrying it off with a little more panache than I was. He had thick gray hair that made for a striking contrast with his still-youthful body, and a gap between his front teeth that women supposedly found irresistible (at least that's what Jeanie used to tell me). His thick gold necklace glinted in the sun, spelling his name to the world.

"You're modeling the proper attitude," Tim told him. "That's all you can do."

The previous fall, a guy named Joe Funkhauser, the father of one of our high school football players, got into an argument with an opposing player's father in the parking lot after a bitterly contested game. Funkhauser beat the guy into a coma and was later charged with attempted murder. The Funkhauser Incident, as the papers called it, attracted a lot of unfavorable attention to our town and triggered a painful round of soul-searching among people concerned with youth sports. In response to the crisis, Tim had organized a workshop for Little League coaches and parents, trying to get them to focus on fun rather than competition, but it takes more than a two-hour seminar to change people's attitudes about something as basic as the difference between winning and losing.

"I don't blame your team for being spooked," I said. "Not after what Lori did to them last time. Didn't she set some kind of league record for strikeouts?"

Carl's grin disappeared. "I've been meaning to talk to you about that, Jack. The strike zone's down here. Not up here." He illustrated his point by slicing imaginary lines across his stomach and throat.

"Right," I said. "And it's six points for a touchdown."

"I don't mean to be a jerk about it," he continued, "but I thought you were making some questionable judgments."

"Funny," I said. "They're only questionable when they don't go your way."

"Just watch the high strikes, that's all I'm saying."

Tim kept smiling stiffly throughout this exchange, as if it were all just friendly banter, but he seemed visibly relieved by the sight of Ray Santelli, the Ravens' manager, returning from the snack bar with a hot dog in each hand.

"Just got outta work," he said, by way of explanation. "Traffic was a bitch on the Parkway."

Ray was a dumpy guy with an inexplicably beautiful Russian wife. A lot of people assumed she was mail order, despite Ray's repeated claims that he'd met her at his cousin's wedding. He ran a livery business with his brother and sometimes kept a white stretch limo parked in the driveway of his modest Cape Cod on Dunellen Street. The car was like the wife, a little too glamorous for its humble surroundings.

"It's those damn toll plazas," observed Tim. "They were supposed to be gone twenty years ago."

Before anyone could chime in with the ritual agreement, our attention was diverted by the appearance of Mikey Fellner, wielding his video camera. A mildly retarded guy in his early twenties, Mikey was a familiar figure at local sporting events, graduations, carnivals, and political meetings. He videotaped everything and saved the tapes, which he labeled and shelved in chronological order in his parents' garage. This was apparently part of the syndrome he had—it wasn't Down's but something more exotic, I forget the name—some compulsion to keep everything fanatically organized. He trained his camera on me, then got a few seconds of Santelli wiping mustard off his chin.

"You guys hear?" Carl asked. "Mikey says they're gonna show the game on cable access next week."

Mikey panned over to Tim, holding the camera just a couple of inches from his face. He wasn't big on respecting other people's boundaries, especially when he was working. Tim didn't seem to mind, though.

"Championship *game*," he said, giving a double thumbs-up to the viewing audience. "*Very* exciting."

LITTLE LEAGUE is a big deal in our town. You could tell that just by looking at our stadium. We've got dugouts, a big electronic scoreboard, and a padded outfield fence covered with ads for local businesses, just like the pro teams (that's how we paid for the scoreboard). We play the national anthem over a good sound system, nothing like the scratchy loudspeaker they used when I was a kid. The bleachers were packed for the championship game, and not just with the families of the players. It was a bona fide local event.

The Wildcats were up first, and Carl was right: his team had a bad case of the jitters. The leadoff hitter, Alex O'Malley, stepped up to the plate white-knuckled and expecting the worst, as if Lori Chang were Roger Clemens. He planted himself as far away from the plate as possible, stood like a statue for three called strikes, and seemed relieved to return to the bench. The second batter, Chris Rigato, swung blindly at three bad pitches, including a high and tight third strike that almost took his head off. His delayed evasive action, combined with the momentum of his premature swing, caused him to pirouette so violently that he lost his balance and ended up facedown in the dirt.

"Strike three," I said, taking care to keep my voice flat and matter-of-fact. I wasn't one of those show-off umps who said *Stee-rike!* and did a big song and dance behind the plate. "Batter's out."

The words were barely out of my mouth when Carl came bounding out of the third-base dugout. He had his arms spread wide, as if volunteering for a crucifixion.

"Goddammit, Jack! That was a beanball!"

I wasn't fooled by his theatrics. By that point, just six pitches into the first inning, it was already clear that Lori Chang was operating at the top of her game, and you didn't need Tim McCarver to tell you that Carl was trying to mess with her head. I should've just ordered him back to the dugout and called for play to resume, but there was just enough of a taste in my mouth from the earlier encounter that I took the bait. I removed my mask and took a few steps in his direction.

"Please watch your language, Coach. You know better than that."

"She's throwing at their heads!" Carl was yelling now, for the benefit of the spectators. "She's gonna kill someone!"

"The batter swung," I reminded him.

"He was trying to protect himself. You gotta warn her, Jack. That's your job."

"You do your job, Carl. I'll take care of mine."

I had just pulled my mask back over my head when Tim came jogging across the infield to back me up. We umpires made it a point to present a unified front whenever a dispute arose.

"It's okay," I told him. "Let's play ball."

He gave me one of those subtle headshakes, the kind you wouldn't have noticed if he hadn't been standing six inches in front of you. "He's right, Jack. You should talk to her."

"You're playing right into his hands."

"Maybe so," he admitted. "But this is the championship. Let's keep it under control."

He was forcing me into an awkward position. I didn't want to be Carl's puppet, but I also didn't want to argue with Tim right there in the middle of the infield. As it was, I could feel my authority draining away by the second. Someone on the Ravens' side yelled for us to stop yapping and get on with the game. A Wildcats fan suggested we'd been bought and paid for by Town Pizza.

"We gotta be careful here." Tim gestured toward the Wildcats' dugout, where Mikey had his video camera set up on a tripod. "This is gonna be on TV."

LORI CHANG smiled quizzically as I approached the mound, as if she couldn't possibly imagine why I was paying her a social visit in the middle of the game.

"Is something wrong?" she asked, sounding a little more worried than she looked.

Lori was one of only three girls playing in our Little League that season. I know it's politically incorrect to say so, but the other two, Allie Reagan and Steph Murkowski, were tomboys—husky, tough-talking jockettes you could easily imagine playing college rugby and marching in Gay Pride parades later in their lives.

Lori Chang, on the other hand, didn't even look like an athlete. She was petite, with a round, serious face and lustrous hair that she wore in a ponytail threaded through the back of her baseball cap. Unlike Allie and Steph, both of whom were fully developed in a chunky, none-too-feminine way, Lori had not yet reached puberty. She was lithe and curveless, her chest as flat as a boy's beneath the stretchy fabric of her Ravens jersey. And yet—I hope it's okay to talk like this, because it's true—there was something undeniably sexual about her presence on the baseball field. She wore lipstick and nail polish, giggled frequently for no reason, and blushed when her teammates complimented her performance. She was always tugging down her jersey in the back, as if she suspected the shortstop and third baseman of paying a little too much attention to her ass. In short, she was completely adorable. If I'd been twelve, I would've had a hopeless crush on her.

Which is why it was always such a shock when she let loose with the high hard one. Unlike other pitchers her age, who struggled just to put the ball over the plate, Lori actually had a strategy, a potent combination of control, misdirection, patience, and outright intimidation. She tended to jam batters early in the count and occasionally brushed them back, though to my knowledge she'd never actually hit anyone. Midcount she often switched to changeups and breaking balls, working on the outside corner. Once she had the batter appropriately spooked and thoroughly off-balance, she liked to rear back and finish him off with a sizzler right down the pipe. These two-strike fastballs hopped and dived so unpredictably that it was easy to lose track of them. Some of the batters didn't even realize the ball had crossed the plate until they heard the slap of leather against leather and turned in angry amazement to see a small but decisive puff of dust rising from the catcher's mitt.

I had no idea where she'd learned to pitch like that. Lori was a newcomer to our town, one of those high-achieving Asian kids who've flocked here in the past decade (every year, it seems, the valedictorian of our high school has a Chinese or Korean or Indian last name). In just a few months, she'd established herself as an excellent student, a gifted violinist, and a powerhouse on the baseball diamond, despite the fact that she could usually be found waiting tables and filling napkin dispensers at Happy Wok #2, the restaurant her parents had opened on Grand Avenue.

"There's nothing wrong," I told her. "Just keep right on doing what you're doing."

Her eyes narrowed with suspicion. "You came all the way out here to tell me that?"

"It's really not that far," I said, raising my mask just high enough that she could see I was smiling.

• • •

BY THE end of the third inning, Lori had struck out eight of the first nine batters she'd faced. The only Wildcat to even make contact was Ricky DiSalvo, Carl's youngest son and the league leader in home runs and RBIs, who got handcuffed by a fastball and dinged a feeble check-swing grounder to second.

Lori's father, Happy Chang, was sitting by himself in the third-base bleachers, surrounded by Wildcats fans. Despite his nickname, Mr. Chang was a grim, unfriendly man who wore the same dirty beige windbreaker no matter how hot or cold it was and always seemed to need a shave. Unlike the other Asian fathers in our town—most of them were doctors, computer scientists, and businessmen who played golf and made small talk in perfect English—Happy Chang had a rough edge, a just-off-the-boat quality that reminded me of those guys you often saw milling around on Canal Street in the city, making disgusting noises and spitting on the sidewalk. I kept glancing at him as the game progressed, waiting for him to crack a smile or offer a word of encouragement, but he remained stone-faced, as if he wished he were back in his restaurant, keeping an eye on the lazy cooks, instead of watching his amazing daughter dominate the Wildcats in front of the whole town on a lovely summer evening.

Maybe it's a Chinese thing, I thought. Maybe they don't like to show emotion in public. Or maybe—I had no idea, but it didn't keep me from speculating—he wished he had a son instead of a daughter (as far as I could tell, Lori was an only child). Like everybody else, I knew about the Chinese preference for boys over girls. One of my coworkers, a single woman in her late thirties, had recently traveled to Shanghai to adopt a baby girl abandoned by her parents. She said the orphanages were full of them.

But if Happy Chang didn't love his daughter, how come he came to every game? For that matter, why did he let her play at all? My best guess—based on my own experience as a father—was that he simply didn't know what to make of her. In China, girls didn't play baseball. So what did it mean that Lori played the game as well or better than any American boy? Maybe he was divided in his mind between admiring her talent and seeing it as a kind of curse, a symbol of everything that separated him from his past. Maybe that was why he faithfully attended her games, but always sat scowling on the wrong side of the field, as if he were rooting for her opponents. Maybe his daughter was as unfathomable to him as my own son had been to me.

LIKE MOST men, I'd wanted a son who reminded me of myself as a kid, a boy who lived for sports, collected baseball cards, and hung pennants on his bedroom walls. I wanted a son who played tackle football down at the schoolyard with the other neighborhood kids and came home with ripped pants and skinned knees. I wanted a son I could take to the ballpark and play catch with in the backyard.

But Jason was an artistic, dreamy kid with long eyelashes and delicate features. He loved music and drew elaborate pictures of castles and clouds and fairy princesses. He enjoyed playing with his sisters' dolls and exhibited what I thought was an unhealthy interest in my wife's jewelry and high heels. When he was seven years old, he insisted on going out trick-or-treating dressed as Pocahontas. Everywhere he went, people kept telling him how beautiful he was, and it was impossible not to see how happy this made him.

Jeanie did her best to convince me that it wasn't a problem; she cut out magazine articles that said he was simply engaged in harmless "gender play" and recommended that we let him follow his heart and find his own way in the world. She scolded me for using words like *sissy* and *wimp,* and for trying to enforce supposedly outdated standards of masculinity. I tried to get with the program, but it was hard. I was embarrassed to be seen in public with my own son, as if he somehow made me less of a man.

It didn't help that Carl had three normal boys living right next door. They were always in the backyard kicking a soccer ball, tossing a football, or beating the crap out of one another. Sometimes they included my son in their games, but it wasn't much fun for any of them.

Jason didn't want to play Little League, but I made him. I thought putting on a uniform might transform him into the kind of kid I would recognize as my own. Despite the evidence in front of my face, I refused to believe you could be an American boy and not love baseball, not want to impress your father with your athletic prowess.

It's easy to say you should let a kid follow his heart. But what if his heart takes him places you don't want to go? What if your ten-year-old son wants to take tap-dancing lessons in a class full of girls? What if he's good at it? What if he tells you when he's fourteen that he's made it onto the chorus of *Guys and Dolls* and expects you to be happy about this? What if when he's fifteen he tells you he's joined the Gay and Lesbian

NINE INCHES | 57

Alliance at his progressive suburban high school? What if this same progressive school allows boys to go to the prom with other boys, and girls to go with girls? Are you supposed to say, *Okay, fine, go to the prom with Gerald, just don't stay out too late?*

I only hit him that once. He said something that shocked me and I slapped him across the face. He was the one who threw the first punch, a feeble right cross that landed on the side of my head. Later, when I had time to think about it, I was proud of him for fighting back. But at the time, it just made me crazy. I couldn't believe the little faggot had hit me. The punch I threw in return is the one thing in my life I'll regret forever. I broke his nose, and Jeanie called the cops. I was taken from my house in handcuffs, the cries of my wife and children echoing in my ears. As I ducked into the patrol car, I looked up and saw Carl watching me from his front stoop, shaking his head and trying to comfort Marie, who for some reason was sobbing audibly in the darkness, as if it were her own child whose face I'd bloodied in a moment of thoughtless rage.

LORI CHANG kept her perfect game going all the way into the top of the fifth, when Pete Gonzalez, the Wildcats' all-star shortstop, ripped a two-out single to center. A raucous cheer erupted from the third-base dugout and bleachers, both of which had lapsed into a funereal silence over the past couple of innings. It was an electrifying sound, a collective whoop of relief, celebration, and resurgent hope.

On a psychological level, that one hit changed everything.

It was as if the whole ballpark suddenly woke up to two important facts: (1) Lori Chang was not, in fact, invincible; and (2) the Wildcats could actually still win. The score was only 1–0 in favor of the Ravens, a margin that had seemed insurmountable a moment ago but that suddenly looked a whole lot slimmer now that the tying run was standing on first with a lopsided grin on his face, shifting his weight from leg to leg like he needed to go to the bathroom.

The only person who didn't seem to notice that the calculus of the game had changed was Lori Chang herself. She stood on the mound with her usual poker face, an expression that suggested profound boredom more than it did killer concentration, and waited for Trevor Mancini to make the sign of the cross and knock imaginary mud off his cleats. Once he got himself settled, she nodded to the catcher and began her windup, bringing her arms overhead and lowering them with the painstaking deliberation of a Tai Chi master. Then she kicked high and whipped a fastball right at Trevor, a guided missile that thudded into his leg with a muffled *whump,* the sound of a broomstick smacking a rug.

"Aaah, shit!" Trevor flipped his bat in the air and began hopping around on one foot, rubbing frantically at his leg. "Shit! Shit! Shit!"

I stepped out from behind the catcher and asked if he was okay. Trevor gritted his teeth and performed what appeared to be an involuntary bow. When he straightened up, he looked more embarrassed than hurt.

"Stings," he explained.

I told him to take his base and he hobbled off, still massaging the sore spot. A chorus of boos had risen from the third-base side, and I wasn't surprised to see that Carl was already out of the dugout, walking toward me with what could only be described as an amused expression.

"Well?" he said. "What are you gonna do about it?"

"The batter was hit by a pitch. It's part of the game."

"Are you kidding me? She threw right at him."

Right on schedule, Tim came trotting over to join us, followed immediately by Ray Santelli, who approached with his distinctive potbellied swagger, radiating an odd confidence that made you forget that he was just a middle-aged chauffeur with a combover.

"What's up?" he inquired. "Somebody got a problem?"

"Yeah, me," Carl told him. "I got a problem with your sweet little pitcher throwing beanballs at my players."

"That was no beanball," I pointed out. "It hit him in the leg."

"So that's okay?" Carl was one of those guys who smiled when he was pissed off. "It's okay to hit my players in the leg?"

"She didn't do it on purpose," Santelli assured him. "Lori wouldn't do that."

"I don't know," Tim piped in. "It looked pretty deliberate from where I was standing."

"How would you know?" Santelli demanded, an uncharacteristic edge creeping into his voice. "Are you some kind of mind reader?"

"I'm just telling you what it looked like," Tim replied.

"Big deal," Santelli replied. "That's just your subjective opinion."

"I'm an umpire," Tim reminded him. "My subjective opinion is all I have."

"Really?" Santelli scratched his forehead, feigning confusion. "I thought you guys were supposed to be objective. When did they change the job description?"

"All right," said Tim. "Whatever. It's my objective opinion, okay?"

"Look," I said. "We're doing the best we can."

"I sure as hell hope not," Carl shot back. "Or else we're in big trouble."

Sensing an opportunity, Santelli cupped his hands around his mouth and called out, "Hey, Lori, did you hit that kid on purpose?"

Lori seemed shocked by the question. Her mouth dropped open and she shook her head back and forth, as if nothing could have been further from the truth.

"It slipped," she said. "I'm really sorry."

"See?" Santelli turned back to Tim with an air of vindication. "It was an accident."

"Jack?" Carl's expression was a mixture of astonishment and disgust. "You really gonna let this slide?"

I glanced at Tim for moral support, but his face was blank, pointedly devoid of sympathy. I wished I could have thought of something more decisive to do than shrug.

"What do you want from me?" There was a pleading note in my voice that was unbecoming in an umpire. "She said it slipped."

"Now, wait a minute—" Tim began, but Carl didn't let him finish.

"Fine," he said. "The hell with it. If that's the way it's gonna be, that's the way it's gonna be. Let's play ball."

Carl stormed off, leaving the three of us standing by the plate, staring at his back as he descended into the dugout.

"You can't know what's in another person's heart." Santelli shook his head, as if saddened by this observation. "You just can't."

"Why don't you shut up?" Tim told him.

Lori quickly regained her composure when play resumed. With runners on first and second, she calmly and methodically struck out Antoine Frye to retire the side. On her way to the dugout she stopped and apologized to Trevor Mancini, resting her hand tenderly on his shoulder. It was a classy move. Trevor blushed and told her to forget about it.

RICKY DISALVO was on the mound for the Wildcats, and though he had nowhere near Lori's talent, he was pitching a solid and effective game. A sidearmer plagued by control problems and a lack of emotional maturity—I had once seen him burst into tears after walking five straight batters—Ricky had wisely decided that night to make his opponents hit the ball. All game long he'd dropped one fat pitch after another right over the meatiest part of the plate.

The Ravens, a mediocre hitting team on the best of days, had eked out a lucky run in the second on a single, a stolen base, an overthrow, and an easy fly ball to right field that had popped out of Mark Diedrich's glove, but they'd been shut out ever since. Ricky's confidence had grown with each successive inning, and he was throwing harder and more skillfully than he had all game by the time Lori Chang stepped up to the plate with two outs in the bottom of the fifth.

I guess I should have seen what was coming. When I watched the game on cable access a week later, it seemed painfully clear in retrospect, almost inevitable. But at the time, I didn't sense any danger. We'd had some unpleasantness, but it had passed when Lori apologized to Trevor. The game had moved forward, slipping past the trouble as easily as water flowing around a rock. I did notice that Lori Chang looked a little nervous in the batter's box, but that was nothing unusual. As bold and powerful as she was on the mound, Lori was a surprisingly timid hitter. She tucked herself into an extreme crouch, shrinking the strike zone down to a few inches, and tried to wait out a walk. She rarely swung and was widely, and fairly, considered to be an easy out.

For some reason, though, Ricky seemed oddly tentative with his first couple of pitches. Ball one kicked up dirt ten feet from the plate. Ball two was a mile outside.

"Come on," Carl called impatiently from the dugout. "Just do it."

Lori tapped the fat end of her bat on the plate. I checked my clicker and squatted into position. Ricky glanced at his father and started into his herky-jerky windup.

On TV, it all looks so fast and clean—Lori gets beaned and she goes down. But on the field it was slow and jumbled, my brain lagging a beat behind the action. Before I can process the fact that the ball's rocketing toward her head, Lori's already said, "Ooof!" Her helmet's in the air before I register the sickening crack of impact, and by then she's already crumpled on the ground. On TV it looks as though I move quickly, rolling her onto her back and coming in close to check her breathing, but in my memory it's as if I'm paralyzed, as if the world has stopped and all I can do is stare at the bareheaded girl lying motionless at my feet.

Then the quiet bursts into commotion. Tim's right beside me, shouting, "Is she okay? Is she okay?" Ricky's moving toward us from the mound, his glove pressed to his mouth, his eyes stricken with terror and remorse.

"Did I hurt her?" he asks. "I didn't mean to hurt her."

"I think you killed her," I tell him, because as far as I can tell, Lori's not breathing. Ricky stumbles backward, as if someone's pushed him. He turns in the direction of his father, who's just stepped out of the dugout.

"You shouldn't have made me do that!" Ricky yells.

"Oh my God," says Carl. He looks pale and panicky.

At that same moment, Happy Chang's scaling the third-base fence and sprinting across the infield to check on his daughter's condition. At least that's what I think he's doing, right up to the moment when he veers suddenly toward Carl, emitting a cry of guttural rage, and tackles him savagely to the ground.

Happy Chang is a small man, no bigger than some of our Little Leaguers, and Carl is tall and bulked up from years of religious weight lifting, but it's no contest. Within seconds, Happy Chang's straddling Carl's chest and punching him repeatedly in the face, all the while shouting what must be very angry things in Chinese. Carl doesn't even try to defend himself, not even when Happy Chang reaches for his throat.

Luckily for Carl, two of our local policemen—Officers Freylinghausen and Hughes, oddly enough the same two who'd arrested me for domestic battery—are present at the game, and before Happy Chang can finish throttling Carl, they've rushed onto the field and broken up the fight. They take Happy Chang into custody with a surprising amount of force—with me they were oddly polite—Freylinghausen grinding his face into the dirt while Hughes slaps on the cuffs. I'm so engrossed in the spectacle that I don't even realize that Lori's regained consciousness until I hear her voice.

"Daddy?" she says quietly, and for a second I think she's talking to me.

MY WHOLE life fell apart after I broke my son's nose. By the time I got out on bail the next morning, Jeanie had already taken the kids to her mother's house and slapped me with a restraining order. The day after that she started divorce proceedings.

In the year that had passed since then, nothing much had changed. I had tried apologizing in a thousand different ways, but it didn't seem to matter. As far as Jeanie was concerned, I'd crossed some unforgivable line and was beyond redemption.

I accepted the loss of my wife as fair punishment for what I'd done, but it was harder to accept the loss of my kids. I had some visiting rights, but they were severely restricted. Basically, I took my daughters—they were eleven and thirteen— to the movies or the mall every other Saturday, then to a restaurant, and then back to their grandmother's. They weren't allowed to stay overnight with me. It killed me to walk past their empty rooms at night, to not find them asleep and safe, and to be fairly sure I never would.

Once in a while Jason joined us on our Saturday excursions, but usually he was too busy with his plays. He had just finished his junior year in high school, capping it off with a starring role in the spring musical, *Joseph and the Amazing*

Technicolor Dreamcoat. People kept telling me how great he was, and I kept agreeing, embarrassed to confess that I hadn't seen the show. My son had asked me not to come and I'd respected his wishes.

A year on my own had given me a lot of time to think, to come to terms with what had happened, and to accept my own responsibility for it. It also gave me a lot of time to stew in my anger, to indulge the conviction that I was a victim, too, every bit as much as my wife and son. I wrote Jeanie and my kids a lot of letters trying to outline my complicated position on these matters, but no one ever responded. It was like my side of the story had disappeared into some kind of void.

That's why I wanted so badly for my family to watch the championship game on cable access. I had e-mailed them all separately, telling them when it would be broadcast, and asking them to please tune in. I called them the day it aired and left a message reminding them to stick it out all the way to the end.

What I wanted them to see was the top of the sixth and final inning, the amazing sequence of events that took place immediately following the beanball fiasco, after both Carl and Ricky DiSalvo had been ejected from the game, and Happy Chang had been hauled off to the police station.

Despite the fact that she'd been knocked unconscious just a few minutes earlier, Lori was back on the mound for the Ravens. She insisted that she felt fine and didn't seem confused or otherwise impaired. She started out strong, striking out Jeb Partridge and retiring Hiro Tamanaki on an easy infield fly. But then something changed. Maybe the blow to the head had affected her more that she'd let on, or maybe she'd been traumatized by her father's arrest. Whatever the reason, she fell apart. With only one out remaining in the game, she walked three straight batters to load the bases.

I'd always admired Lori's regal detachment, her ability to remain calm and focused no matter what was going on, but now she just looked scared. She cast a desperate glance at the first-base dugout, silently pleading with her coach to take her out of the game, but Santelli ignored her. No matter how badly she was pitching, she was still his ace. And besides, the next batter was Mark Diedrich, the Wildcats' pudgy right fielder, one of the weakest hitters in the league.

"Just settle down," Santelli told her. "Strike this guy out and we can all go home."

Lori nodded skeptically and got herself set on the mound. Mark Diedrich greeted me with a polite nod as he stepped into the batter's box. He was a nice kid, a former preschool classmate of my youngest daughter.

"I wish I was home in bed," he told me.

The first pitch was low. Then came a strike, the liveliest breaking ball Lori had thrown all inning, but it was followed by two outside fastballs (Ricky's beanball had obviously done the trick; Lori wasn't throwing anywhere near the inside corner). The next pitch, low and away, should have been ball four, but inexplicably, Mark lunged for it, barely nicking it foul.

"Oh, Jesus," he whimpered. "Why did I do that?"

So there we were. Full count, bases loaded, two out. Championship game. A score of 1–0. The whole season narrowing down to a single pitch. If the circumstances had been a little different, it would have been a beautiful moment, an umpire's dream.

But for me, the game barely existed. All I could think of just then was the smile on Happy Chang's dirty face as the cops led him off the field. I was kneeling on the ground trying to comfort Lori when Happy turned in our direction and said something low and gentle in Chinese, maybe asking if she was all right or telling her not to worry. Lori said something back, maybe that she was fine or that she loved him.

"Easy now," Santelli called from the dugout. "Right down the middle."

Lori tugged her shirt down in back and squinted at the catcher. Mark Diedrich's face was beet red, as if something terribly embarrassing had already happened.

"Please, God," I heard him mutter as Lori began her windup.

I should have been watching the ball, but instead I was thinking about Happy Chang and everything he must have been going through at the police station, the fingerprinting, the mug shot, the tiny holding cell. But mainly it was the look on his face that haunted me, the proud and defiant smile of a man at peace with what he'd done and willing to accept the consequences.

The ball smacked into the catcher's mitt, waking me from my reverie. Mark hadn't swung. As far as I could determine after the fact, the pitch appeared to have crossed the plate near the outside corner, though possibly a bit on the high side.

I guess I could have lied. I could have called strike three and given the game to the Ravens, to Lori Chang and Ray Santelli. I could have sent Mark Diedrich sobbing back to the dugout, probably scarred for life. But instead I pulled off my mask.

"Jack?" Tim was standing between first and second with his palms open to the sky. "You gonna call it?"

"I can't," I told him. "I didn't see it."

There was a freedom in admitting it that I hadn't anticipated, and I dropped my mask to the ground. Then I slipped my arms through the straps of my chest protector and let that fall, too.

"What happened?" Mark Diedrich asked in a quavery voice. "Did I strike out?"

"I don't know," I told him.

Boos and angry cries rose from the bleachers as I made my way toward the pitcher's mound. I wanted to tell Lori Chang that I envied her father, but I had a feeling she wouldn't understand. She seemed relieved when I walked past her without saying a word. Mikey Fellner was out of the dugout and videotaping me as I walked past second base and onto the grass. He followed me all the way across centerfield, until I climbed the fence over the ad for the Prima Ballerina School of Dance and left the ballpark.

That's what I wanted my ex-wife and children to see—an umpire walking away from a baseball game, a man who had the courage to admit that he'd failed, who understood that there were times when you had no right to judge, had responsibilities you were no longer qualified to exercise. I hoped they might learn something new about me, something I hadn't been able to make clear to them in my letters and phone calls.

But of course I was disappointed. What's in your heart sometimes remains hidden, even when you most desperately want it to be revealed. I remembered my long walk across the outfield as a dignified, silent journey, but on TV I seem almost to be jogging. I look sweaty and confused, a little out of breath as I mumble a string of barely audible excuses and apologies for my strange behavior. If Jeanie and the kids had been watching, all they would have seen was an unhappy man they already knew too well, fleeing from the latest mess he'd made: just me, still trying to explain.

KIDDIE POOL ·······➤

IN A LIGHT RAIN, AT A LITTLE AFTER THREE IN THE
morning, Gus Ketchell stood on his back stoop in slippers
and shorty pajamas, holding a bulky cardboard box and staring uncertainly at his next-door neighbors' garage.

Come on, he told himself. *You can do this.*

No one would ever know. The Simmonses' house was dark,
the old air conditioner wheezing away in the second-floor
bedroom window. He pictured Peggy alone on the bed, snor-
ing heavily, nearly comatose from the industrial-strength
sleeping pills she'd been taking since Lonny's sudden death a
month ago. Gus could probably break down the front door
with a sledgehammer, turn on every light in the house, and
make himself a ham sandwich without disturbing her.

Gus's own wife, Martha, was also asleep, but even awake
she wouldn't have registered his absence at this ungodly hour;
aside from the occasional hotel room, they hadn't shared a
bed in years. There were no longer any dogs in the immediate

neighborhood to sound an alarm, either, not since Fred Di-Mello had been forced to put down his ancient, slobbering basset hound last October. Fred had buried Sadsack in his backyard, and Gus often saw him staring forlornly at the circle of rocks he'd placed in the ground to mark the gravesite.

So the coast was clear. But still Gus hesitated.

He just didn't like the idea of trespassing—breaking and entering, to be precise—even in a place so close to home, where he'd once been welcome. It would have been so much easier—so much more *civilized*—if he could just have rung the Simmonses' doorbell in the morning and said, *Hey, Peg, sorry to bother you, but I need a favor.* And Peggy would have said, *Sure, Gus, you name it. But why don't you sit down and have a cup of coffee first?*

Once upon a time, the Ketchells and the Simmonses had been those kinds of neighbors, back when everyone was young and their kids moved between the two yards as if they were all part of one big family. Lonny Simmons sometimes borrowed Gus's wheelbarrow and extension ladder without asking; Gus did the same with Lonny's ratchet set and Weed-wacker. The Ketchells had an open invitation to swim in the Simmonses' built-in pool, a bona fide luxury when it was installed in the early seventies, one of maybe a half dozen in the whole town. The two families barbecued together, went on camping trips, swapped babysitting, and took turns shoveling each other's sidewalk when it snowed.

Somewhere along the way, though, it all went sour. The kids grew up and went away. Lonny filled his swimming pool with concrete, said the damn thing was too much trouble. Peggy got fat and haughty; she made some remarks that

Martha hadn't appreciated. There were grievances—a missing drill bit, a motion light that shined into a bedroom window. Gus and Lonny fell out of the habit of shouting jocular greetings to each other when they were both out in their yards. After a while, they stopped waving.

Nonetheless, relations between the two households had remained reasonably civil until about three years ago, when the Simmonses got a bee in their bonnet about the old oak tree in the Ketchells' yard, which overhung both properties. Lonny and Peggy thought it was diseased and demanded that it be cut down before falling limbs damaged their precious garage. After a couple of tense discussions, Gus and Martha reluctantly agreed to get some estimates. They hadn't even had time to make their initial calls when the mail carrier arrived with a registered letter containing vague threats of legal action if the tree was not cut down "with all due dispatch."

A registered letter! From their next-door neighbors! Gus went ballistic. He scribbled a choice obscenity on the envelope and shoved it under the Simmonses' front door, right back where it came from. From then on, it was War.

OF ALL the unpleasant memories, one particular episode still rankled. Last July, Gus's three-year-old twin granddaughters had come for a visit during a wicked heat wave, the worst of the summer. Knowing how hard it was to entertain three-year-olds in the best of circumstances, he had purchased an inflatable kiddie pool from Costco, the biggest one they had. It came with something called a "high-volume hand pump," which Gus had been assured was "extremely efficient."

With an air of grandfatherly self-assurance, he removed the heavy vinyl liner from the box and spread it out on the grass. Squatting in the merciless sun, he pumped without making any visible headway, until his right hand was too raw to continue, then switched to his left. When that gave out—the pool still lay as flat as a rug on the parched grass, billowing slightly at its edges—he had no choice but to continue blowing up the damn thing with his mouth, while two whiny, pink-cheeked girls in swim diapers and bikini tops looked on with increasing impatience, criticizing his technique and questioning his competence.

At some point in the midst of this fiasco, Gus became aware of Lonny watching him from his own backyard. The cocky bastard was reclining shirtless on a lounge chair in the shade of a dogwood—unlike Gus, Lonny had retained a lean, youthful physique well into his golden years, and he liked showing it off—sipping a cold beer and casting sly glances in the direction of his garage, where he kept an air compressor that could have inflated the pool in seconds. Gus had used it numerous times in the past, effortlessly pumping up basketballs, bike tires, air mattresses, whatever. But he was damned if he was going to ask Lonny for help, and Lonny was damned if he was going to offer it. So Gus just kept on huffing and puffing and sweating, mentally cursing his neighbor the whole time. Finally, more than two hours after he'd begun, he turned on the hose and began filling the pool with water.

Well, Lonny was dead now, and the grandkids were coming for another visit. And that compressor was still just gathering dust in the garage, not doing a damn bit of good for anyone.

• • •

BALANCING THE pool box on his hip, Gus lifted the latch on the gate and slipped into his neighbors' yard. A misty drizzle drifted across his face as he circled around the gas grill, onto the carpet of AstroTurf Lonny had laid on top of what used to be the swimming pool.

The Simmonses' garage was detached from the house, set way back at the rear of the property. The original structure had barely been big enough to accommodate a car and a lawn mower, but Lonny had expanded it in the mid-eighties, turning the squat little box into an attractive and comfortable cottage, complete with a wood-burning stove, a stereo system, and a half bathroom.

He had conceived of the refurbished garage as a sort of clubhouse for his teenaged sons, and for a couple of years they'd actually used it that way, hanging out with their buddies, blasting heavy metal on the stereo, and turning themselves into expert Ping-Pong players. But it didn't last; the boys got driver's licenses, and their attention shifted to the world beyond their backyard. After his sons left, Lonny began spending more and more time in the garage himself, drinking beer and watching ball games, playing epic eight-ball tournaments against himself on the pool table he'd bought for a song when the Limelighter Café went belly-up. In recent years, Gus had often noticed the light on late at night and wondered what Lonny was up to. A couple of times this spring, he'd seen his former friend emerging from the garage at daybreak, looking rumpled and bewildered as he shuffled across the turf to his house.

Gus heard the branches of the oak groaning ominously in the breeze and couldn't help looking up into the dark canopy of leaves that hovered over the garage like an enormous fist. Lonny had been deeply alarmed by the symphony of creaks and squeals produced by the massive limbs; he'd insisted to Gus that the whole tree was ready to come toppling over in the next big storm, trunk and all, as if it were no longer rooted to the ground.

But the tree's still here, Gus thought. It was Lonny who had fallen, brought down by a massive heart attack during an afternoon nap in the garage. Gus would have considered it an ideal way to go—no suffering, no medical bills, no burdens placed on your loved ones—except that he'd been within listening range of Peggy's hysterical shrieks upon finding the body and had witnessed the frozen look of devastation on her usually proud face as she followed the stretcher out to the ambulance.

The garage door was locked, but that wasn't a problem—Lonny kept a spare key in a secret compartment at the bottom of a thermometer he'd mounted on the wall above his woodpile. Gus knew this because he and Martha had given Lonny the trick thermometer as a fiftieth-birthday gift, back in the days when everyone got along and the passage of time still seemed like cause for celebration.

THE FIRST thing that struck Gus as he stepped inside the garage was the smell of cigar smoke. Not a faint stale whiff of it but a concentrated gust, so strong that he expected to turn on the light and find Lonny leaning on the pool table, squinting at the cue ball through a cloud of grayish fumes from the El Producto clamped between his teeth.

But all he saw, when his groping hand finally found the switch, was a large open room, the geography of which was instantly, and deeply, familiar. The workshop along the left wall—the wrenches, screwdrivers, and hammers all neatly suspended from the pegboard. Some metal storage shelves full of paint cans, power tools, and miscellaneous crap. Beyond that, the old refrigerator where Lonny kept the beer he bought by the case at the Liquor Warehouse. The bathroom in the corner, just past the snowblower, which was covered for the season with a brown plastic tarp.

In the middle of the garage, Lonny had created a makeshift den, a few pieces of cast-off furniture—foldout sofa, easy chair, end table with a little portable TV on it—arranged in a semicircle around the Franklin stove. The game area filled the remaining space: Ping-Pong table, pool table, foosball. The whole place gave the impression of a finished basement that had doggedly burrowed its way above ground.

As his eyes adjusted to the light, it gradually occurred to Gus that the garage must have remained untouched since the day of Lonny's death. He told himself to stop gawking, to just inflate the pool and get the hell out, but he couldn't seem to make himself move. He felt a small hard ball of grief rise up from his throat, growing as it moved, then burst out of his mouth in a series of sobs that shook his whole body.

"Oh, Lonny," he heard himself cry. "Oh, Jesus."

• • •

FEELING A bit shaky, Gus sat down on the easy chair and tried to get hold of himself. He wasn't sure what it was about being here that upset him so much. He wasn't a superstitious man, didn't believe in ghosts. Nor did he have any kind of sentimental attachment to the garage itself. Except for one long-gone summer, he had rarely set foot in here for more than a few minutes at a time.

It must have been 1989, he thought. That was the year Martha got laid off from Honeywell, and things got tense between them. Lonny wasn't working, either. He was recovering from knee surgery and was bored out of his skull, puttering around the house all day.

For a short time—a month, maybe just a couple of weeks—Gus had fallen into the habit of joining Lonny in the garage after supper and staying for several hours, not heading home until he was pretty sure that Martha was asleep, or at least too tired to pick a fight.

What had he and Lonny done on those lazy summer nights? Watched the Yankees, drunk beer, knocked the balls around on the pool table. Listened to country music, which Lonny loved (he had driven an eighteen-wheeler as a young man and considered himself an honorary Southerner) and Gus usually hated. But for some reason, he didn't mind it so much in Lonny's garage, all those songs about hard luck and heartbreak, how everybody got their share.

A couple of times, though, late at night, they got to talking, man-to-man, about more serious subjects—the deaths of their parents, their worries about their kids, the everyday indignities of walking around in an aging body, what their lives added up to more than halfway down the road.

And they talked about their marriages, too, something they had never done before. Lonny complained bitterly about Peggy—how she'd let herself go and lost her sense of fun, how critical she'd become of everyone they knew, as if she'd somehow been promoted to a higher station of life. On top of everything else, their sex life had gone down the tubes. She practically made him beg for it; he was lucky if they had relations once a week.

"I don't know what happened," he confessed. "She used to love it, used to put these little notes in my lunch box."

The notes weren't dirty, Lonny explained. *I can't wait for bedtime,* she'd write, or *You are entitled to a free gift. Details at eleven.* Just cute little things like that. But man, they sure got him going.

"Now I'm lucky if I get a sandwich," he said, grimly scrutinizing his cigar. Gus must have been thrown off by Lonny's candor; he must have felt obligated to confide a secret of his own. Or maybe he just needed to unburden himself. Whatever the reason, once he got started on the subject of Martha, it all came tumbling out. Her frustration with him, with the fact that, intelligent as he was, he was never going to amount to anything more than shipping supervisor at Precision Bearings. For years she'd been bugging him about going to night school, taking some courses in computers or accounting, but he always had some excuse. And now—it was as if both of them had woken up on the same gray morning and realized the same thing—it was too late. They'd turned a corner. Their lives were their lives. Nothing was going to change.

"It wasn't so bad when she was working," Gus explained. "But now that she's home all day, she broods about it."

After years of stoical silence, Martha had turned into a fountain of complaints. She wanted to travel, drive a nice car, to own a vacation house on the water, to look forward to a fun and prosperous retirement, but it wasn't gonna happen. Because of him—his passivity, his cowardice, his willingness to settle for second best. He could see the disappointment in her face every time she looked at him, and it had done something to his head. Well, not just his head.

"Between the sheets," he told Lonny. "You know. It's not working like it's supposed to."

"Ouch." Lonny gave a sympathetic wince. "That's a tough break."

And of course Martha held *that* against him, too. He didn't get it. She claimed to have lost respect for him as a man, but somehow still expected him to perform like one.

"At least she's still interested," Lonny pointed out.

"Lotta good it does me," muttered Gus.

All these years later, Gus wasn't quite clear why he and Lonny had stopped spending their nights together in the garage. All he remembered for sure was that Martha had gone back to work the following September—she found a secretarial position at Merck, a job she'd keep until retirement—and their marriage slowly returned to an even keel. She stopped complaining, lost interest in making him accept responsibility for her unhappiness. His "problem" had continued, but after they moved to separate bedrooms, it no longer seemed to upset her so much.

GUS HAD the compressor warming up and the deflated pool spread out on the cement floor when he suddenly became aware of a hitch in his plan, such an obvious one that he was embarrassed not to have considered it until now: if he inflated the pool in here, he'd never be able to get it out. Lonny's garage was equipped with a roll-up door wide and high enough to admit a car, but Gus hadn't seen it in its raised position for years, not since the day the pool table had been delivered. Lonny had apparently decided to treat the big door as if it were a wall, blocking it up from the inside with an impressive collection of junk. It would have taken a half hour of hard labor just to clear a path to the handle, and Gus would have to put everything back when he was finished.

No, the only practical way in and out of the garage was the regular door, maybe seven feet high by three feet across; the kiddie pool had a nine-foot diameter. After a moment's thought, he arrived at what seemed like a reasonable solution. All he needed to do was drag the pool liner directly outside the door, with the air valve facing in; that way he'd be able to inflate it from the doorway without exposing himself to the rain—it had gotten quite a bit heavier in the past few minutes—and without removing the compressor from the garage.

The plan would have worked perfectly except that the electrical cord on the compressor turned out to be too short. Gus checked all the obvious places—the drawers on the worktable, the tool chest, the storage shelves—before his gaze finally landed on a fat orange extension cord, neatly coiled, resting on the card table where Lonny kept his record player, a clunky wood-veneer Kenwood that had to be at least thirty years old. *At Folsom Prison* was on the turntable, and Gus couldn't help smiling. That was Lonny's favorite record, and it seemed like a blessing that it should have been the last music he had ever heard.

A handful of familiar, timeworn albums were stacked on the table, a rogues' gallery of men in cowboy hats. Gus flipped through the collection—Johnny Cash, Marty Robbins, Merle Haggard, George Jones, Tom T. Hall—the essential sameness of the portraits making it that much more jarring when he reached the bottom of the pile and found himself looking at a hazy, romantic photo of a woman with an elaborate fifties hairdo sniffing a spray of flowers.

Bouquet, the cover said. *The Percy Faith Strings in Stereo.*

A startled laugh escaped from Gus's mouth, followed by an odd feeling of relief, the sense of a small mystery being solved long after he'd stopped wondering about it.

SHORTLY AFTER he'd retired from Precision, Gus returned from his annual physical with a free sample of Viagra that had been urged on him by his doctor. When he sheepishly mentioned this to Martha, she surprised him with a willingness to give it a try.

"I've missed all that," she told him.

"Me, too," he said.

They tried not to make too big a deal about it, taking the plunge on Saturday night after a pleasant dinner at Applebee's and a game of Scrabble. They went upstairs and undressed in the dark, shy as newlyweds, before slipping under the covers. For a few seconds, as they pressed against each other in a tentative, slightly anxious embrace, Gus imagined that things would be better between them from now on, that they'd found a cure for what ailed them, the *real* problem lurking at the bottom of everything else.

This feeling of optimism lasted only long enough for his vision to adjust to the darkness, at which point his wife's face came slowly into focus. Her eyes were wide-open, and she was staring up at him with an expression of such profound sadness that Gus felt all the air go out of him.

"Martha," he said. "Honey?"

She started at the sound of his voice, as if she'd forgotten he was there.

"Is this okay?"

"Yeah," she muttered in an unconvincing voice. "It's fine."

"Are you sure?"

"It's fine," she repeated, in the clipped, slightly annoyed tone she would have used if a waitress had spilled a drink in her lap. "Don't worry about it."

Confused, but trying to make the best of it, Gus pressed on to the finish. Martha kissed him on the cheek—he was grateful for the kindness—then immediately turned onto her side, facing away from him. He wanted to say something, to get some reassurance about what had just happened, but he didn't know where to start, and she wasn't helping him. He lay beside her for a long time, until her breathing turned soft and regular, then got up and shuffled across the hall to his son Mark's old room, where he'd been sleeping for the past several years. He felt pretty downhearted at first, but upon reflection, he decided that they'd taken a real step forward. It was foolish to imagine that they could fix their marriage in one night. They'd probably have to work at it for a while. But at least the pill had done its job, and they were officially unstuck from their rut.

Their anniversary was coming in a few weeks; that would be a good time to try again. This time he would do it right—flowers, a nicer restaurant, and then at home, soft music and champagne. They could dance a little beforehand; that had always gotten Martha in the mood.

One step at a time.

In the morning he went down to the TV room to look for the old album she loved so much, the one they used to play sometimes when the kids were asleep. But he couldn't find it, despite the fact that all the LPs were neatly alphabetized, everything in its place. The absence of this one particular record disturbed him, as if it were a symbol of all the romance that had vanished from their marriage.

"Honey," he said at breakfast, "have you seen *Bouquet*?"

"*Bouquet*?"

"The Percy Faith record? The one with 'Tenderly' on it?"

"Not recently," she said, not even glancing up from *The Star-Ledger*. "Why?"

After a brief hesitation, he spelled out his plans for their anniversary, and how the Percy Faith record might fit into them.

"I want it to be a special night," he said. "I feel like I haven't been trying hard enough."

Martha put down the paper. There was a tenderness in her gaze that he hadn't seen for a long time. She reached across the table and took his hand.

"You know what?" she said. "I really don't think it's a good idea."

• • •

THE LONGER Gus contemplated the album cover, the more puzzled he became. There must have been some kind of reasonable explanation for how it migrated from his TV room to Lonny's garage, but for the life of him, Gus couldn't imagine what it might be.

One thing was certain: there was no way Lonny had purchased his own copy of *Bouquet*. From the beginning, he had mocked Gus's fuddy-duddy taste in "elevator music" with every bit as much disdain as Gus's own children had. No, Lonny must have borrowed the Percy Faith album at some point in the misty past, but when? And why? And even if he had—which in itself seemed pretty unlikely—why hadn't he returned it? Why was it sitting out on a table in the garage, along with a bunch of country-and-western records?

While he pondered these questions, Gus tipped the album cover, letting the record come sliding partway out of its sleeve, as if the grooved black vinyl might offer some helpful clues. But something else fell out as he did so, a Polaroid that landed faceup on the table, an image so utterly unexpected that Gus barked a harsh chuckle of amazement at the sight of it.

In the photo, Martha had been surprised in the act of clipping a pink rose from a bush in their backyard. She looked radiant, but this effect wasn't a product of youth (she appeared to be around fifty in the picture) or beauty (though she'd aged well, Martha had never been the kind of woman a stranger would have described as "pretty") but of surprise itself. Her eyes were bright with pleasure and her mouth was slightly open. Gus could almost hear her saying *Hey!* in a playfully scolding tone.

You could see the chain-link fence in front of her and

Gus's toolshed in the back, which meant that the picture had to have been taken from the Simmonses' backyard. Gus's hands trembled as he turned the photo over. What he saw on the flip side was somehow even harder to fathom than what was on front: a simple invitation in his wife's graceful Catholic-school cursive, the same handwriting he saw when she sent him to the store to buy broccoli, flank steak, Grape-Nuts, Lysol.

Gimpy, she had written. *Will you dance with me?*

He studied the photograph for a long time, absorbing the unpleasant truth in his wife's joyfully startled expression. Once again his mind was forced back fifteen years, to that tense, awkward summer when Martha had lost her job and Lonny had undergone surgery for a torn ligament. It was humiliating to think that the betrayal was already under way on those nights when Gus had bared his soul in the garage, but even more awful, in a way, to think that it wasn't, that "Gimpy" had made overtures to Martha only *after* learning of Gus's inability to perform in the bedroom.

But if that was when it started, when had it ended?

They must have broken it off at some point before the oak-tree dispute, he thought, because Martha had stood by his side through the whole ordeal. If anything, she'd seemed angrier at the Simmonses than he had. The memory of Lonny's death was still fresh in Gus's mind, and he had no recollection of Martha's reacting like a heartbroken lover. She'd been shocked and saddened by the news of their neighbor's passing, but not excessively, and no more than Gus had. They had decided, as a couple, not to attend the wake and had instead written a polite note of condolence to Peggy. It was

Gus—not Martha—who had woken up on the morning of the funeral overcome by feelings of guilt and sadness. At breakfast he told her they really should go to the cemetery to pay their respects.

"It's the least we can do," he said. "He was our friend for a long time."

"You go ahead," she told him. "I just don't feel like I'm welcome there."

Gus considered making an appearance on his own, but in the end he stayed away, haunted all day by the feeling that he was in the wrong place, doing the wrong thing. He burst into tears twice, once in the shower, and again at CVS, while waiting for a prescription to be filled. Martha, on the other hand, seemed strangely composed, as if it were a day like any other. Gus had felt almost relieved that evening, stepping into the house after his ritual two-mile walk around the high school track, to find her sobbing like a lost child at the kitchen table, a half-peeled potato in her hand. He tried to embrace her and tell her it was okay, but she asked him not to touch her.

"I'm fine," she said. "Please just leave me alone."

THE RAIN was coming down full force now, battering the garage from all sides, as if someone were spraying a fire hose against the walls and dropping bucketloads of gravel on the roof. He'd been so distracted by the Polaroid that he'd forgotten all about the kiddie pool, which was still lying outside the garage, awaiting inflation. He opened the door, startled by the force of the storm, and began hauling it in, flapping the plastic to drain the rainwater that had puddled on its surface. It seemed amazing to him now—amazing and pathetic—that all he'd wanted from this night was to fill the damn thing with air while no one was looking.

He folded the liner as carefully as if it were a flag, then laid it back in its box, thinking as he did so that what really got to him wasn't that he'd been cheated on by his wife—that could happen to anyone. What really bothered him was that he could have spent so much time on earth—he was sixty-eight years old, for God's sake—and understood almost nothing about his own life and the lives of the people he was closest to. It was as if he were still a child, a little boy sitting at the big table, listening to the grown-ups talk in their loud voices, laughing whenever they did, without having the vaguest idea of what was supposed to be so funny.

Well, at least now he knew the right questions to ask. All he had to do was go home and wait for Martha to wake up and come downstairs. He could show her the picture and demand that she tell him everything, the whole sorry history of her deception. But the thought of doing that just then—of leaving the garage and trudging back across Lonny's yard in the pouring rain to have a conversation that was going to break his heart—suddenly seemed impossible, way beyond his strength. It was close to five in the morning, and he was just too tired.

Instead of going home, he turned off the light and climbed into the sofa bed. The mattress was thin and lumpy, but it felt good to be off his feet. He didn't mind that this was the bed on which Lonny had died, the bed his wife had shared with another man. Right now, it was just a place to rest. He drew the sheet up to his chin, closed his eyes, and waited for sleep to come.

Everything would have been fine if it weren't for the oak tree
rustling and scraping overhead, groaning as though in pain. A
few times Gus thought he heard a distinct cracking sound, as
if one of the big limbs were splitting off from the trunk, about
to come crashing down through the roof. He pulled the sheet
all the way over his head and began humming to drown out
the noise. It wasn't a song, just a random succession of notes—
hum dee dum dee dee dee do—and he couldn't help wondering
if Lonny had done something similar near the end of his own
life, on those nights he'd spent in the garage. Because he was
an old man, and he was scared. Because he was alone out here,
and no one was coming to comfort him.

NINE INCHES ·········➤

ETHAN DIDN'T WANT TO GO TO THE MIDDLE SCHOOL
dance, but the vice principal twisted his arm. He said it was
like jury duty: the system only made sense if everybody stepped
up and nobody got special treatment. Besides, he added, you
might as well do it now, get it over with before the new baby
comes and things get even crazier.

Ethan saw the logic in this, but it didn't make him feel any
less guilty about leaving the house on Friday evening with the
dishes unwashed and Fiona just getting started on her nightly
meltdown—apparently her busy-toddler day wasn't complete
unless she spent an hour or two shrieking her head off before
bedtime. Donna smiled coldly at him from the couch, as if
he'd volunteered to be a chaperone out of spite, just to make
her life that much more difficult.

"Don't worry about us," she called out as he buttoned his
coat. "We'll be fine."

She had to speak in a louder-than-normal voice to make

herself heard over Fiona, who was standing in the middle of the living room in yellow Dr. Denton's, her fists balled and her face smeared with a familiar glaze of snot, tears, and unquenchable fury.

"No, Daddy!" she bellowed. "You stay home!"

"I'm sorry," Ethan said, not quite sure if he was apologizing to his wife or his child. "I tried to get out of it."

Donna scoffed, as if this were a likely story. She was usually a more understanding person, but this pregnancy wasn't bringing out the best in her. Only five months along, she had already begun groaning like a martyr every time she hoisted herself out of a chair or bent down to tie her shoe. She was also sweating a lot, and her face had taken on a permanent pink flush, as if she were embarrassed by her entire life. Ethan couldn't say he was looking forward to the next several months. Or the next several years, for that matter.

"Love you guys," he said, inching toward the door.

HIS SPIRITS lifted as he got into his car. It was a crisp March night with a faraway whiff of spring sweetening the breeze, and he couldn't help noticing what a relief it was to be out of the house, going somewhere—anywhere—in the dark on a weekend. He just wished his destination could have been a little more exciting.

When Ethan first got hired at the Daniel Webster Middle School, teachers weren't expected to babysit the kids at social functions. But that was back in a more innocent time, before the notorious Jamaican Beach Party of 2009, a high school dance that degenerated into a drunken brawl/gropefest and scandalized the entire community. Six kids were arrested for fighting, three for misdemeanor sexual assault, and two for pot; eight more were hospitalized for alcohol poisoning. Cell-phone videos of some shockingly dirty dancing made their way onto the Internet, causing severe embarrassment for several senior girls-gone-wild who had stripped down to bikinis during the festivities and become the focus of unwanted attention from a rowdy group of varsity lacrosse and hockey players. Dances were canceled for an entire year, then reinstated under a host of strict new rules, including one that required the presence of faculty chaperones, who would presumably impose the kind of professional discipline that had been lacking in the past.

Ethan thought the new rules made sense for high school, where the kids were old enough and resourceful enough to get into real trouble, but it felt like overkill to extend it to the middle school, one more burden added to a job that already didn't pay nearly enough, though he knew better than to complain to anyone who wasn't a teacher. He was sick and tired of people reminding him that he got summers off and should therefore consider himself lucky.

Yeah, he didn't have to teach in July and August, but so what? It wasn't like he got to while away eight weeks at the beach or lounge in a hammock by the lake. He didn't even get to sit home reading fat biographies of the founding fathers or take his kid to the playground. He was a thirty-two-year-old man with a master's degree in history, and he still spent his summer vacations the same way he had when he was sixteen—standing behind the counter of his father's auto parts store, ringing up wiper blades and air filters to make a little extra cash.

• • •

FOR THE second time in less than twelve hours, he parked in the faculty lot and made the familiar trudge around the side of the building to the main entrance, where a crowd of boisterous seventh- and eighth-graders had already begun to gather; there was no such thing as being fashionably late to a dance that went from seven to nine-thirty. Ethan was popular with the kids—he was, he knew, widely considered to be one of the cool teachers—and a number of them shouted out his name as he passed: *Mr. Weller! Hey, it's Mr. Weller!* Oddly gratified by the recognition, he acknowledged his fans with a quick wave as he approached the double doors, onto one of which someone had taped a single sheet of red paper, its message printed in big black letters: THIS IS HOW WE PARTY.

The main hallway was deserted, faintly ominous despite—or maybe because of—the Mylar balloons taped to classroom doorknobs and the festive hand-lettered signs posted on the walls to mark the big occasion: DREAM BIG! THE SKY'S THE LIMIT!! PREPARE TO MEET YOUR FUTURE!!! Ethan was a little puzzled by these phrases—they seemed off-message for a dance, more like motivational slogans than manifestos of fun—but he wasn't all that surprised. The kids at Daniel Webster were products of their time and place, dogged little achievers who were already taking SAT prep courses and padding their résumés for college. Apparently they were ambitious even when they danced.

As far as he knew, the other chaperones on duty were Rudy Battista and Sam Spillman, so he wasn't sure what to make of it when he spied Charlotte Murray checking her reflection in the glass of a vending machine outside the cafeteria. She turned at the sound of his footsteps, looking unusually pleased to see him. Her expression changed as he got closer, her mouth stretching into a comical grimace of despair.

"Help," she cried, flinging her arms around his neck as if he were a long-lost relative. "I'm trapped at an eighth-grade dance!"

Charlotte was an art teacher, a bit of a Bohemian, one of the more interesting women on the faculty. Ethan patted her cautiously on the upper arm, struck by how pretty her reddish-gold hair looked against the green of her sweater. There was a nice clean smell coming off her, a humid aura of shampoo and something faintly lemony.

"I'm filling in for Sam," she explained upon releasing him. "His father's back in the hospital."

Ethan nodded solemnly, trying to show the proper respect for his colleague's ailing parent. Secretly, though, he was delighted. Sam was a social black hole, the kind of guy who could buttonhole you in the teachers' lounge and kill your whole free period telling you about the problem he was having with his dishwasher. Trading him for Charlotte was a major upgrade.

"It's your lucky day," she said, as if reading his mind.

"No kidding."

They smiled at each other, but Ethan couldn't help noticing a slight awkwardness in the air. He and Charlotte had been good friends during his first year at Daniel Webster. He was single back then, always up for a movie or a drink, and she was separated from her husband. For a little while there—this was five years ago, ancient history—they seemed on the verge of maybe getting involved, but it didn't happen. She went back to Rob, he met Donna, and their lives headed off on separate tracks. These days they only saw each other at school and limited their conversation to polite small talk.

"So how are you?" she asked.

"Okay." Ethan pronounced the word with more emphasis than it usually received. He was suddenly conscious of his thinning hair, the weight he'd put on since knee surgery had ended his pickup-basketball career. He was three years younger than Charlotte, but you wouldn't have guessed it from looking at them. "You know, not bad. How about you?"

"Great," she replied, making a face that undercut the word. In the past year or so, she'd taken to wearing oval, black-framed eyeglasses that made her look like a college professor in a Van Halen video. "Nothing too exciting. How's your little girl?"

"Adorable. When she's not screaming."

Charlotte took this as a joke; Ethan didn't bother to correct her.

"And you're having another?"

"Yeah, figured we should do it now, before we get used to sleeping through the night."

She said she was happy for him, but he could see it took some effort. Kids were a sore spot in her marriage. She wanted to start a family, but her husband—he was a struggling scrap-metal sculptor, deeply devoted to his art—refused to even consider the possibility. This had been the cause of their separation, and nothing seemed to have changed since they'd gotten back together.

They were saved from this tricky subject by the arrival of Rudy Battista, barely recognizable in khakis, a brown turtleneck, and a checkered blazer, a far cry from the crinkly nylon sweatsuits he wore to teach gym every day.

"Look at you," Charlotte called out. "Got a date?"

Rudy adjusted his lapels, his face shining with health and good humor. "It's a special occasion. I believe it calls for a certain elegance."

"I wish you'd told me that an hour ago," Charlotte complained, but Ethan thought she looked just fine in her simple skirt-and-sweater combo, the black tights and ankle-high boots adding a slightly funky touch to the ensemble. He was the slacker of the group in his relaxed-fit jeans and suede Pumas. At least his shirt had buttons.

"I brought you guys a present." Rudy reached into his pocket and produced two identical strips of soft yellow measuring tape, the kind favored by tailors. He handed one to each of his colleagues. "Exactly nine inches long."

"Are you serious?" Ethan asked. The vice principal had briefed him on the Nine-Inch Rule a couple of days ago—it stipulated that students had to keep their bodies at least that far apart while dancing—but it didn't seem like the kind of thing that was meant to be taken literally. "We're actually supposed to measure?"

"Just during the slow songs," Rudy explained. "The kids think it's funny."

Charlotte shot a skeptical glance at Ethan, who shrugged and stuffed the measuring tape into his pocket. She pulled her own piece taut in front of her face and pondered it for a couple of seconds.

"If that's nine inches," she said, "someone's got some explaining to do."

...

ETHAN SPENT the first half hour of the dance manning the table outside the cafeteria, taking tickets, checking IDs, and crossing names off a master list, while a uniformed cop hulked in the doorway behind him, scrutinizing the kids for signs of drug or alcohol abuse. Lieutenant Ritchie was an older guy—he had to be pushing sixty—with a brushy white mustache and none of the mellowness you might have expected from a small-town cop coasting toward retirement. He introduced himself as a special departmental liaison to the school board, appointed to oversee security at dances and sporting events. He said the position had been created specially for him.

"One of my nieces got caught up in that Jamaican mess," he said, shaking his head as if the trauma were still fresh. "We let that thing get outta hand."

Ethan had to turn away two kids at the door, but not because they'd been partying: Carlie Channing had forgotten her ID, and Mike Gruber hadn't realized that the tickets had to be purchased in advance. Both of them begged for onetime indulgences that Ethan would have been happy to provide, but Lieutenant Ritchie made it clear that no exceptions would be permitted on his watch. He seemed to take it for granted that he was the final arbiter, and Ethan had no reason to assume otherwise. Carlie left in tears, Mike in sullen bewilderment.

"It's a good lesson for them," the Lieutenant observed. "Follow the rules, you got nothing to worry about."

Ethan nodded without enthusiasm, vaguely ashamed of himself for knuckling under so easily. Carlie returned ten minutes later with her ID, but he was haunted for the rest of the night by the thought of poor Mike wandering the empty streets, exiled from the fun on account of a technicality.

IT WAS a relief to slip into the cafeteria, where the lights were low and the music was loud. Assuming an affable, don't-mind-me expression, Ethan joined his colleagues at their observation post by the snack station. Every few songs one of them would venture out on a leisurely reconnaissance mission, but mostly they just nibbled on chips and Skittles while commenting on the action unfolding around them.

"Look at that." Rudy directed their attention to Allie Farley, a leggy seventh-grader teetering past them in high heels and an alarmingly short skirt. "That can't be legal."

Charlotte craned her neck for a better look. She was the chaperone in charge of dress-code enforcement.

"It wasn't that short when she came in. She must've hiked it up."

Allie was chasing after Ben Willis, a shaggy-haired, delicate-looking kid who was one of the alpha jocks of Daniel Webster. When she caught up, she spun him around and began lecturing him on what appeared to be a matter of extreme urgency, judging from the slightly deranged look on her face and the chopping gesture she kept making with her right hand. Similar conferences were taking place all over the cafeteria, agitated girls explaining to clueless boys the roles they'd been assigned in the evening's dramas.

For his part, Ben just stared up at her—she had at least half a foot on him—and gave an occasional awestruck nod, as if she were some supernatural being, rather than a classmate he'd known since kindergarten. Ethan sympathized; Allie had gone a little crazy with the eyeliner and lipstick, and he was having trouble connecting the fearsome young woman on the dance floor with the giggly, fresh-faced girl he taught in fourth-period social studies. She seemed to have undergone some profound, irreversible transformation.

"I wish I could've worn something like that when I was her age," Charlotte said. "I had scoliosis, and back then you had to wear this awful body brace. It looked like I was wearing a barrel."

"I didn't know that," Ethan said.

"I never told you?" Charlotte seemed surprised. Back when they were pals, they'd stayed out late drinking and talking on numerous occasions and had covered a fair amount of personal history. "Junior high was a nightmare."

"Must've been tough," Rudy said.

"Long time ago," Charlotte said with a shrug.

Allie turned away from Ben and began signaling to Amanda DiCarlo, a petite, dark-haired girl who was standing nearby. Eyes widening with horror, Amanda clapped one hand over her mouth and shook her head. Allie beckoned again, this time more emphatically, but Amanda wouldn't move. She was wearing a white lab coat with a stethoscope slung around her neck, an outfit that marked her as a member of the Social Activities Committee, the group that organized the dances. The SAC apparently insisted on picking a theme for each event—tonight's was Dress as Your Future, which at least explained the cryptic signs in the hallway—but no one seemed to know or care about the theme except the committee members themselves. In addition to the cute physician, a basketball player, a ballerina, a CEO, and a female astronaut were circulating throughout the cafeteria, looking a bit sheepish as they interacted with their uncostumed peers.

Overcome with impatience, Allie seized Amanda by the arm, forcibly tugged her over to Ben, then scampered off, leaving the newly constituted couple to fend for themselves. They barely had time to exchange blushes before "Umbrella" began to play and Amanda's shyness suddenly vanished. It was like she became another person the instant she started dancing, mature and self-assured, a pretty medical student just off work and out to have a good time. Ben hesitated a few seconds before joining her, his movements stiff and a bit clunky, eyes glued on his partner as dozens of classmates surged onto the floor, surrounding and absorbing them into a larger organism, a drifting, inward-looking mass of adolescent bodies.

Ethan wasn't sure why he found himself so riveted by the spectacle of his students dancing. Individually, most of the kids didn't look graceful or even particularly happy; they were far too anxious or self-conscious for that. Collectively, though—and this was the thing that intrigued him—they gave off an overwhelming impression of energy and joy. You could see it in their hips and shoulders, their flailing arms and goofy faces, the pleasure they took in the music and their bodies, the conviction that they occupied the absolute center of a benign universe, the certainty that there was no place else to be but right here, right now. He couldn't remember the last time he'd felt like that.

He was so busy staring that it took him a little while to notice Charlotte's arm brushing against his. She was swaying in place, her elbow knocking rhythmically against his forearm, lingering a second or two before floating away. When he turned to smile at her, she responded with a long, quizzical look. In the forgiving darkness of the cafeteria, she could've easily been mistaken for twenty-five, a young woman full of potential, a stranger to disappointment. She leaned in closer, bringing her lips to his ear.

"You okay?" she asked. "You seem a little sad."

THE TROUBLE started during a moment of deceptive calm, a lull he recognized too late as the eye of the hormonal hurricane. It was a little before nine o'clock—the home stretch—and Ethan was feeling loose and cheerful. If pressed, he might even have been willing to admit that he was enjoying himself. The kids had prevailed upon the teachers to join them for a few line dances—the Electric Slide, the Cotton-Eyed Joe, the Macarena—and he felt like he'd survived the ordeal not only with his dignity intact but with his good-guy reputation enhanced. Then he'd been invited to preside over the raffle, pulling names out of a Red Sox cap and bestowing gift certificates for pizza and frozen yogurt on winners who couldn't have been more excited if he'd been handing out iPods.

He was making his way back to the snack station when a vaguely familiar slow song began to play; Charlotte later told him it was "Chasing Cars" by Snow Patrol. He felt something stirring among the kids, a sudden sense of urgency as they scanned the room for prospective partners. At the same time, the DJ turned on his special-effects machine, a revolving sphere that shot off an array of multicolored lights, painting the cafeteria and everyone in it with a swirling psychedelic rainbow.

There must've been something hypnotic about the combination of that song and those lights, because Ethan stopped in the middle of the dance floor and let it wash over him. All around him, kids were forming couples, moving into each other's arms, and without fully realizing what he was doing, he found himself scanning the room, searching for Charlotte. It wasn't until he located her—she was wandering among the dancers, checking for compliance with the Nine-Inch Rule— that Ethan finally emerged from his trance, remembering that he had a job to do. For the first time since Rudy had given it to him, he reached into his pocket and withdrew his yellow tape.

There'd been slow dances earlier in the evening, but the kids hadn't seemed too interested. Relatively few couples had ventured onto the floor, and the ones who did had been extremely well behaved. This time, though, maybe because the night was winding down, Ethan sensed a different mood in the cafeteria. Most of the dancers still kept a safe distance, but a significant minority were inching closer, testing the limits of what was permissible, and a handful had gone into open rebellion, pressing together with moony looks on their faces and no daylight between them.

When Ethan came upon one of these pairs, he tapped both partners on the shoulder and held up the measuring tape as a helpful reminder. He was pleased to discover that Rudy was right—the kids seemed to enjoy the intervention, or at least not mind it. Some smiled guiltily, while others pretended to have made an honest mistake. In any case, no one protested or resisted.

The song must have been about halfway over by the time he spotted Amanda and Ben. They had drifted away from the herd, creating a small zone of privacy for themselves on the edge of the dance floor. Even at first glance, something seemed strange about them, almost forbidding. The other couples had at least made a show of slow-dancing, but these two were motionless, clinging to each other in perfect, almost photographic stillness. Amanda was melting against Ben, arms wrapped tight around his waist, her face crushed into his chest. His eyes were closed, his lips slightly parted; he appeared to be concentrating deeply on the smell of her hair.

Ethan knew what he was supposed to do, but the role of chaperone suddenly felt oppressive to him. They just looked so blissful, it seemed wrong even to be watching them—almost creepy—but for some reason he couldn't manage to avert his eyes, let alone move.

He wasn't sure how long he'd been staring at them before Lieutenant Ritchie appeared at his side. Ethan nodded a greeting, but the Lieutenant didn't reciprocate. After a moment, he jutted his chin at the young lovers.

"You gonna do something about that?"

"Probably not," Ethan replied. "Song's almost over."

The Lieutenant squinted at him. Bands of red, yellow, and green light flickered across his face.

"That's a clear violation. You gotta break it up."

Ethan shrugged, still hoping to run out the clock. "They're not hurting anybody."

"What are you, their lawyer?"

By this point, Rudy and Charlotte had arrived on the scene, the combined presence of all four adults creating an official air of crisis. Ethan could feel the attention of the whole dance shifting in their direction.

"What's going on?" Rudy asked. He was all business, like a paramedic who'd happened upon an accident.

Lieutenant Ritchie glared at Ben and Amanda, who remained glued together, oblivious to anything beyond themselves. Charlotte looked worried. The damn song just kept on going. Ethan knew when he was beat.

"It's okay," he assured his colleagues. "I'm on it."

LATER, IN the bar, Ethan tried to describe the look on Amanda's face right before he pried her away from Ben. The way he remembered it, her expression wasn't so much angry as uncomprehending; he'd had to call her name three times just to get her to look up. Her eyes were dull and vacant, like she'd been jolted out of a deep sleep.

"I don't think she even knew where she was," Ethan said.

"She's a sweet kid," Charlotte pointed out.

"Tell that to the Lieutenant."

"Ugh." Charlotte's mouth contracted with disgust. "I'm surprised he didn't use his pepper spray."

Lieutenant Ritchie had insisted on formally ejecting Ben and Amanda from the dance, a punishment that carried a mandatory two-day suspension and required immediate parental notification. Ben's dad had at least been polite on the phone—he apologized for his son's behavior and promised there would be consequences at home—but Amanda's mother treated the whole situation like a joke. *It was a dance,* she told Ethan, pronouncing the words slowly and clearly, as if for the benefit of an imbecile. *They were dancing at a dance.* She made him explain the Nine-Inch Rule in great detail, correctly sensing that he found it just as ridiculous as she did.

"I still remember the first time I danced like that," Ethan said. They were working on their second drink—Rudy had joined them for the first round, but left after receiving a phone call from his wife—and the bourbon was having a welcome effect on his jangled nerves. "Must've been seventh grade, with Jenny Wong. She was just a friend, a girl from down the block, but it was such an amazing feeling to have her pressed up against me like that, with all those people around. One of the highlights of my life."

"You're lucky," Charlotte said, sounding like she meant it. "When I was that age, I used to sit alone in my room and make out with my arm."

"Really?"

"It wasn't so bad." She glanced tenderly at the crook of her elbow. "I still do it sometimes. When nothing else is going on."

Ethan smiled. It felt good, being here with Charlotte. Mc-Nulty's had always been their bar of choice—they'd sat more than once at this very table—and he couldn't quite shake the feeling that the past five years had never happened, that they were right back where they'd left off. He had to make an effort not to blurt out something inappropriate, like how much he missed talking to her, how wrong it was that such a simple pleasure had vanished from his life.

"By the way," he said, "I really like your glasses."

"Thanks." Her smile was unconvincing. "I prefer contacts, but my eyes get dry."

He studied her irises—they were hazel with golden flecks—as if checking on their moisture level.

"Something wrong?" she asked.

"Not really. This is just kinda weird, isn't it?"

Charlotte looked down at the table. When she looked up, her face seemed older, or maybe just sadder.

"I don't know if you heard," she said. "Rob and I are getting divorced."

"No, I hadn't. I'm sorry."

She shrugged. "We've been thinking about it for a while. At least I have."

Ethan hesitated; the air between them seemed suddenly dense, charged with significance.

"To tell you the truth," he said, "I never understood why you went back to him."

Charlotte considered this for a moment. "I almost didn't. I was all set to leave him for good. That night I slept on your couch."

He didn't have to ask her to be more specific. She'd slept on his couch exactly once, and he remembered the occasion all too well. Her thirtieth birthday. He'd made lasagna and they'd killed a bottle of champagne. They both agreed she was too drunk to drive home.

"I waited for you all night," she told him. "You never came."

A harsh sound issued from his throat, not quite a laugh.

"I wanted to. But we had that long talk, remember? You said you still loved Rob and couldn't imagine being with anyone else."

"I was stupid." Charlotte tried to smile, but she seemed to have forgotten which muscles were involved. "I was so sure we were going to sleep together, I guess I overcompensated. Rob and I had been together since freshman year of college. I just wanted you to know what you were getting into."

"You've gotta be kidding." A bad taste flooded into Ethan's mouth, something sharp and bitter the whiskey couldn't wash away. "I was dying for you. That was the longest night of my life."

"I thought you'd abandoned me."

"But you said—"

"I was confused, Ethan. I needed you to help me."

"You went back to him two days later."

"I know." She sounded just as baffled as Ethan did. "I just couldn't bear to break his heart."

"So you broke mine instead."

Charlotte shook her head for a long time, as if taking inventory of everything that might have been different if he'd just come out of his bedroom.

"I'm the one who lost out," she reminded him. "Everything worked out fine for you."

Ethan didn't argue. This didn't seem like the time to tell her about the weeks he'd spent on his couch after she went back to her husband, the way his world seemed to shrink and darken in her absence. He didn't go on a date for almost a year, and even after he met Donna—after he convinced himself that he loved her—he never lost the sense that there was a little asterisk next to her name, a tiny reminder that she was his second choice, the best he could do under the circumstances.

Charlotte wasn't making any noise, so it took him a few seconds to realize she was crying. When she took off her glasses, her face seemed naked and vulnerable, and deeply familiar.

"I don't know about you," she said as she wiped her eyes, "but I could use another drink."

IT WAS late when he pulled into his driveway, almost one in the morning, but he wasn't tired. He wasn't drunk either, not anymore, though he'd felt pretty buzzed after his third drink, pleasantly unsteady as he made his way down the long, dim hallway to the men's room. There were ice cubes in the urinal, an odd echo of his bourbon on the rocks, and an old-school rolling cloth-towel dispenser, the kind that makes a thump when you yank.

He wasn't too surprised to find Charlotte waiting in the hallway when he stepped out of the bathroom—it was almost like he'd been expecting her. A peculiar expression was on her face, a mixture of boldness and embarrassment.

"I missed you," she said.

Kissing her just then felt perfectly normal and completely self-explanatory, the only possible course of action. There was no hesitation, no self-consciousness, just one mouth finding another. He ran his fingers through her hair, slid his palm down the length of her back, then lower, tracing the gentle curve of her ass. She liked it, he could tell. He spread his fingers wide, cupping and squeezing the soft flesh.

Voices made them pull apart, two young women on the way to the ladies' room.

"Excuse me," one of them said, turning sideways to slip by.

"Don't mind us," chuckled the other.

It was no big deal, just a brief, good-natured interruption, but for some reason they never recovered from it. When they started kissing again, it felt forced and awkward, like they were trying too hard. Charlotte pulled away after only a few seconds.

"Oh, God, Ethan." Her glasses were askew, her face pink with shame. "What are we doing?"

"It's okay," he told her. "We're just having a good time."

She didn't seem to hear him. Her voice was barely audible. "I better go."

"Come on. You don't have to do that."

"I do."

She turned swiftly, heading for the exit. He followed her out to the parking lot, pleading with her to stay for one more drink, but nothing he said made any difference. She just kept muttering about his pregnant wife and child, and how sorry she was, all the while fumbling in her purse for her car keys.

"You have to forgive me," she said in a pleading voice. "I'm just going through a hard time. I'm really not the kind of person who—"

He grabbed her by the shoulders, forcing her to look at his face.

"I love you." The words just popped out of his mouth, but in that moment they felt true, undeniable. "Don't you understand that?"

She shook her head. The only thing in her eyes was pity.

"You need to go home, Ethan. Just forget this ever happened. Please?"

Then she got in her car and drove off, her face ashen, her eyes fixed straight ahead. He thought about chasing after her, but he knew it would be useless. There was nothing to do but go home, just like she told him.

Now that he was here, though, he couldn't seem to get out of the car. Maybe in a minute or two he'd unbuckle his seatbelt and head inside, into the house where his wife and child were sleeping. In the meantime he was happy enough to stay right here and think about kissing Charlotte outside the men's room and the dreamy look on Amanda's face when he showed her the measuring tape and explained that she and Ben were dancing too close, the way she just smiled and closed her eyes and let her head fall back onto her partner's chest, as if the two of them were the only people who mattered in the world, as if they had no one to answer to but themselves.

SENIOR SEASON ·········➤

IT'S PRETTY QUIET WHEN I LEAVE FOR SCHOOL, NOT A neighbor in sight except for Mrs. Scotto, who likes to get an early start on her yardwork. She's out there every morning in her bathrobe and slippers, cleaning up the leaves that fell overnight. She doesn't bother with a rake; she just bends over, plucks them off the ground one by one until she has a handful, then straightens up as best she can and drops them into a bag that says YARD WASTE. She does this all day long, from Labor Day to Thanksgiving, into December if necessary. People around here call her the Leaf Lady.

I have no idea how old she is. All I know is that she seemed ancient when we moved here twelve years ago, and she hasn't gotten any younger. She's a permanent part of the autumn scenery on Grapevine Road, a stooped, birdlike woman endlessly patrolling her front yard, her entire existence devoted to that little patch of grass. And she gets the job done, you have to give her that. It's late September now,

NINE INCHES | 111

but even in mid-November, when the whole town's blanketed with dead foliage, you can count on Mrs. Scotto's lawn to be spotless.

People around here admire her work ethic, or at least they pretend to. They all say the same thing when they walk by: *Come to my house when you're done.* Mrs. Scotto always laughs and says she charges twenty bucks an hour. Then she makes some friendly comment about the weather or asks about the person's family. She's a sweet old lady, not nearly as creepy as you might expect.

She's just lonely, my mother likes to remind me. *She lost her husband and her kids moved away.* And then my mother gives me one of her looks, like she hopes I'm filing that away for future reference.

I never paid much attention to Mrs. Scotto in the past. I was always busy and happy, and she was always just *there,* living her strange elderly life on the sidelines of my own. This fall, though, she's been getting on my nerves. I can't even look at her without feeling a little sick to my stomach, wondering how she can stand it. But she always smiles and waves in old-lady slow motion when I drive by, and I always wave right back. I'm sure it's one of the highlights of her day.

WHEN I get to school, Megan's standing in front of my locker, looking kinda nervous, and I know in my gut she's gonna break up with me. It's been coming for a while now. She was gone most of the summer, working at a camp in New Hampshire, and things have been weird between us ever since she came home, like she secretly resents me for ruining her senior year, like I'm some sad sack of shit she has to drag around while she's supposed to be having the time of her life.

I can't say I blame her for that.

What I do blame her for are those denim cutoffs, cuffed way up above what the dress code allows, and those teetery wedge sandals that make her muscly legs look longer and thinner than they really are. It just doesn't seem necessary, getting all dressed up like that to break my heart, a nice big *Fuck you* with a cherry on top.

"Okay," I tell her, tensing my stomach like I'm about to get hit. "Just get it over with."

"What are you talking about?" She smiles like I'm the old Clay, the boyfriend she deserves. "I just want to know if you're busy after school."

"Busy?" I laugh, but even that sounds pissed off. "Busy doing what?"

"That's what I thought." She runs her fingertip down the center of my chest, stopping just above my belt. "Then you won't mind a little company?"

I can feel my brain working away, trying to catch up. I didn't used to be this stupid.

"What about your practice?"

Megan's co-captain of the cheerleading squad, which is a major deal in our school. They go to regional tournaments and usually do pretty well. Most of the girls are trained gymnasts; they don't mind getting tossed in the air. They like to brag about how, statistically speaking, cheerleading is even more dangerous than football. Girls supposedly break their necks all the time.

"I can blow it off." She's still smiling, but I can see how closely she's studying me, like this is some kind of test. "I miss you."

Her legs are really smooth, except for a coin-shaped scar on her left knee, a circle of shiny pink. She fell on blacktop when she was a kid, an older boy cousin pushing her from behind when she was about to beat him in a race.

"You look hot in those shorts," I tell her.

MEGAN'S PRETTY cheerful in the car after school. She told Ms. Lambert—the cheerleading advisor—that she had a dentist appointment, and Ms. Lambert just nodded and said, *Okay, see you tomorrow.* It was that easy.

"That would never happen on the football team," I tell her. "Coach Z. used to say that dead guys were excused from practice, but only if they brought a note from the undertaker."

"That sounds like him."

"It was a joke, but it was kinda serious, too. Nobody ever missed practice, not unless they were on crutches."

Megan switches the radio from my hip-hop to KISS 108, the only station a self-respecting cheerleader will listen to. It's their tribal music, the soundtrack of high school popularity. Within seconds she's bobbing her head and singing along, doing that seated dance that girls do in cars, all hands and hair and puckered lips.

"I *love* this song," she tells me.

"You love every song."

"Nuh-uh. Just this one."

I smile back, happy to see her so happy, to know that she can still feel that way with me. And it's a beautiful day on top of it, the sky blue and the windows open, the trees turning color and those cuffed-up shorts.

"Ooh, look," Megan says, like she's pointing out a tourist attraction. "There's the Leaf Lady."

Mrs. Scotto's standing in the middle of her lawn, beneath the big oak tree that's the bane of her existence, gazing up at the branches with a worried expression. She's wearing regular clothes now—baggy jeans and a man's shirt and a floppy tan sun hat—which means she at least went inside long enough to get changed. There are days, I swear, when she's still out there in her robe and slippers when I come home in the afternoon.

"Crazy old bitch," I mutter, not quite under my breath.

Megan looks surprised. "I thought you liked her."

"It's just kinda depressing, you know? Like picking up those leaves is her only reason to live."

"She's keeping busy. It's way better than sitting in the house all day, watching the shopping channel. That's what my grandma does."

"I guess." I pull into my driveway a little faster than I should and scrape the bottom of the bumper. "Just be nice if there were some other options."

"There are," Megan reminds me. "She could be dead or in a wheelchair or not even remember her own name. When you're that age, you're lucky to be picking up leaves."

"I guess," I say again, and shut off the engine.

• • •

THE GIRLS on our cheerleading squad have a reputation for being kind of slutty, and from what I hear, some of them actually live up to it. Megan's an exception. The first time we hooked up, way back in sophomore year, she explained that she was a virgin and planned on staying that way until her wedding night.

Don't worry, she told me, right before she stuck her tongue in my ear. *There's lots of other things we can do.*

That was a bit misleading, because it turns out that she doesn't go for oral, either, so *lots of other things* really just means a steady diet of kissing and underwear humping and using our hands. Most of the time I'm okay with it. But it's been a while since we were alone like this, and I can't help hoping when we get to the bedroom that maybe today will be different, that maybe something happened over the summer at Camp Hiawatha that changed her mind about what she will and won't do. Something that had possibly caused the distance between us, but might also bring us back together.

It's just wishful thinking. Everything's like always, all the old boundaries still in place. The shorts come off, but the panties stay on. The Trojan remains in the drawer, hidden inside a pair of socks.

"You're a great guy," she whispers, slipping her lotiony hand into my boxers. "I'm really proud to be your girlfriend."

Megan's not too big on the dirty talk. Mostly she just says lots of sweet things while she jerks me off, complimenting me on the way I smell, and the stubble on my chin, and my broad shoulders. But she says this stuff in a low, breathy voice, her eyes locked on mine. Usually it gets me pretty turned on.

Today, though, I'm a little distracted. She keeps working away, murmuring about my triceps and my teeth, but for some reason, all I can think about is Mrs. Scotto, and what it must feel like to be eighty-something years old, nothing left to do but pick up dead leaves and put them in a bag. Megan must sense it because her hand stops moving and her eyes get all worried.

"Clay?" she whispers. "Is something wrong?"

"It's okay," I tell her. "Keep going."

SATURDAY'S A home game against Mansfield, and I have to force myself to go to the stadium. I like to imagine that it would be a minor local scandal if I didn't show up, that people would speculate about my absence in hushed and anxious tones: *What happened to Clay? Why isn't he here?* But really, they probably wouldn't even notice. The team's doing just fine without me.

Coach Z. asked if I wanted to stay on the roster, which would have allowed me to travel on the team bus to away games and stand on the sidelines in my Cougars jersey. He said maybe I could do something useful—hold a clipboard, keep track of offensive formations, make sure there were enough paper cups for the Gatorade—but I told him no thanks, that I'd just watch from the bleachers like everybody else.

So that's what I do. I line up with the civilians, show my ID, plunk down three bucks for a ticket. Then I make my way to the student section and take my place with the rowdy senior guys. I know a lot of them—varsity soccer and lacrosse players, mostly, hard partyers, loudmouths who like to give the refs and opposing players a hard time—and I do my best to blend in, show a little spirit. I clap my hands and join the chants, pumping my fist like I'm not dying inside every time the ball gets snapped and the bodies crash together without me.

RIGHT BEFORE halftime I go for a hot chocolate. It feels like I'm trapped in a moving spotlight, everybody in the bleachers watching like I'm some kind of tragic celebrity. *There he is,* I can almost hear them whisper. *There's Clay Murphy.* My face heats up; I can't afford to look anywhere but straight ahead.

I manage not to talk to anybody until I get on line at the refreshment stand and find myself standing right behind Mr. Makowski, my old Pop Warner coach, a big bald guy with a belly hanging over his belt like a sack of cement mix. His son Bobby's taking my place at right inside linebacker, doing a great job, really stepping up. Everybody says so. There was an article about him in the *Patch* just the other day: "Makowski Making Waves, Getting Noticed."

"Clay," he says, smiling the way you do when you visit someone in the hospital. "How you doing?"

"All right, I guess."

"Back to normal?"

"Almost. The doctor says it takes time."

There's a roar from our side of the bleachers. We both turn, a little too late to see what happened. It must have been a third-down stop because our defense is trotting off the field, the punt-return unit heading in from the sidelines. Mr. Makowski pats me gently on the shoulder, like he's afraid I might break.

"You're a tough kid," he tells me. "Keep your chin up, okay?"

PARTS OF last year are pretty foggy, but I have a clear memory of the play that messed me up. It was a third-quarter goalline stand against Bridgeton, the next-to-last game of the season. We were up 20–6, but a touchdown would've put them right back in the game. So our defense was pumped. We stopped them three times in a row from the two-yard line.

On fourth down, their tailback—a kid named Kenny Rodriguez—took the handoff, and somehow I just knew what was gonna happen. That's the beautiful part of football, those moments that unfold like a dream, a little slower and brighter than real life. You're reacting, but it doesn't really feel that way. It feels like you're predicting, or somehow even controlling the action.

Kenny launched himself off the ground, trying to dive for the touchdown, and I did the same thing at exactly the same time. People said it was an amazing hit, two human missiles colliding in midair. I remember the *crack* of our helmets, the *oof* of air leaving my body as I slammed into the turf. Then just a hum, like a refrigerator in a quiet house.

EVERYBODY ASSUMED that Kenny got the worst of it. I was just dazed; he was the one who got knocked out, the one who left the field on a stretcher with a collar around his neck. But he was back in the lineup the following week, even scored a touchdown. He shook it off, the way you're supposed to.

I wasn't so lucky. For months afterward, I had stabbing headaches and blurry vision; I couldn't concentrate on anything. I missed a lot of school, but staying home was its own kind of hell, because there was nothing I could do to pass the time that didn't make me feel worse. I couldn't read or look at a computer screen, couldn't watch TV, couldn't play video games or make out with Megan, couldn't even listen to music. A lot of the time, I didn't even feel like eating.

I'd torn my ACL freshman year and had spent the whole spring recuperating, so I understood what it meant to be patient, to give my body the time it needed to heal. But when you hurt your knee, you know exactly what's wrong and so does everybody else. You get the surgery, you get the crutches and the brace, you do the PT. You get a lot of sympathy from your buddies and attention from girls. When you hurt your brain, you don't really know what's going on, and nobody else does, either. One day you feel pretty decent, the next you're a wreck. Some headaches come and go; others stick around and get comfortable.

"It's a software problem," Dr. Koh explained. "There's a glitch in your operating system."

IT WASN'T until springtime that I finally began to feel a little better. The headaches got less frequent and less intense, and my short-term memory started to improve. I had fewer blackouts in class, and found that I could read for fifteen or twenty minutes at a stretch, do a handful of math problems, even play *Call of Duty* without feeling like I was going to throw up every time something exploded.

I started hitting the weight room after school, trying to make up for lost time. It was such a relief to be back in the flow, pumping iron with my boys, swapping insults, laughing at stupid shit. It was all good—the soreness in my arms and chest, the occasional dizzy spells, the sweaty clothes in my gym bag, the familiar BO funk of the locker room. Even the return of my athlete's foot felt like cause for celebration.

I knew my mom didn't want me to play anymore, but I wasn't too worried about that. She'd tried to make me quit after my knee operation, and I figured I'd win this battle the way I won that one, by wanting it so bad she wouldn't have the heart to say no. And I honestly didn't think I was asking for all that much. I already knew I wasn't gonna play in college—I'm too small to be a linebacker at that level, and too slow for defensive back—so all I had left was one more season. Ten games, maybe a couple more if we were lucky and made it into the playoffs.

"You're not serious," she said, when I handed her the permission slip for my senior season.

"I'm better now."

"You still get headaches."

"Just little ones."

"You're not yourself, Clay. I can tell."

"I'm fine."

"Let's see what the doctor says."

Dr. Koh didn't come right out and say I couldn't play. That's not how they do it. He just said we needed to weigh the risks and benefits and make an informed decision based on the available scientific evidence, blah, blah, blah. According to Dr. Koh, there were a lot of risks: cognitive impairment, academic problems, chronic fatigue, serious depression, paranoia, early dementia, stuff you don't even want to think about. He showed us an article about ex-NFL players living with post-concussion syndrome, guys who couldn't get out of bed in the morning, couldn't spell their names or remember the way home from the grocery store; guys who jumped out of moving vehicles or tried to fix their teeth with Krazy Glue. One guy killed himself by drinking antifreeze.

These were athletes in the prime of their lives, he told us. *But they had the brains of old men.*

"It's okay if you hate me for a while," my mother told me on the way home. "I'm pretty sure I can live with that."

I TOOK the permission slip to my father, wondering if there was anything he could do. We were sitting on his front stoop, watching my stepmother and the twins blow soap bubbles in the driveway.

"I'm not your legal guardian," he reminded me. "I couldn't sign this if I wanted to."

"I just thought maybe you could talk to Mom."

"I already did." He folded the slip and handed it back to me. "I think she made the right call."

That wasn't what I was expecting. My dad loves football just as much as I do, maybe even more. It's our thing, the glue that held us together through the divorce and all the weirdness that came after, when he moved out of town and started a whole new family without me. In all the years I played, he never missed a single game, not even the one that took place twelve hours after the twins were born. My stepmother still hasn't forgiven him for that.

"I'm sorry, Clay."

He put his arm around my shoulder and left it there. I knew he still loved me, but I couldn't help wondering what we were gonna talk about for the rest of our lives.

WHEN MEGAN finally breaks up with me, she does it by text, on a Sunday afternoon in early October: *i tried really hard but im tired of being the only one in this relationship xxoo m.* She's mad because I skipped last night's victory celebration at Amanda Gill's, which turned out to be the best party of the season so far. Something must've been in the punch: there were stupid fights and scandalous hookups; on the dance floor, girls were flashing their boobs like it was spring break. This morning, a bunch of bras were hanging from the apple tree in Amanda's front yard. I saw a picture of it on Facebook.

Megan's not the only one who missed me. My football buddies—Rick, Keyshawn, and Larry—kept calling my cell, telling me to get my ass over there. *Dude, it's unbelievable! It's gonna turn into an orgy any minute!* They actually came to my house around midnight, waking my mom with the doorbell. She wasn't as mad about it as I thought she'd be. She just came down to the bottom of the stairs, squinted at the guys for a few seconds, then went back up to bed.

"Come on, bro," Larry told me. He's the left inside line-backer, my former partner in crime. "You gotta come to this party."

"I don't feel like it."

"We miss you," Keyshawn told me. He's a wide receiver, one of our captains. "It's not as much fun without you."

I didn't know what to say. These guys have been my posse since we started playing Pop Warner in middle school. We still hang together when we can, but it's not like it used to be.

"What's the matter with you?" Rick asked. He was smiling, but in a mean-drunk kind of way. He used to be starting nose tackle, but a sophomore took his job a couple weeks ago, and it's killing him. "You're not the only guy who ever got hurt, you know."

"I guess I'm just a douchebag," I said, smiling right back.

FOR A while after she dumps me, Megan stays in pretty close touch. She texts me on a regular basis and stops by my locker at least once a day to see how I'm doing.

"I'm worried about you," she tells me, but she sounds more annoyed than concerned, like she doesn't have time for this, but is going to do it anyway, because she's a nice person. "Are you sure you're okay?"

"I'm fine."

"We should talk, Clay."

"We're talking now."

"No, I mean really talk. You want to get coffee or something?"

But I don't feel like talking. Not to Megan, not to my mother, not even to my buddies. All I want to do is hunker down and get through the rest of the fall. I'm pretty sure I'll feel a lot better when December comes and I don't have to think about football anymore.

It'll be over soon. That's what I remind myself when I can't sleep, when I'm just lying there in the dark, feeling cheated. *Just a few more games and it'll be over for everyone.*

HALLOWEEN CATCHES me by surprise. Not because I don't see it coming—pumpkins and skeletons and fake headstones are all over the place—but because it doesn't seem like anything I need to worry about.

It's just not that big a deal in our school. People are allowed to wear costumes, but hardly anyone does except Mr. Zorn, a chem teacher who puts on a Superman suit and gives a supposedly hilarious lecture about Kryptonite, and a handful of freshman and sophomore girls who can't resist the chance to dress up as sexy kittens and French maids. Also, the girl cheerleaders come to school in football uniforms.

That's the thing I forgot about.

It's pretty funny, actually. They don't just get jerseys from the varsity guys, they borrow shoulder pads and helmets, too. Everything's way too big—the shirts hanging past their knees, the pads askew, the helmets loose, with lots of pretty hair spilling out. Most of the girls are grinning behind their facemasks, like they know exactly how cute they are, but a few try to scowl and swagger like tough guys, holding their arms out like they're carrying buckets of sand, and grunting at everyone they pass.

Somehow I manage not to see Megan until fifth-period lunch. She's standing on line in the cafeteria with her best friend, Brianna, both of them nodding frantically, like they're having a contest to see which of them can agree the hardest. Brianna's not a cheerleader, so she's just wearing regular clothes.

Megan's wearing shoulder pads and a Cougars jersey, number 55, which belongs to Bobby Makowski. She must've gotten tired of the helmet because she's taken it off and placed it on top of the tray she's pushing down the line toward the steam table.

"Clay," she says, when she sees me standing there. She's got black war paint under her eyes and it gives her a fierce look, but I can see how nervous she is. "How are you?"

I can't take my eyes off her chest, those two big 5s, bright white against the blue mesh fabric. Last year she wore my jersey, number 51.

"Wow," I say. "So you're with Bobby now?"

I guess I'm hoping she'll deny it, assure me that it's just a coincidence, that she just grabbed the shirt out of a random pile. But we both know it doesn't work that way.

"I'm sorry," she says, after exchanging an *Oh, shit* look with Brianna. "I wanted to tell you."

"There's a lotta guys on the team. It didn't have to be Bobby."

"It just happened," she explains. "I didn't do it to hurt you."

"Are you gonna fuck him?" It's a stupid thing to ask, but I can't help myself.

She squints at me in disbelief. "Don't be an asshole, Clay. It's not like you."

By now, the whole line's stopped and everybody's watching us like we're a TV show. There's space in front of Megan, but she doesn't move, not even when Brianna touches her on the shoulder, trying to nudge her forward.

I don't know what else to do, so I grab Bobby's helmet off the tray. There are paint smears all over the surface, little smudges of green and red and black, the residue of a season's worth of combat. My old helmet looked a lot like this at the end of last year.

I spread the earholes and tug it over my head. It's a little tight around my temples, but otherwise a decent fit. I buckle the chinstrap, staring at her through the grid of Bobby's face-mask. It feels good to wear a helmet after all this time, like I'm suddenly myself again. Megan's shaking her head, very slowly, and I can see that she's close to tears.

"Please don't do this," she whispers.

AFTER THE clocks change, the cold gets under your clothes. Dead leaves are everywhere, like scraps torn from a huge pile of brown paper bags.

I go to school in the dark and come right home in the afternoon. Sometimes it seems like Mrs. Scotto and I are the only two people living on Grapevine Road.

The team's playing well, leading the division, on the way to their first play-off berth in years. People talk about it all the time in school.

That's great, I say. *Good for them.*

Megan and Bobby are out in the open now, walking hand in hand down the hall, looking smug and cheerful, so proud of each other. He must've pumped a ton of iron over the summer because he's huge across the chest and shoulders, way bigger than he used to be. I'm not working out and my own muscles are shrinking. It's like I have a slow leak in the top of my head, like all the air's going out of me.

I see them kissing in the parking lot one morning. She's up on her tiptoes, her hand jammed into the back pocket of his jeans.

I'm having trouble in math class again, but I really don't think it's because something's wrong with my brain.

I'm pretty sure I just suck at math.

I play Xbox until my eyes feel like marbles.

I surf a lot of porn, too, find my way to stuff I don't want to see, but can't take my eyes off. Some of the girls look so lost, like they don't know where they are or what they're doing. It's like watching zombies.

Never again, I tell myself.

Then I wash my hands and start cooking dinner. My mother's always so pleased when she comes home from work and there's water boiling on the stove.

Thank you, Clay. You're a really big help.

You're welcome, Mom.

It's a long month.

THEY HOLD the bonfire pep rally the night before Thanksgiving. It's a famous local tradition, one of the biggest social events of the year. Hundreds of people show up, including lots of college kids home for the holiday.

I leave my house around seven-thirty, walking because it's impossible to park anywhere near the blaze. It's a damp raw night, and I'm surprised to see Mrs. Scotto still on the job, dragging one of her YARD WASTE bags from the garage to the curb. It must be pretty heavy because she has to stop every few steps to catch her breath and adjust her grip. I keep my head down, pretending not to notice when she waves.

I don't want to go to the rally, but I promised my buddies I'd make an appearance. They're already pissed at me for blowing off the last two games, tired of hearing me blame it on Megan, even though it's true: I can't bear to see her shaking her pom-poms, looking so pretty, so totally focused, like she's doing the one thing she was put on earth to do, biting her knuckles when the team's down, jumping for joy when they score a touchdown. The guys don't say so, but they think I'm being a pussy, wasting my senior year.

Fuck her, they told me at lunch. *You're better off without her. Forget about Megan. There's tons of cute sophomores.*

It's the bonfire, dude. Whaddaya gonna do? Sit home and whack off all night?

I TAKE the long way around to avoid the crowd, entering the park at East Street, cutting through the woods and across the soccer fields toward the smoke and the noise. I stop at the top of the sledding hill, looking down on the fire, which they build on the infield of the softball diamond below.

It's pretty impressive, a ten-foot tower of lumber with a festive mob gathered around, watching the flames lick their way up from the bottom of the structure, a modest blaze building slowly into an inferno. There's an ambulance and a fire truck parked on the outfield grass, not far from the marching band. They're not marching, though—too dark, I guess— just standing in place as they play the Gary Glitter song, the whole crowd shouting "Hey!" in unison and punching at the air, just like at a game. I remember what it feels like to be down there by the flames, the heat and the music and the flushed faces, people you don't even know slapping you on the back, telling you to go get 'em, get out there tomorrow and kick some ass.

I can see the team from here. They're gathered in a clump near third base, a lot of big guys in dark jerseys, their numbers clearly visible in the fireglow. There's Rick and Keyshawn and Larry and the rest of them, mingling with cheerleaders and parents and random kids from school. It looks like a good time.

All I have to do is walk down the hill and join the party. I know I'm welcome: the guys have told me so a hundred times. But I can also see Bobby down there—the numbers on his jersey seem a little too bright, almost radioactive—and a dim shape beside him that must be Megan, so I just stay where I am, watching sparks fountain into the sky every time a piece of wood shifts position.

Around nine Coach Z. picks up a bullhorn and tells the world how proud he is of all his guys, the amazing courage and heart they've shown, turning the season around after a rocky start, winning seven of their last eight games, earning a well-deserved spot in the playoffs. He says he has nothing but respect for every one of these individuals, nothing but love and admiration. And then he names the whole varsity squad, starting with the sophomores and moving all the way up through the seniors. He speaks solemnly, pausing between each name, giving the crowd a chance to roar its approval. It's a long, excruciating process. And that whole time I just stand there, waiting in vain to hear my own name rising up through the darkness.

THERE'S A ten o'clock curfew on game nights, so the players make their exit around nine-thirty, when the blaze is at its peak. It hurts to watch them file out, everyone applauding as they make their way across the outfield to the parking lot and board a waiting school bus. They'll be quiet on the way back to the high school, everybody serious and focused, thinking about the job they need to do tomorrow against Woodbury. It's a good feeling, riding in the dark with your teammates, knowing the whole town's behind you.

The crowd thins out after that, but the band keeps playing and a fair number of people stick around. The bonfire usually lasts until midnight, when the Fire Department hoses down the embers. There's nothing stopping me from joining the stragglers—it's just a party now, nothing to be embarrassed about—but instead I turn around and leave the way I came.

I don't feel like going home, so I just walk for a long time, trying to clear my head, zigzagging through the residential streets on the south side of town, turning this way and that, going nowhere in particular. At least it feels that way, right up to the moment when I find myself standing on the corner of Franklin Place, the little dead-end street where the Makowskis live, and it suddenly occurs to me that I've been heading here the whole time.

I'm not surprised to see Megan's mother's Camry in Bobby's driveway, right next to Mr. Makowski's pickup. Megan used to come to my house on game nights, to keep me company after curfew. Mostly we just watched TV with my mom, but for some reason I felt especially close to her then, sitting on the couch with our fingers intertwined. It makes sense that she'd do the same thing for Bobby, but it pisses me off, too.

I stand across the street, leaning against a tree trunk, looking at the front of Bobby's house. At least the cheerleaders haven't decorated it yet. That'll happen later, after he's asleep. In the morning, he'll wake up to toilet-paper streamers on the branches and inspirational messages taped to the door, soaped on the windows of his family's cars: WE LUV U BOBBY MAK!!! BEAT WOODBURY!!! GO #55!!! I used to get so stoked, stepping outside on Saturday morning, knowing what I'd find, but always pleasantly surprised anyway.

It's ten-thirty, and I'm hoping Megan won't stick around much longer. The players are supposed to be in bed by eleven, and with me she always made it a point to leave before then, even when I begged her to stay a little longer, hoping for a little alone time after my mom went up to bed.

You need your rest, she'd tell me. *We can stay up late tomorrow.*

I'm relieved when the front door opens at ten forty-five, but it's not Megan who steps out. It's Mr. Makowski, wearing a Carhartt jacket over his pajama bottoms. He walks across the street with his hands jammed into his pockets. He looks tired and annoyed.

"What the hell are you doing?" he asks me.

"Nothing," I tell him.

"Well, you better go home. Don't make me call the police."

"I'm not hurting anyone."

"You're scaring people. Standing out here like a stalker."

That's not fair. I'm not stalking Megan. I don't want to talk to her, don't even want her to know I'm here. I just want to see her leave, to know she's not giving Bobby those few extra minutes she denied me. I'm not sure why it matters, but it does.

He waits, but I don't move. Mr. Makowski steps closer and slaps me lightly on both cheeks, the way you do when you're putting on aftershave.

"Son," he says, "you better pull yourself together."

ONE OF the things I learned last year is that it helps sometimes to project yourself into the future, to allow your mind to turn the present into the past. That's what I try to do on the way home from Bobby's.

A year from now, I tell myself, none of what I'm feeling right now will even matter. I'll be in college, living in a dorm, surrounded by people from other towns and other states, kids who don't know Megan and Bobby and don't give a crap about the Cougars or the playoffs or our big Thanksgiving rivalry with Woodbury. I'll lose some more bulk and grow my hair long; none of my new friends will even know that I used to be a football player, or that I got hurt, or that they're supposed to feel sorry for me. I'll just be the laid-back dude from down the hall, the guy everybody likes. Maybe I'll join the Ultimate Frisbee team, just for fun, get myself in shape. I see myself jumping like a hurdler, snatching the disc out of the air, flicking it way downfield before my feet even touch the ground.

Damn, they'll say. *Where'd he come from?*

This fantasy keeps me occupied all the way to Grapevine Road, right up to the moment when I turn the corner and see the wall of brown bags arranged in front of Mrs. Scotto's house. It's such a strange and upsetting sight, I can't help crossing the street for a closer look.

There are twenty-eight bags in all, lined up along the curb like headless, limbless soldiers, stretching the entire length of her property. It must've taken her all night to drag them out here. They're not light, either. I give one of them an experimental kick, and my foot barely makes a dent, as if the bag is packed with sand instead of YARD WASTE. I kick it harder the second time, and that does the trick: the toe of my sneaker breaks the skin, leaving a neat little puncture wound that gets bigger with each successive blow until the whole thing just splits open, and all the guts come spilling out, way more leaves than you can imagine from looking at it.

I pause for a second, a little freaked-out by what I've done. I don't know why I'm breathing so hard, why my face feels so hot and my heart so jumpy. I don't know why I'm still standing here, why I don't just turn around and run.

Son, I think, right before I go ballistic on the second bag, *you better pull yourself together.*

IT'S THANKSGIVING Day, and the sun's barely up, but Mrs. Scotto doesn't seem all that surprised to see me crossing the street with a rake in my hand. She's in her robe, standing in the middle of the mess I made, the disaster area that used to be her perfect lawn.

"Clay?" she says. "Did you do this?"

I take a moment to survey the damage, a season's worth of dead leaves scattered on the grass, along with the carcasses of so many broken bags. Some of the leaves are relatively fresh, bright flashes of red and yellow and orange; others are dark and slimy, fragrant with decay. They're distributed unevenly across the yard, shallow drifts and rounded clumps marking the spots where bags got overturned, once I got tired of kicking them. I can't understand why I didn't get caught, why nobody stopped me or called the police.

"I'm sorry," I tell her. "I had a really bad night."

She considers this and gives a little nod, as if she knows this is as good an explanation as she's ever going to get. Then she bends down and scoops up a handful of leaves, which she deposits in a brand-new YARD WASTE bag. There's a big stack of them on the front stoop.

"Well, I must say, you did a very thorough job." Her voice is croaky and frail, but not as angry as I expected. "I thought I was dreaming when I looked out the window."

"Don't worry," I tell her. "I'm gonna help you clean it up."

"Thank you," she said. "That would be nice."

I use the rake at first, but it doesn't feel right, so I put it down and follow Mrs. Scotto's example, stooping and snatching up the leaves with my bare hands. It's a little gross at first, but pretty soon it starts to feel normal.

"My nephew's supposed to pick me up at noon," she tells me. "I'm invited to his house for Thanksgiving dinner. But I guess I'll have to cancel."

"You go ahead," I tell her. "I can finish up on my own."

"That's okay." Mrs. Scotto's face looks younger when she smiles. "I don't like my nephew very much."

"We're going to my uncle's," I say. "But not until four o'clock."

"Isn't there a football game today?" she asks.

I nod and leave it at that. There's a game, but it doesn't have anything to do with me. The sun gets brighter and warmer as we work. My back starts to hurt, but I do my best to ignore the discomfort. I try not to think about anything but the leaves on the ground, and the slow progress we're making, me and Mrs. Scotto, getting everything back to the way it's supposed to be.

ONE-FOUR-FIVE ·········➤

IN THE TURBULENT, LONELY MONTHS THAT FOLLOWED the collapse of his marriage, Dr. Rick Sims became obsessed with the blues. It started simply enough; he was driving home from work, half-listening to one of the classic-rock stations preset into the SiriusXM unit on the Audi A4 he was pretty sure he could no longer afford, when a song snagged his attention—"Born Under a Bad Sign," not the original and far superior Albert King version that he would later come to love, but the white-bread cover by Cream. Its main riff sliced through the fog of his guilt and shame, a simple, plodding phrase that repeated itself with slight variations throughout the song:

Ba-DA-da-DA-da-DA/ba-da-da-DA-da . . .

Hey, he thought, though he hadn't picked up a guitar in years. *I bet I could play that.*

When he got home—home being the grim condo he'd rented after Jackie had evicted him from their comfortable, five-bedroom house on Finnamore Drive—he unearthed his old Yamaha acoustic from its dusty case, tuned it as best he could, and started fooling around on the low strings, trying to re-create the riff from memory. Something wasn't right, so he turned to the Web for assistance, discovering a treasure trove of helpful links: tablature sites, free lessons on YouTube, and a vast archive of live-performance videos, not just King and Clapton and Hendrix tearing it up, but a bunch of random dudes playing along with the record in their bedroom or basement. Some of these amateurs were dishearteningly good, but others could barely play a note. It was like some weird form of masochism, the way they flaunted their ineptitude, inviting the cruelty of anonymous commentators:

no offense but you suck ass
Worst. Guitar. Player. Ever.
Hey not bad for a deaf retard
Holy S**t that was AWFUL!!!
Jimi just choked on his vomit again.

Sims hated to admit it, but he took a shameful pleasure in the abuse, watching the poor saps take their punishment. *Better you than me, brother.* It was a tough world out there, and you were a fool to reveal your weakness. He wondered if maybe these losers were so desperate for human contact that insults from total strangers seemed like a step in the right direction, an upgrade from complete invisibility. In any case, it was oddly encouraging to see the whole spectrum of human talent laid out like that, to discover that, even now, rusty as he was, he was nowhere near being the worst guitar player in the world.

138 | TOM PERROTTA

It was after ten o'clock when he closed the laptop and
stowed away the Yamaha, which meant that he'd been working on that one simple song for almost three hours. His fin-
gertips hurt and his mind was buzzing, but it was a healthy
change of pace, doing something constructive instead of pin-
ing for his kids, or dozing off in front of some lame TV show,
or masturbating to obscure fetish porn that made him feel
dirty and hollow when he was finished. He ate a sandwich,
watched the news for a bit, and then went to the bathroom to
brush his teeth. Sims usually had trouble sleeping in the
condo—the mattress was too soft, and he could hear the traffic on Route 27—but that night he drifted off right away, a
weary blues riff echoing in his head like a lullaby.

JUST A few weeks earlier, Sims had been an enviable man, a
proverbial pillar of the community—husband, father, home-
owner, soccer coach, churchgoer, Audi driver, pediatrician.
And now he was something else—an outcast, an adulterer, an
absentee dad, the costar of a sordid workplace scandal. It didn't
seem to matter that he'd devoted his entire life to constructing
the first identity; it had been erased overnight, on account of a
single, inexplicable transgression. He wanted to say it wasn't
fair, but he'd stopped believing in fairness a long time ago. As
far as he could tell, it didn't matter who deserved what: people
got what they got and they pretty much had to take it.

On the morning of his life-altering fuck-up, Sims had attended the funeral of a former patient, a five-year-old chat-
terbox named Kayla Ferguson, who'd been diagnosed with
inoperable brain cancer—diffuse pontine glioma, to be

exact—at the ripe old age of three and a half. Over the course of her illness—long after he'd referred the case to a pediatric neuro-oncologist—Sims had stayed in close touch with Kayla's mother, fielding her distraught calls at all hours of the day and night. He hadn't just briefed Heather Ferguson on her daughter's increasingly dire prognosis, translating Dr. Mehta's dense (and heavily accented) medical jargon into plain English, he'd become her friend and advisor, listening patiently to marathon rants about her worthless ex-boyfriend, her heartless boss, and her implacable insurance company, offering sympathy and encouragement when he could, doing his best to keep her spirits up through the long and punishing ordeal. Toward the end, she called so frequently that Sims's wife started to get annoyed, and even a bit jealous, suggesting more than once that he might not have been quite so attentive if Heather Ferguson had been a forty-year-old in roomy mom jeans rather than a twenty-three-year-old single mother who just happened to be "cute like a cheerleader," which was how Sims had described her in a regrettable moment of candor.

"She's upset," he would say. "The least I can do is listen."

"At two in the morning?"

"Come on, Jackie. Her daughter's dying."

Her daughter's dying. That was his trump card and he played it for all it was worth. Because it was true, of course, but also because Jackie was right: Sims *was* smitten. He was having all kinds of crazy feelings for Heather Ferguson—he wanted to cook her dinner and pay her medical bills and take her to a luxury spa for a weekend of pampering. He wanted to drive to her house in the middle of the night and make love to her—slowly and tenderly, to distract her from her pain—and then hold her while she cried, and he needed to remind himself every chance he got that it was impossible, because he was a doctor and *her daughter was dying*. It hadn't been easy—one night she'd called from her bathtub at three in the morning, midway through her second bottle of wine—but Sims had kept his urges in check, always conducting himself in a professional and ethically responsible manner.

So his conscience was clear when he arrived at the funeral home and made his way into the viewing room, which was packed with people who must have been Heather's relatives, coworkers, and former classmates, far more of them than he'd expected, given her frequent laments about being alone in the world. Sims took a seat in the last row of folding chairs, relieved to see that the little white coffin was closed. It appeared to be floating on a bed of flowers and stuffed animals; a framed photo of Kayla was resting on the lid, taken before she got sick, a little girl smiling sweetly at the world, waiting in vain for the world to smile back. The memorial service was mercifully short, just a gut-wrenching slide show followed by a generic eulogy, a young minister gamely theorizing that Kayla was an angel now, sitting on a heavenly throne beside a God who loved her so much he couldn't bear to be apart from her for another day.

When it was over, Sims waited on line to pay his respects to the family. Heather was stationed in front of the coffin, greeting each mourner with a brave, heavily medicated smile, nodding intently at whatever the person said to her, as if she were memorizing a series of secret messages. She was sharing the place of honor with Kayla's father, a hard-partying roofer who was two years behind on his child support. Sims moved quickly past the deadbeat dad, shaking his hand and offering a few mechanical words of condolence before turning to Heather, his throat constricting with emotion. She looked lovely in her black dress, almost radiant, though her face was dazed and slack with grief.

"Oh, God," he said, opening his arms. "I am so sorry."

He stepped forward for the hug—there was no doubt that they would hug, not after everything they'd been through—but instead of accepting the embrace, she shoved him in the chest, an angry, two-handed thrust that made him grunt with surprise.

"Don't you touch me!" Her voice was shrill and indignant, trembling on the edge of hysteria. "Don't you dare fucking touch me!"

Sims was too shocked to speak. He wondered if she'd mistaken him for someone else, an old boyfriend, maybe, a jerk who'd hurt her in some unforgivable way.

It's me, he wanted to tell her. *It's Rick. Dr. Sims.*

"You *asshole!*" She shoved him again, harder than the first time, like a schoolboy starting a fight. She looked almost feral, her face contorted with rage and revulsion. "Why'd you let her die?"

"I didn't—" Sims began, but he had no idea how to finish. "We did everything we could."

"Oh, yeah." She nodded in bitter agreement. "You did a great job."

Heather turned toward the coffin, that adorable picture of Kayla, and lost her train of thought for a second or two. When she finally spoke, her voice was softer, more bewildered than angry.

"Really fucking awesome, Dr. Sims. Thanks for all your help."

"Heather, please . . ." But by then he was already being led away by an apologetic man in a dark suit, an employee of the funeral home, who escorted him to the front door and ejected him, politely, from the premises.

THAT SAME evening, Sims attended a retirement party for Irene Pollard at the Old Colonial Inn. It was an anomaly—he rarely socialized with the admin staff and wasn't all that friendly with the guest of honor, a grandmotherly receptionist whose incompetence was legendary around the Health Plan. But he was still a bit shaken by the incident at the funeral home and thought a drink or two might help wash away the bitter taste in his mouth.

The party broke up early, but Sims was detained on his way out by Eduardo Saenz, a gay physical therapist who'd helped him with a shoulder problem a couple of years earlier. Eduardo greeted him with boozy enthusiasm and invited him to share a pitcher of margaritas with some colleagues who'd relocated to a booth in the back room. Sims accepted without hesitation—he still wasn't ready to go home—and was delighted to discover that the colleagues in question were Olga Kochenko and Kelly Foley, two of his most attractive co-workers. Sims didn't know either of them very well, but they welcomed him like an old buddy, skipping right past the small talk and inviting him into their conversation.

"We were just talking about threeways," Kelly informed him from across the table. She was an athletic, short-haired blonde, a nurse practitioner from Cardiology. "There's a little difference of opinion."

"Oh, yeah?" Sims nodded sagely, as though he were an expert on the subject. "What's the problem?"

"Kelly doesn't like them," said Olga, a pharmacist whose short skirts and ridiculously high heels made her a frequent topic of lunchtime conversation among the male doctors of Sims's acquaintance. "She thinks they're tacky."

"I never used that word," Kelly protested. She had the planet Saturn tattooed on the inside of her right forearm, and a pink star outlined in black on the back of her left hand. "I'm just over it, you know? There's too much to keep track of."

"Girl, you gotta learn to multitask," Eduardo told her.

"I can walk and chew gum," Kelly assured him. "It's the other people I'm worried about. All those arms and legs flailing around. I'm sick of getting kicked in the face."

"I'll tell you what I hate," Olga volunteered. She was sitting next to Sims, wearing a low-cut peasant blouse that revealed a hint of cleavage, just enough that he felt gallant for averting his gaze. "When you never even signed up for a threeway? Like a few weeks ago, I went home with this hot girl from my Zumba class? We're in her bedroom, just getting started, and the next thing you know there's this naked body-builder dude standing in the doorway, stroking his dick and filming us with his iPhone. I'm like, *Hello? Who the fuck are you?* And she's like, *Oh, that's Benjamin. I hope you don't mind if he joins us.*"

Kelly rolled her eyes and said she'd been there, more than once. Eduardo wanted to hear a little more about Benjamin, but Olga turned her attention to Sims, sizing him up with a playful expression. She had a cute, slightly doughy face that she spiced up with dramatic eye shadow and long fake lashes.

"What about you, Doctor? What's your professional opinion?"

"About threeways?" Sims made a slow motorboat noise with his lips. "You're asking the wrong guy. I'm married with six-year-old twins. These days it's pretty much a miracle if I get a two-way."

Olga laughed and touched her glass to his. "You're funny."

Sims figured they'd move on to a different subject, but they were just getting started. Kelly said she'd had her first threesome back in high school, when she got seduced by a couple whose toddler she was babysitting, which meant that she actually got paid for it. Olga claimed that she'd once started making out with her dental hygienist right in the middle of a cleaning, and that the dentist eventually wandered in and joined the fun. Sims kept saying, *Come on, that didn't happen,* but what did he know? Just because he'd washed up on a sexual desert island, that didn't mean everybody else was stranded, too, doomed to a lifelong diet of coconuts. Some people were living it up on the party boat, enjoying the big buffet.

"You did one together, right?" Eduardo asked.

"Oh, God." Kelly hid her face in her hands. "That was a disaster."

"You were fine," Olga said. "It was totally my fault."

"She got the giggles," Kelly told Sims. "And then I got them, too, and we just couldn't go through with it. The guy got so mad."

"Who was he?" Sims wanted to know.

Kelly shrugged, like the guy was just an extra in their movie. "Some asshole we met on vacation. Really full of himself."

"It's weird," Olga observed. "I thought it would be nice, 'cause we know each other so well. But when push came to shove, it was like, *Yeah, she's my best friend, but there is no way I'm gonna eat her pussy.*"

"Your loss," Kelly said, and they all laughed.

Sims's phone buzzed, delivering yet another text from his wife asking when he planned on coming home. *Soon,* he responded for the third time, grateful for the elasticity of the word, the way it renewed its promise with each passing moment, even as the thought of actually going home grew more and more oppressive. He could picture his arrival, the humiliating interrogation at the door, the way he'd have to account for his whereabouts and grovel for forgiveness, like a teenager who'd broken curfew. It was just too *boring* to contemplate, such a soul-killing exercise, and it made him wonder if Jackie felt as trapped as he did, as if they'd been cast in a bad play they'd never even auditioned for.

EDUARDO LEFT around ten-thirty, but Sims stuck around to polish off the pitcher. Even in retrospect, he found it hard to blame himself for what happened next. He wasn't flirting with either of his new friends—not even with Olga, who was sitting so close, her knee bumping companionably against his beneath the table—nor did he possess even the remotest hope of getting laid. He was just happy to be there, killing time, postponing the inevitable return to real life. And he certainly wasn't making a sexual overture when he stood up and announced that he was off to the men's room.

"Want some company?" Olga asked.

"Excuse me?" Sims was pretty drunk by then and wasn't sure he'd heard right.

Olga held his gaze. "I asked if you wanted some company."

"In the men's room?"

"Not this again," Kelly groaned. "What is it with you?"

"I'm curious," Olga explained. "I just want to see what's it like in there."

"It's really not that great," Sims assured her.

"All right." Olga held up both hands in a gesture of surrender. "If it makes you uncomfortable . . ."

He heard the taunt in her voice, the junior high challenge to his manhood.

"I don't mind," he said. "You want to go, let's go."

"You sure? I wouldn't want to put you in an awkward position . . ."

"It's a free country," Sims told her. "You can do whatever you want."

Olga flashed a victorious grin at Kelly as she slid out of the booth. Even in heels Olga was tiny, at least six inches shorter than Sims, but he felt like a little boy as she took him by the hand and led him through the deserted restaurant. They turned down a narrow hallway alongside the kitchen and stopped in front of a door marked GENTLEMEN. Sims pushed it open and stepped inside, with Olga following close behind. To his great relief, he saw that it was empty.

"Welcome." He gestured at their humble surroundings—the side-by-side sink and urinal, the lone stall with its swinging door, the overflowing trash can, the dingy tile floor. In the eternal contest between piss and disinfectant, the smell of piss had a slight edge. "I wasn't expecting visitors."

"It's lovely," she observed. "If I had a men's room, it would look just like this."

"I'm glad you like it." Sims smiled uncertainly. "But if you don't mind, I kinda have to use the facilities."

"Go right ahead," she told him. "I'm just a fly on the wall."

He could have ducked into the stall, but the dare, as he understood it, required him to use the urinal. He was just drunk enough not to be embarrassed as he unzipped and made the necessary adjustments, turning his body at a slight angle to preserve his modesty. Once he was under way, he glanced over his shoulder and saw Olga standing against the wall beside the hand dryer, watching him with friendly, non-prurient interest. It was a strangely intimate moment, and Sims could feel himself blushing as he turned around and finished his business. Neither of them said a word as he washed and dried his hands, then followed her out of the restroom.

Kelly was gone when they returned to the table. Sims left a tip, then walked Olga out to her car, a Mini Cooper parked at the dark end of the lot. They kissed for a few seconds, and then he bent her over the hood, tugged her panties out of the way, and fucked her from behind, clutching a fistful of her dark hair to steady himself. They didn't have a condom, so he pulled out; she turned around and knelt uncomplainingly on the gravel, smiling up at him like a suitor about to pop the question.

Sims experienced a powerful moment of euphoria in the run-up to his orgasm—it was almost as if his soul had levitated from his body—but it passed too quickly and he returned to himself with a thud, as if he'd fallen from the sky. He thought suddenly of Jackie—*Oh, shit!*—and then of Heather, standing in front of her daughter's coffin. *Really fucking awesome, Dr. Sims.* When he came, it felt like a rush of sorrow, as if he were pumping molten sadness into Olga's mouth, though she later remarked that it tasted pretty good, a little sweeter than average.

SIMS REALIZED pretty quickly that the music he wanted to play required an electric guitar. Money was tight—he was paying the condo rent on top of his jumbo mortgage—so he focused on used equipment, checking Craigslist every day, making frequent visits to Rosedale Discount Music and the Guitar Center at the mall, hoping to stumble on a bargain. He came across a few decent instruments in his price range, but nothing that was anywhere near as good as the candy-apple Stratocaster he'd owned back in high school.

About a month into his search, a sympathetic clerk at the Guitar Center told him about Drogan's, this under-the-radar shop in Gifford that specialized in repairing and rebuilding vintage guitars. The owner was a legendary figure in the rock world, a former roadie who'd worked with lots of famous people.

"It's pretty funky," he said. "Definitely worth a look."

Drogan's didn't have a website, but Sims found a listing in the white pages and stopped there on his way home from work the following evening. It was an off-putting place, a low stucco building that could just as easily have housed a machine shop or a XXX video store, squatting between an ugly office complex and a tuxedo rental outlet on a godforsaken stretch of Lake Avenue. There was no signage and only one small window facing the street, nothing to identify the business or suggest that a visitor might be welcome. Sims entered through the side door, startling the guy behind the counter, a middle-aged hipster who'd just taken the first bite out of a monster burrito. He gazed at his visitor in mute apology, eyes wide and cheeks bulging.

"Jush secon," he mumbled, his mouth full of beans and guacamole.

"Take your time," Sims told him.

Still chewing, the guy put down the burrito and slid off his stool, wiping his hands on the front of his jeans. He was around Sims's age, probably early forties, big and soft in the middle, with thinning hair and Civil War muttonchops.

"Sorry, man. You caught me in flagrante. Don't get much business this time of night."

"I didn't mean to interrupt your dinner."

"No worries." The guy took a sip of bottled water, washing down his food. "I'm Mike Drogan, by the way."

"Rick Sims."

They shook hands across the counter.

"What can I do for you, Rick?"

Sims hesitated. There were musical accessories inside the display case—strings, picks, capos, tuners, straps—but no instruments in sight.

"I'm looking for a used electric guitar. Not too expensive. But maybe this isn't—"

"Don't worry, you're in the right place." Mike pointed to a gray metal door, on which the words INNER SANCTUM had been carefully stenciled in black paint. "We keep the guitars in there. It's easier to control the humidity. Why don't you take a look while I finish my dinner."

Sims glanced at the overstuffed burrito on the counter. It was standing upright, protruding from its foil wrapper like a fat banana from a shiny metal peel. A few grains of rice had spilled from the ruptured tortilla onto the glass below.

"Where's that from?"

Mike seemed pleased by the question. "You know Ernesto's? Over by the train station? They got this truck that stops by the office building next door, when the cleaning people are there. I basically live on these things."

"Looks pretty good."

"Best burrito ever." Mike tugged on a wiry sideburn, pondering Sims with a knowing expression. "You hungry? I could cut it in half."

"No, no. I'm not gonna—"

"I'm happy to share," Mike insisted. "I always stuff myself and then I regret it. You'd be doing me a favor."

Sims was tempted. He didn't have any dinner plans, figured he'd stop at Wendy's on the way home, his last resort on nights like this. Mike's burrito looked way more appetizing than an industrial chicken sandwich. But it seemed wrong, somehow, taking food from a guy he'd just met.

"That's okay. I'm gonna check out the guitars."

"Your call," Mike said with a shrug. "Just give me a shout if you need anything."

• • •

DROGAN'S HAD a limited inventory, maybe twenty guitars hanging on the walls of the Inner Sanctum, but Sims could see right away that it was an impressive collection, one instrument more valuable than the next. There were no price tags, just index cards identifying the year and model, with a concise descriptive phrase scrawled below—1957 Telecaster ("a true classic"), 1973 Deluxe Goldtop Les Paul ("Jimmy Page Favorite"), 1968 Chet Atkins Nashville ("all-original hardware"). The only one that seemed remotely in Sims's ballpark was a 1995 Epiphone SG ("reliable Korean workhorse"), with a white body and black pickguard.

Mike had told him it was okay to handle the merchandise, so he lifted the SG from its hanger and gave it a test drive. It was a lot heavier than the Fenders he'd been considering, but the action was light and fast, and the chunky neck fit nicely in his hand. He strummed the chords to "Down by the River," and finger-picked the intro to "Stairway to Heaven," which he'd learned in high school and never forgotten. He was working his way through "One Way Out," the quick, stuttering riff he hadn't quite mastered, when he noticed Mike standing in the doorway, looking faintly amused. Sims stopped playing.

"I'm not very good. I'm just getting back into it."

"Sounds okay to me," Mike said. "But you gotta plug that thing in and make some noise. It sounds really sweet through this Marshall over here."

At the other stores he'd visited, Sims had refused to play through an amp. There was always an element of performance when you did that, a sense that you were being watched and judged. The only guys brave enough to do it were the ones who could shred like Steve Vai or Eddie Van Halen, the guys who'd been practicing for years in their bedrooms.

"No thanks." Sims tried to smile, but his lips felt unnaturally tight. "I'm really not—"

"Tell you what." Mike tossed him a cable. "Let's just jam a little. Start with an E blues."

Sims's face got hot, as if there were an electrical coil implanted beneath the skin. "I don't know how."

"Sure you do." Mike took a hollow-body Gibson off the wall and plugged it into a small beige amp. "Just play a one-four-five."

Sims shook his head, a stranger in a strange land.

"It's your basic blues progression," Mike explained. "You've heard it a million times."

He started strumming some chords, and Sims recognized the changes right away, the backbone of every Chuck Berry song he'd ever heard. Just an E and an A and a B. He played along until he had it down, at which point Mike broke off for a solo, improvising some tasty licks while Sims struggled to maintain the chug-a-chug rhythm, repeating those three chords over and over, the old one-four-five. Then Mike showed Sims a pattern he could use to play his own solo, a simple five-note scale. Sims's fingers were slow and clumsy, but it didn't matter. The notes were right, and they meshed with the chords in gratifying, sometimes magical ways. He felt like he'd cracked some ancient code.

"Jesus," he said. "It's almost like I know what I'm doing."

"You got a nice feel for the music," Mike told him. "That's what counts. It's not about who plays the fastest."

He showed Sims a basic shuffle, then added some flourishes. They played a slow blues in a minor key and even took a shot at "Born Under a Bad Sign," with Mike growling the lyrics over Sims's slightly erratic accompaniment. Sims felt exhausted and exhilarated by the time they called it a night.

"I like this guitar," he said, carefully replacing the SG on its hook. "Can I ask you what it costs?"

"I'm not sure," Mike confessed. "Let me check with my uncle."

"Your uncle?"

"He's the owner. I'm just helping out."

"Don't you have a price list or something?"

"It's all in his head," Mike explained. "I'll try to talk to him tomorrow."

THE SEX with Olga was quick and dirty. It couldn't have lasted for more than a couple of minutes. When it was over, she straightened her skirt, dusted off her knees, and kissed him on the cheek.

"See you around," she told him.

On the way home, Sims didn't spend a lot of time thinking about what had happened, or what it meant, because he was pretty sure it hadn't meant a thing. It was just dumb luck, as if he'd stumbled upon a bank robbery and somehow ended up with a bag of money in his hand. He wasn't innocent, he understood that, but he wasn't exactly guilty, either, or at least not as guilty as he looked. He was mostly just concerned with avoiding a scene at home, figuring out a way to get past Jackie without telling too many lies.

As it turned out, he didn't need to tell a single one because she'd given up and gone to bed. She barely stirred when he slipped in beside her, just mumbled, *That you?* and went back to sleep. In the morning she acted like everything was fine, bustling around the kitchen in her robe, making lunch for the twins, giving him the usual rundown of her daily schedule—ten o'clock yoga, shopping at Whole Foods, and then she had to take the boys to the Rock Gym for their climbing class, the later session, which meant that she wouldn't be able to start dinner until six at the earliest, so maybe it would be better if they did some kind of takeout. It wasn't until Trevor and Jason went upstairs to get dressed that she dropped the act.

"What the hell happened last night?"

"Sorry," he muttered. "I had a little too much to drink. I should've called."

To his surprise, she didn't press for details.

"Are you hungover?"

"Nothing a few cups of coffee can't fix."

She managed a tiny smile, but he could see that it cost her something.

"Please don't do that again, Rick. It's really disrespectful. Not just to me—to the boys, too. They kept asking me when you were coming home."

"Don't worry. It won't happen again."

That was it, nothing like the third-degree he'd been dreading. He dropped the boys at school, grabbed a venti latte at Starbucks, and continued on to the Health Plan, wondering if there would be any awkwardness with Olga. It had been a

NINE INCHES | 155

long time since Sims had had drunken sex with someone he barely knew, and he had no idea what sort of morning-after protocol was currently in effect. You were probably just supposed to send a friendly text—*Thx!! That was fun!!!*—but he was old-school, so he headed straight to the Pharmacy to say hello, only to discover that he'd been let off the hook for the second time that morning.

"Olga's not in," said the assistant, a young Muslim woman in a headscarf. "She called in sick."

"I hope it's nothing serious."

"Food poisoning." The assistant smiled wryly. "Olga gets that a lot. Especially after parties."

By mid-afternoon, Sims had begun to wish he'd taken the day off himself. His head was throbbing and his mouth felt parched, no matter how much water he drank. And there was always one more kid to examine, another tongue to depress, another scrawny arm to jab with a needle. And all the while, the sound of his own droning voice.

How's fourth grade treating ya? Wearing your seatbelt? Any trouble concentrating? No, that's perfectly normal. Just a sprain. An ingrown hair. Let me take a look. Try not to scratch that, okay, champ?

He rallied toward the end of the day and was feeling a little better as he exited the building. It was a sunny afternoon in early April; a fresh, blustery wind swept across the parking lot like a promise of better things to come. Sims was tired and a little distracted—he was debating whether to pick up some flowers for Jackie—so it didn't even occur to him to be alarmed when he saw the stranger waiting by his Audi: a man, probably in his late fifties, balding and thickly built, wearing a rumpled gray suit.

"Are you Sims?" he inquired, the slightest trace of a foreign accent in his voice.

"I'm Dr. Sims. Can I help you?"

The man smiled and extended his hand. Even as he reciprocated, Sims felt the first vague inklings of trouble.

"I'm Yevgeny Kochenko," the man said, squeezing Sims's hand with more than the usual pressure. "Olga's my wife."

"What?" Sims laughed in spite of himself. He tried to extricate his hand, but Yevgeny's grip seemed to be tightening. "Olga's not married."

"You think it's okay to fuck my wife?" Yevgeny asked in a weirdly calm voice as he crushed Sims's hand in his own. "How you like it if I fuck your wife? Maybe I fuck her in the ass? How about that, Dr. Sims?"

Sims flashed back to the night before, trying to remember if Olga had been wearing a ring or had said anything to suggest that she had a husband. He was sure she hadn't—she'd seemed pretty damn single to him—but even if she had, he would have pictured a much-younger, better-looking man with a full head of hair.

"You sure you're married to Olga?" he said, but instead of answering the question, Yevgeny punched him in the stomach and then in the face, and that was just the beginning.

LUCKILY FOR Sims, there was a fair amount of activity in the parking lot. Several people witnessed the assault and started screaming; two security guards rushed out of the building

NINE INCHES | 157

and intervened before Yevgeny could inflict any irreparable damage. Sims was taken to the ER at Rosedale General, where he was treated for facial lacerations—twelve stitches under the right eye, seven more on the chin—and diagnosed with a mild concussion. The doctor kept him under observation for a couple of hours before letting him go.

Jackie didn't say much in the hospital, and she was just as quiet on the way home. She could barely look at him, didn't seem the least bit concerned about his condition or curious to know why he'd been attacked by a sixty-year-old Russian jewelry-store owner whose much-younger wife worked in the Health Plan Pharmacy. The silence was unnerving, and Sims couldn't stand it for more than a couple of minutes.

"It wasn't an affair," he said, trying to move his puffy lips as little as possible. His whole mouth hurt, even his fucking tongue, which he'd accidentally bitten at some point in the proceedings. "It was just one time. Last night at the retirement party."

"I don't care, Rick. I really don't want to know."

Sims switched the ice pack from his left cheek to his right. The Percocet was starting to wear off.

"We were drinking and she followed me into the men's room."

That got her attention.

"You had sex in the men's room?"

"No. She just stood there and watched me pee."

"Is that some kind of turn-on?"

"I don't know. We were drunk."

"So where'd you do it?"

"In the parking lot. Up against her car."

"Congratulations." She gave him a big thumbs-up. "Did you at least use a condom?"

Sims winced. "There wasn't a lot of planning."

"Terrific. Now we can both get herpes."

"I'm sorry," he said. "It was really irresponsible."

"Or maybe she'll get pregnant!" Jackie upped the volume on the fake enthusiasm. "Wouldn't that be cool? One big happy family."

"That's not gonna happen. I didn't—"

"Really?"

"No, I mean . . ." Sims knew he was talking too much, but he couldn't seem to stop. Maybe it was the medication, or maybe just the feeling that it didn't matter anymore, since he'd already been punished for his sins. "In her mouth."

Jackie made a face. That was one thing she could do without. "You're such a stud. I'm glad you enjoyed yourself."

Sims moved the ice bag to his shoulder. He couldn't remembering being punched or kicked in the shoulder and had no idea why it hurt so much.

"I swear to God," he said. "I didn't know she was married."

"But she knew you were."

"Yeah."

"Well, I hope you said nice things about me. Like how I cook your dinner and wash your underwear and take your kids everywhere they need to go."

"Jackie, please. You have to understand. I was a mess yesterday. This really fucked-up thing happened at the memorial service."

He told her about Heather Ferguson, the way she'd shoved him and cursed him in front of the coffin, in front of all those people, how he'd been kicked out of the funeral home and forbidden to go to the cemetery.

"Can you believe that? After everything I did for her. All those phone calls and hospital visits, all the time and energy I gave to that poor little girl. To get treated like I was the bad guy . . ."

Sims fell into a brooding silence. He wondered if he would ever see Heather again, how much time would have to go by before he could call and ask how she was doing. Maybe they could get together for coffee, he thought, maybe talk a little about what had happened, if she was feeling up to it. It would help to know what she'd been thinking, to have some kind of an explanation, if not the apology he deserved.

"I loved her," he said, surprised not just by the words, but by the fact that he'd blurted them out, and the terrible realization that they were true. "And she broke my heart."

Jackie didn't say anything after that, didn't even look at him. She kept her eyes straight ahead, leaning forward and squinting through the windshield as though she were driving through a blizzard. She seemed okay when they got home: she paid the babysitter, got Sims settled into bed with a fresh ice pack, and gave him another Percocet. Then she kissed him on the forehead with a little more tenderness than he might have expected.

"As soon as you're feeling a little better," she told him, "you're gonna have to find someplace else to live."

IT WAS harder than Sims anticipated to get a price quote on the SG. Mike's uncle Ace—he was the famous ex-roadie, friend of Stephen Stills and Boz Scaggs, and lots of other notables—was suffering from early-stage Alzheimer's, and he wasn't always sharp enough to talk business. Mike said it was tough to see him like that; he'd always been bigger than life, an ageless, incorrigible hippie who rode a chopper and chased younger women well into his sixties. Now Uncle Ace was fading away at the Golden Orchard Assisted Living Community, surrounded by decrepitude, losing touch with himself and his hard-rocking past. He didn't care about his guitar collection anymore; half the time he didn't even recognize his favorite nephew.

"Used to be he had good and bad days," Mike said. "But lately it's more like bad days and worse days."

Sims didn't mind the delay; it gave him a standing excuse to stop by the store on his way home and ask if there was any news. Mike always seemed to happy to see him and was always up for a little jamming.

"You're getting a lot better," he'd tell Sims. "You must be practicing."

It gradually turned into a regular thing, three or four nights a week. They'd grab a burrito from the truck, talk a little while they ate, then retire to the Inner Sanctum to play those amazing guitars through those vintage amps, as loud as they wanted. The store was pretty well soundproofed, and there were no neighbors to disturb in any case.

"Check this out," Mike would say, and he'd launch into the intro of "Hey Joe" or "Texas Flood," whatever song they'd decided to work on. "Is that sweet or what?"

Mike was a talented musician—he'd been playing in bands since he was twelve—and a patient, generous teacher. He

guided Sims through a host of classic tunes—"Mannish Boy,"
"You Shook Me," "One Bourbon, One Scotch, One Beer"—
stopping when necessary to expound on any theoretical or
technical issues that arose. The amount of new information
was overwhelming at times—the major and minor pentaton-
ics, the chord inversions, the double stops and slurs and
whole-note bends—but it was exactly what Sims needed, a
musical boot camp, an intensive, ongoing tutorial in the art
of blues guitar. He tried to formalize the arrangement a couple
of times, offering to pay the going rate for lessons, but Mike
wouldn't hear of it, though he did let Sims buy the burritos
and keep the mini-fridge stocked with beer.

When they were done, they would sit around for another
hour or two, listening to Roy Buchanan and Buddy Guy and
Hubert Sumlin, marveling at the precision and raw passion
these artists brought to the music, and that indefinable *something* that made each one unique.

"*Holy shit!*" Mike would say when something really great
happened, a blinding solo run, or a single, piercing note at the
crucial moment. He sounded incredulous, even a little pissed
off. "*Motherfucker!*"

It was usually pretty late by the time Sims left, and he
always felt a little melancholy heading out to his car, partly
because the thought of going home to the condo depressed
him, but mainly because he felt bad for Mike, who wasn't going anywhere. For the past six months, he'd been living in the
store, sleeping on a couch in the back office, showering at a
gym down the road. *Talk about the blues,* he said. He'd been
out of work for two and a half years, ever since he got laid off

from his IT job when the market imploded and everything went south.

His marriage fell apart a year later, though he insisted it had nothing to do with his employment situation. The real deal-breaker was the Chester A. Arthur facial hair he'd decided to cultivate in an attempt to cheer himself up. He thought his new sideburns-and-mustache combo looked pretty cool, but his ex-wife begged to differ. She said it creeped her out and refused to have sex with him until he got rid of it. Sims didn't say so, but he could see her point. Mike's muttonchops were bushy and reddish gray, with a disconcertingly pubic texture, and the pointy tips extended all the way to the corners of his mouth.

"What happened to the mustache?" Sims asked.

"I got rid of it," Mike replied. "As a peace offering. But that wasn't good enough for Pam."

"You really got divorced because of your sideburns?"

Mike made an ambiguous bobbing motion with his head.

"We had some other problems," he admitted.

"Did you ever go to counseling?"

"We didn't have the right insurance. But I don't think it would've helped much."

Sims was curious because he and Jackie had recently tried couples counseling themselves. Jackie kept insisting that Sims had stopped loving her because she'd gained so much weight during pregnancy and hadn't been able to lose it. In her mind, that was the key to everything—the reason why their sex life was so unrewarding, the reason why he never listened to a word she said, and the reason he'd fallen in love with Heather Ferguson, who was so much younger and thinner than she was. Sims kept trying to tell her that it wasn't the extra weight that bothered him, it was her complete lack of interest in sex, her attitude of pained resignation every time he touched her. She said she only acted like that because of the way he looked at her, the disgust that he didn't even bother to conceal.

"I can't forgive you for that," she told him. "All those years you made me feel like shit."

They gave up after three sessions when it became clear that talking about their problems just made things worse. It was a relief to throw in the towel, or at least it would've been if not for the boys, and the knowledge that his relationship with them was broken, too, that he'd never get a chance to be the kind of father he'd hoped to be.

He told Mike about their seventh birthday party, to which Jackie had grudgingly invited him. It wasn't one of those fancy parties—no magicians or ponies or cotton-candy machines—just a bunch of neighborhood kids running around the yard in goofy hats, climbing on the cedar play structure that Sims had assembled from a kit three years earlier. He tried chatting with some of the other parents, but they treated him with strained, wary politeness, as if he carried some sort of communicable disease. But at least his boys were happy to have him there. Trevor, the bigger and sweeter of the twins, kept running over to Sims and jumping into his arms, the way he had when he was a toddler. Jason, smaller and more verbally adept, kept telling Sims that he loved him, though he also kicked him in the shins a couple of times, completely out of the blue, with what felt like genuine animosity. Both boys cried when Sims said good-bye—Trevor kept begging him to stay for a sleepover—and when Sims got back to the condo, he opened a bottle of bourbon and drank himself to sleep.

"Tell me it gets better," he said. "Tell me I'm not gonna feel like crap for the rest of my life."

Mike stroked his upper lip, the bare skin where his mustache used to be. He had two kids of his own, both in high school.

"It helps to play the guitar," he said. "That's the only thing that works for me."

IN EARLY September, six months after they'd separated, Jackie invited Sims to Trastevere, the new Italian place in the center of town. He figured she wanted to talk about the divorce settlement, though as far as he knew, there wasn't a whole lot left to discuss. According to Sims's lawyer, the negotiations were substantively complete, just a few remaining i's to dot and t's to cross, nothing too momentous. The process had been surprisingly amicable; both he and Jackie had acted like responsible adults, keeping the best interests of the kids front and center, neither of them picking petty fights or making unreasonable demands. Sims had grumbled a bit about the custody arrangement—he would only get the twins on Wednesday and Saturday, and only Saturday would be an overnight—but Jackie had convinced him that the boys needed as much stability and continuity as possible during this difficult time of transition. And besides, he knew how much space they required, how much they loved kicking the soccer ball in the backyard and playing Wii sports on the big-screen TV in the basement rec room. He had no doubt that the condo would feel as cramped and depressing to them as it did to him.

Jackie was ten minutes late, and Sims almost didn't recognize her when she finally showed up. She was wearing a black-and-gray dress that he'd never seen before, very flattering, but it was more than that; it was the confidence with which she approached the table, the enigmatic smile and subdued little wave she gave him when their eyes met. He'd been aware of subtle changes in her appearance over the past few months—she'd lost weight, colored her hair, done something new with her makeup—but he hadn't registered the cumulative effect until she sat down across from him. This was a new Jackie, a far cry from the frumpy, defeated woman he'd been living with.

"Wow," he said. "You look great."

"Thanks." She studied him for a moment, her eyes narrowing with maternal concern. "You, too."

He knew she was lying. Bachelor life had been hard on him. He'd put on fifteen pounds—too many burritos, too much beer—and hadn't spent nearly enough time outdoors. His skin was pasty, and he'd grown a salt-and-pepper soul patch that Mike liked a lot, but that had earned him a lot of good-natured ribbing at the Health Plan. His colleagues called him Jazzman and Dr. Beatnik and asked if they could borrow his bongo drum.

"I gotta lose some weight," he said. "I eat too much junk."

"You should hire a personal trainer," she suggested. "That's the only thing that worked for me."

"Trainers are pretty expensive. I don't think I can afford one."

If Jackie heard the implicit criticism—after all, it was Sims's money that had paid for her newly toned physique, not to mention the haircut and the pretty dress—she chose to ignore it.

"It's worth it, Rick. Not just for your appearance, you know? Just for the way you feel about yourself. About the whole world. It's makes such a difference if you feel good about yourself."

Sims couldn't stop staring at her lips. They seemed so much fuller and more sensual than he remembered. Maybe it was the lipstick, he thought. She hadn't worn lipstick for years.

"I've been playing a lot of guitar," he said. "Getting pretty good, actually. I practice every night. It's kinda what's keeping me sane."

"That's great," she said, opening her menu. "It's good to have a hobby."

Sims hated that word—*hobby*. Music wasn't a *hobby*. It was a basic human activity, as essential as language or religion, though he didn't imagine that Jackie saw it like that. Music had never meant much to her, not even when she was young. As far as Sims knew, she'd never had a favorite band, only went to concerts when she was dragged along by school friends or guys she was dating. It had been a rift between them, the fact that he had a musical life and she didn't.

"How are the kids?" he asked. "Everything okay at school?"

"Jason's doing fine, but Trevor's struggling with the math, as usual. I think he's gonna need a tutor."

Sims nodded grimly, adding another fifty or a hundred bucks a week to his mental tally. But what could you do? If the kid needed a tutor, he needed a tutor.

"What about you?" he said. "Anything new?"

"Well . . ." She hesitated for moment. "I think I'm gonna start studying for my real estate license."

"Really?"

"I probably won't make a lot of money at first, but there's a lot of potential in the long run. Especially if the market picks up."

"Hey, that's great. I bet you'll be good at that."

The waitress came and took their orders. Sims kept staring at Jackie as she pored over the menu. She reminded him of someone, though he wasn't exactly sure of whom. But then she smiled and said she'd like the scallops, and suddenly it was clear: the new Jackie reminded him of the Jackie he'd met ten years ago, the woman he'd fallen in love with and proposed to on the Staten Island Ferry. It was like she'd gone up to the attic and taken her old self out of storage, not just the face and the body, but that glow, that fresh, lovely glow that a woman gets when she knows she's loved and desired. Sims hadn't seen that glow for a long time.

She must have been reading his mind because she smiled sadly when the waitress left and said there was something else she needed to tell him, a pretty big thing, actually: she'd been seeing someone for the past three months, a high school assistant principal named Paul Gutierrez, and they'd just gotten engaged over the weekend. She held up her left hand so he could see the diamond ring, right there where Sims's bigger diamond had once glittered.

"Paul's a sweet guy," she told him. "And the boys really like him."

"Wow." Sims kept his eyes on her finger. It was a lot easier than looking at her face. "That was quick."

"When you're our age, there's not much reason to wait."

"Wow," he said again. "How the fuck did that happen?"

• • •

SIMS TOOK the news pretty hard. It was bad enough to think about Jackie sleeping with another man, but what killed him was the idea of this Paul guy living in *his* house, raising *his* kids. It was a weird, demoralizing feeling, knowing that this stranger would be helping Jason and Trevor with their homework, dropping them off at school, picking them up from soccer practice. Paul would play catch with them in the yard and take them on beach vacations, where they'd body surf and collect shells and little pieces of colored glass, and in the evening he'd take them out for pizza and ice cream. Maybe he'd take them on a day trip to the amusement park, where he'd ride the roller coaster, screaming along with the boys, and years later they'd all think back to that vacation and remember how great it was, how much they'd felt like a real family.

Mike's ex-wife had a boyfriend of her own, so he knew exactly what Sims was going through.

"His name is *Denny*." Mike shook his head, as if the name were too much to bear. "The kids talk about him all the time. Denny this, Denny that. Denny drives a Honda Element. That's his big claim to fame."

"This guy Paul, I'm sure he's perfectly nice. But I just want to beat the crap out of him, you know? Just on principle."

Mike scowled approvingly, as if watching a mental movie of the beatdown.

"Denny's a graphic designer. But he plays rugby for fun. Who the fuck plays *rugby*?"

The only consolation for Sims was financial. He wasn't sure how much money an assistant principal made, but he figured it had to be a pretty decent amount, which meant that Jackie and the boys would be able to maintain the standard of living they were accustomed to without relying solely on Sims. And who knew? Maybe Jackie would get her real estate career off the ground one of these days. That would give him even more breathing room if he ever decided to make a career change. It was just too stressful being a pediatrician, his stomach clenching up every time he examined a sick kid, not knowing which of his patients was the next Kayla Ferguson, the one holding the unlucky ticket. He just wanted to do something else for a while, a job that didn't involve telling a mother that her child was going to die.

What he really wanted to do was start a blues band with Mike, find a drummer and a bassist, play a few local gigs, and see where it led. They'd been talking about it for a while, and Mike had been putting out feelers, checking around with some of his musician buddies to see if anyone was available. In the meantime, they'd been working hard on some songs, mostly covers, but a couple of originals, too, music by Mike, lyrics by Sims.

When they knew they were ready, they went into the Inner Sanctum, plugged in their guitars, and made a cell-phone video of "Born Under a Bad Sign," playing along with a backing track Mike had recorded on his laptop. They did six takes before they nailed it, Sims holding down the rhythm without a hitch, Mike singing with bitter conviction and adding some sizzling lead guitar. When they were finished, they bumped fists and uploaded their file to YouTube. After that, there was nothing to do but sit back, crack open a cold one, and wait for someone to notice. On the whole, Sims was proud and hopeful—he thought they'd done an excellent job with the song—but there was a faint current of dread running beneath his optimism, because good things turned to shit all the time, and you couldn't always see it coming.

THE CHOSEN GIRL   ········➤

ROSE'S FRONT WINDOW LOOKS OUT ON THE BUS STOP across the street. Despite the ferocious early March cold—the radio says it's eight degrees with the wind chill—the middle school kids have assembled as usual in their sacklike jeans and ski jackets, clapping their gloves and stamping their fancy sneakers against the frigid ground, snorting plumes of vapor as they crane their necks for a glimpse of yellow down at the far end of Sycamore. It's only seven-forty—the bus won't be here for another five minutes. Rose presses her cheek against the warmth of her coffee mug, releasing an involuntary shudder of sympathy for the Chosen girl. Five minutes can feel like forever on a morning like this, even when your parents haven't sent you out of the house without proper clothing.

The Chosen girl stands off to one side, over by the fire hydrant, her primly old-fashioned outfit—long skirt, drab woolen sweater, simple cotton kerchief—intensifying her isolation, making her seem even farther away from the other kids than she already is. There's a look of vacancy on her face, as if she's unaware that she's the only one at the bus stop not wearing a coat. Her brother and two other Chosen boys are dressed for the weather, bundled into nice bulky parkas that let them blend into the scenery at first glance, though they, too, stand apart from the others, a cluster unto themselves. As far as Rose knows—and she's the first to admit that she doesn't know much about these strangers who have become such a conspicuous and disturbing presence in her town—the Chosen just don't seem to believe in coats for the women and girls, though it's hard to imagine something like that could actually be part of their religion.

Watching the girl, Rose can't help thinking of the expensive winter jacket—her grandson's Christmas present—that's been gathering dust in her hall closet since November, a two-tone monstrosity emblazoned with the ugly logo of a team called the San Jose Sharks. It would be too big for her, of course. The girl—Rose imagines her name to be Rachel or Sarah, something plain and biblical—is such a scrawny little thing; the coat would just swallow her up, the garish mall colors mocking her sickly complexion, the dishwater pallor of her lank hair. It would be warm, though, and Rose pictures herself carrying it across the street, draped across her arms like a sleeping child, wordlessly offering it up to the half-frozen girl. Would she take it?

Would you? she silently inquires.

As if she's heard the question, the Chosen girl looks up, tugging nervously at her kerchief. Her expression darkens, but it's not anger on her face, just an adolescent petulance that makes Rose smile in spite of herself. At almost the same instant, the familiar bulk of the school bus slides into view, coughing dirty exhaust. It lurches away a few seconds later, leaving behind a forlorn vista of blacktop, sidewalk, and trampled grass. Rose remains seated in her chair by the window for a long time afterward, still staring at the spot where the girl had been, the coffee mug going cold in her hands.

MANY YEARS earlier, when her son had waited at the same bus stop, Rose had not been allowed to stare out the window like this. Instead she'd had to flatten herself against the wall, peering through the narrow crack between the blind and the window, seeing without being seen. She'd done this to humor Russell, who'd been mortified by the sight of her face pressed against the glass, her benevolent gaze trained on him as he went about his business in the world.

"Stop spying on me," he'd told her a few days into his new life as a fifth-grader. "It's embarrassing."

"I'm not spying. I'm just seeing you off."

"Well, cut it out. The kids are making fun of me."

Rose would have liked to laugh at his concerns, but she knew what a sensitive boy he was, how easily wounded. It was hard enough being smaller and smarter than the other kids; he didn't need to be ridiculed as a mama's boy on top of that. So she'd compromised, retreating behind the lowered blind, actually becoming the spy he'd accused her of being in the first place.

This arrangement worked out pretty well until the morning the boys stole Russell's hat. It seemed like a joke at first, a dopey prank. Russell was standing by himself as he often did, not bothering anyone, his face hidden beneath the bill of his brand-new Yankees cap, when Lenny Barton came tiptoeing up behind him. Lenny was an older boy, husky and boastful and unaccountably popular, despite the fact that he was repeating sixth grade and rarely washed his hair. As far as Rose knew, he and Russell had never had any trouble before.

Lenny snatched the hat quickly and cleanly. When Russell rushed at him to grab it back, Lenny began backpedaling, waving it in the air just out of the smaller boy's reach. It broke Rose's heart to see her son jumping for his precious hat like a dog being taunted with a stick. Lenny tossed the hat to another boy, who tossed it to another, causing Russell to careen madly in pursuit, always reaching his target a second too late.

Rose closed her eyes and reminded herself that it was all harmless play, but it was no use. When she opened them again, the game had gotten worse. Some girls were in on it now, and she could hear their squealing laughter rising above the mocking chatter of the boys. Russell was exhausted, stumbling and flailing, and when she saw him go down—it was hard to say if he'd fallen or been tripped—Rose had finally had enough. She was out the door and halfway across the street before she realized that she was only wearing a nightgown and slippers, but by then it was too late.

"Stop it!" she shouted, her voice sounding shrill and hysterical in her own ears. "Just stop it right now!"

The whole bus stop froze at the sight of her, a grown woman standing by the curb in a flimsy peach nightgown, her hands raised as if for a fistfight. Rose looked at the faces of her son's tormentors as they traded glances and fought off smirks. Already she knew that she'd made a terrible mistake.

Before she could say anything, the hat came fluttering out of the crowd—she hadn't seen who threw it—and landed near her feet. Rose bent down to pick it up, pressing one hand against the collar of her nightgown to conceal her breasts, which felt huge and pendulous and all but naked in the cool morning air. It wasn't until she straightened up that she dared look at Russell.

"Here's your hat," she said, slapping it against her leg a couple of times to dust it off.

He was standing about ten feet away, close enough to Lenny Barton that you might have mistaken them for friends. Rose was in her late thirties then and still considered herself an attractive woman, but something in her son's eyes made her wonder if she'd gotten old and ugly without realizing it.

"Go inside," he snapped, as if commanding a dog. It was a voice she'd never heard from him before, though she'd become quite familiar with it in later years. "Go inside and put some clothes on."

SHE FINDS the skirt in the attic, tucked away in a cardboard box. It's only calf length, and plaid to boot, but it's the longest one she owns. It still fits, more or less, just as long as she leaves it unzipped.

It's harder to find a kerchief. Rose hasn't worn one in years, though she remembers a time when they were not at all uncommon. On rainy days you'd see women all over town using them to protect their hairdos. Women had hairdos then. They wore curlers. Now even the words sound funny: *hairdos, curlers*. Rose once had beautiful hair, chestnut with auburn highlights. Pat used to love watching her brush it when they were first married. It's cut short these days, and she's stopped coloring it now that he's not around to tease her about looking like an old lady.

On the way out she examines herself in the hall mirror. The outfit looks awful, even worse than she imagined. The brown and tan of the skirt clash with the peculiar maroon of Pat's bulky pullover, and the thing on her head—it's a torn vinyl rain bonnet, decorated with a print of faded purple daisies—barely even qualifies as a kerchief.

Oh my, she thinks, laughing softly as she slips out of the mirror's grasp. *Am I really going to do this?*

The cold attacks her the instant she steps out the door, stabbing through her sweater, swarming under her skirt, doing its best to drive her back inside. She hesitates for a second or two on the stoop, mustering courage, reminding herself that it's only a five-minute walk to the supermarket.

The sidewalks are empty. Nobody around here walks anymore, not even when it's nice out. Rose leans into the heartless wind, thinking how nice it would have been to invite the girl inside for a cup of tea, to get to know her a little better.

I watch you, she would confess. *Through the windows.*

I know, the girl might reply, sniffing suspiciously at the tea. *I don't mind.*

Go ahead and drink, Rose would say. *It'll warm you up.*

We're not supposed to. It's a sin.

A sin? Rose starts to laugh, then stops herself. *I don't think it's a sin to drink something warm on a cold day.*

The girl thinks it over, then brings the cup slowly to her lips, allowing herself only the tiniest of sips. She looks up at Rose.

It's good, she says, the blankness of her face giving way to shy pleasure. *Thank you very much.*

ROSE DOESN'T know if the Chosen girl is forbidden to drink tea. The idea just popped into her head, and she's not sure if she's confusing the Chosen with some other strange religion. She's heard so many rumors since they began moving into town four or five years ago, she doesn't know what to believe: they're Mormons, they're Quakers, they're ex-hippies making it up as they go along, the men have multiple wives, the women aren't allowed to speak in public, they don't own televisions, they keep large sums of money hidden in their mattresses, and so on. All she really knows is what she's seen with her own eyes and read in the paper about their zoning dispute with the town two years ago.

The Chosen bought a house on Spring Street, in a nice residential area, and applied for a permit to turn it into a place of worship. After a lot of angry debate and letters to the editor—some of the neighbors were concerned about traffic and noise and parking problems—a compromise was finally arrived at in which the Chosen agreed to sell the property and use the proceeds to buy a house in a mixed commercial/residential zone, where they wouldn't cause so much of a disturbance. Since then a lot of the tension has died down, and the Chosen seem to have been accepted as a more or less permanent part of the community, both of it and apart from it at the same time.

Rose didn't realize how accustomed she had become to their presence until Russell's last visit, when he stopped by for a day at the tail end of a conference in New York City. Driving back from Home Depot, they pulled up at a red light in the center of town, right in front of a teenaged Chosen boy who was standing on the corner in a business suit, shouting at the top of his lungs the way they sometimes did, testifying to the passing traffic. Rose barely gave him a second thought, but Russell lowered the driver's-side window and began gesturing to the boy, asking him what was wrong, did he need any help? The boy stepped closer—he was tall and good-looking, like most of the Chosen boys (the girls, for some reason, were another story)—and bent forward until his face was almost inside their car.

"They betrayed him!" the boy was screaming. There was a note of genuine outrage in his voice, as if the betrayal had happened just a second ago, and he wanted someone to call the police. "They betrayed him!"

"What?" demanded Russell. "Who?"

"The son!" the boy wailed. "They betrayed the son!"

By the time Russell figured out what was going on, the light had changed, and some of the drivers behind them had started honking. Russell stepped on the gas, glancing in bewilderment at his rearview.

"Jesus Christ," he said. "What was that all about?"

"The Chosen," she replied, enjoying his confusion more than she would have liked to admit. "They do that sometimes."

"The Chosen?"

"You've been away too long," she told him.

• • •

ROSE TAKES a cart and starts off for the produce section, ignoring the hostile and questioning glances some of the other shoppers seem to direct at her. It's mostly old people at this time of day, and she feels suddenly depressed to find herself in their company. *I should be working,* she tells herself. *I should never have stopped.* But they had kept changing the computers around on her at the office, and then her arthritis started flaring up. On top of everything else, her boss was replaced by a younger man who talked to her like she was stupid, and one morning she simply couldn't bring herself to climb aboard the train. Now she's here, part of a small army of retirees who watch the cashiers like hawks and stand motionless in the parking lot, poring over receipts as if they're love letters from the glory days.

"Rose?"

Startled, Rose looks up from the bananas in her hand and sees an old woman peering at her with an expression halfway between confusion and concern. A dirty-faced toddler is crammed into the child seat of the woman's cart, sucking regally on a lollipop.

"Rose, honey, is that you?"

Rose has to force herself to look from the child to the grandmother, to work her way past the mask of age to the real face underneath. *Janet,* she realizes. *Janet Byrne.*

"It's me," Rose confesses.

"My God." Janet looks her up and down, smiling as if Rose has just told an unsuccessful joke. Janet leans forward, lowering her voice to a whisper. "I thought you were . . . one of them."

Rose shakes her head, overcome by a sudden wave of embarrassment. She'd like to explain herself to Janet, to tell her about the Chosen girl—*I just wanted to know how cold she was*—but it all seems crazy now, nothing she feels free to discuss at the Stop & Shop. She turns her attention back to the baby, who is gazing up at her with glassy, placid eyes.

"Isn't she precious?"

"I'm too old for this." Janet shakes her head, but Rose can see the happiness in her eyes as she reaches forward to stroke her granddaughter's cheek. "You forget how much work it is."

Rose wants to tell her that she envies her fatigue, that it's better to be tired from doing something than from doing nothing at all, but she and Janet have never been more than passing acquaintances.

"Such a pretty girl," she says instead.

"How many do you have?" Janet asks.

"Just one. Cody. He's eleven now. I don't see him enough."

"Cody." Janet makes a face. "The names they give them. This one's Selena."

"Selena." Rose wishes she'd had a little girl of her own to dress up and fawn over. Eliza they could have called her. Eliza Geraldine. They would have stayed friends, the way Rose had with her own mother. She would have kept close to home. "Such a pretty name."

"You son's in California, right?"

"Beverly Hills."

"I hear he does face-lifts."

Rose nods, though Russell's actual specialty is breasts.

"Will he give me a discount?" Janet laughs merrily, tugging back the skin on both cheeks. For a disconcerting second, her former face rises to the surface, the slyly pretty young mother Rose remembers from Little League and PTA, the chain smoker with peasant blouses and tinted glasses.

"He's coming for a visit soon." Rose wants to smile, but her mouth won't cooperate. "We're going to celebrate Christmas in April."

"That's nice," Janet replies, as her face surrenders to the forces of gravity. "That'll be nice for you."

"He's very busy," Rose adds. "His wife doesn't like the cold weather."

"You must be proud of him." Janet smiles, but it's an effort of will. Her boy, Bobby, had a drug problem and now works the stamp counter at the post office. "My son the doctor."

"I don't want to be a burden," Rose explains, her voice coming out louder than she means it to. "Come when you want, that's what I tell him. Whenever it's convenient."

The baby whimpers impatiently. Janet touches Rose lightly on the shoulder.

"We better go," she says. "You take care of yourself."

Without asking permission, Rose bends down and kisses the baby on the forehead.

"So precious," she whispers.

RUSSELL AND his family aren't coming for another month, but the blizzard on Saturday morning inspires her to put up the Christmas tree. It'll be nice to have the company, a visible symbol of the holiday to lift her spirits and keep her mind focused on the visit. And besides, it's something to do right now, something to keep her occupied through the otherwise empty hours. She doesn't know why, but Saturday is always the longest day of the week, the day she most misses Pat's company, though all he did the last few years of his life was lie on the couch and complain.

The plastic spruce is taller than she is, bottom-heavy and unwieldy, and Rose struggles to drag it down from the attic. It was Pat's idea, the artificial tree. Rose always preferred real ones, fire hazard or not. But when you celebrate Christmas in April, it's pretty much fake or nothing. At least there's no assembly required.

After getting the tree righted in the stand—another tough job—Rose makes several trips back to the attic for boxes of ornaments, tinsel, lights, and the little wooden Nativity scene she received as a wedding present from her great-aunt Margaret. She would have preferred to wait for Cody to trim the tree, but she knows from her last visit to California—most of which he spent wearing headphones and playing video games—that he's past the age of enjoying it.

The decorating goes slowly at first. Rose tries to ignore the lurking sense that something's missing, that she's performing a common household task rather than a holiday ritual, when it finally dawns on her: she forgot the music. You can't trim a tree without music.

She opens the cabinet, finds the ancient Bing Crosby album—he's looking pleased with himself on the cover, sporting a rakish little elf's hat—and sets it lovingly on the turntable. That was one thing that got Cody's attention, the fact that she owned a record player and still used it. He was as amazed as Russell had been, at about the same age, to learn that his own grandmother had killed chickens with her bare hands, snapping their necks with no more thought than he would have given to twisting off a bottle cap.

Once Bing starts crooning, everything falls into place. Suddenly it's Christmastime, a curtain of snow falling slant-wise outside the window. The individual ornaments emerge like old friends from their tissue-paper cocoons. Before long the fake tree becomes the real thing, or at least close enough to believe in. Stepping back to admire her handiwork, Rose finally admits to herself how cheated she's been feeling the past few months, how bitterly she resents her daughter-in-law for canceling the holiday at the last minute.

It's all right, she thinks. *We'll pretend it never happened.*

THEY DECIDED *to go to Hawaii instead,* Rose imagines say-ing. She'd keep her tone neutral, let the facts speak for them-selves. *Can you imagine?*

The Chosen girl would nod, eyes full of sympathy. *Did he give a reason?*

He said his wife was stressed-out. She needed a little down-time.

Stressed-out? The Chosen girl repeats the phrase as if she'd never heard it before.

She was working too hard. The real estate market is booming where they live. That's what she does—sells real estate. She used to be a nurse. That's how she met Russell.

Do you like her? The girl asks the question without gossipy intent. She seems to be trying to work something out.

Rose isn't sure how to answer. It's as if there are two El-lens, one the mousy-haired girl from Freehold who somehow snagged herself a plastic surgeon, the other a platinum-blond businesswoman who couldn't be bothered with anything that didn't involve making and spending lots of money. The last time Rose saw her, she had a new Mercedes and new breasts to go with it, plus a wardrobe of revealing clothes to call attention to the upgrade, including a bikini meant for a much younger woman.

She changed a lot, Rose would explain. *After they moved to California. They live in Beverly Hills.*

That sounds pretty, says the Chosen girl.

It is. Rose smiles. *Nothing like here. Sunny and beautiful every day of the year.*

The girl seems perplexed. *So why did they need to go to Hawaii?*

Rose had wondered the exact same thing. She'd wondered it many, many times.

You'll have to ask them, she says with a sigh. *I try not to interfere.*

WHEN THE tree is finished, she wraps presents in the cheerful glow of the blinking lights: a low-fat cookbook for Ellen, a nice travel kit and bathrobe for Russell, a bathing suit and package of socks for Cody. All that's left is the Sharks jacket, but her heart sinks as she removes it from the closet. It's a ridiculous gift, she sees that now—a warm coat in April for a boy who lives on a street lined with palm trees. She wonders if the store will let her exchange it for something that makes more sense, a baseball glove or maybe some computer games, but she needs to consult Russell before doing anything. For all she knows, her grandson already owns three baseball gloves and every computer game known to man.

She picks up the phone, punches in the numbers, then hangs up before it has a chance to ring, her heart pounding erratically. She can't understand why she's so nervous; all she wants is to ask a simple question. Can't a mother ask her son a simple question?

Rose hasn't spoken to Russell for two weeks, since the Saturday morning when she caught him on his way out to play golf. He said he'd call her back that night, but something must have come up. The time difference makes it hard for them to connect sometimes, especially with Russell's busy schedule. *I'll tell him about the snowstorm,* she thinks, *and running into Janet Byrne. I'll tell him about the tree.* She presses redial, breathing slowly and deeply, her heart beating at a more manageable rhythm.

"OH, JESUS," Russell mutters. "I said *that*? Are you sure?"

"Russell," she says weakly. For a moment, Rose wonders if she's losing her mind, if she imagined a conversation with her son the way she's been imagining conversations with the Chosen girl, but in her heart she knows it's not true. She understands the difference between being lonely and being crazy, and she remembers what he told her. "You said we'd have Christmas in April."

"My memory's a little fuzzy on that, Ma. What I do remember is you saying we should come when it's convenient, and next month really isn't convenient."

"Isn't it Cody's school vacation?"

"Yeah, but that's not the problem. It's Ellen. She's going into the hospital on the ninth."

Rose catches her breath. "The hospital? Oh my God."

"Don't worry, Ma. It's no big deal."

"Is she sick?"

"She's fine. It's an elective procedure."

"Female trouble?" Rose whispers.

"Just some contouring," Russell explains after a brief hesitation. "She hasn't felt good about her thighs for a long time."

Contouring? Rose stares dumbly at the tree across the room, the red and blue lights blinking on and off with monotonous regularity. *You stupid woman,* she thinks. *You stupid, stupid old woman.*

"Mom?" Russell says. "Are you there?"

THE TREE seems lighter as she drags it over the rug and into the hallway, though it should by rights feel a lot heavier, weighted down as it is by the metal stand and its full array of ornaments, a number of which have by now fallen from the branches and gone skittering across the floor. A small part of Rose is shocked by what she's doing—this shaky voice in her head keeps pleading with her to stop, to get hold of herself—but the rest of her just keeps tugging and shuffling toward the door, intent on getting the thing out of the house, out of her sight.

Squeezing backward through the doorway is the hardest part—she's got to prop the outer door open with her hip while bending and yanking at the same time—and she's so caught up in the logistics of this maneuver that she doesn't even remember the snow until her slipper sinks into the drift on the front stoop, and she yelps in surprise. Still, there's nothing to do but keep going, finish what she's started.

NINE INCHES | 187

She descends gingerly, holding on to the railing with both hands, testing her foothold before committing to the next step. Once she's made it down, she seizes the tree by its top branches and yanks it off the stoop in a single violent motion, scattering a spray of ornaments onto the white-blanketed lawn. After that it's easy: she drags the tree like a child's sled down the front walk and heaves it up onto a bank of curbside snow, where the garbagemen will be able to get it on Monday morning.

Her feet are cold and she's not wearing a coat, but she can't bring herself to turn around and go back inside. The snow's coming down hard, falling in clumpy flakes that cling to her eyelashes and have to be blinked away like tears.

I'm alone, she thinks, staring down at the gaudy corpse of the tree, the candy-cane ornament she got at Woolworth's, the little train she picked up at a yard sale, the gingerbread man who's been around so long he doesn't have any buttons left. Her mouth is open, her breathing fast and shallow. *No more Christmas for me.*

A stiff wind kicks up, but she barely notices. She's thinking of her mother at the end, sitting with an attendant in the TV room of the nursing home, watching a program in Spanish. She's thinking of Pat putting down his newspaper, telling her his chest feels funny. She's thinking of her last visit to California, the inhuman bulges beneath Ellen's tight blouse, the pride and tenderness with which Russell offered her up for inspection.

"Don't they look great?" he asked. "We should have done this years ago."

• • •

IT FEELS like a dream at first, the Chosen girl materializing out of the snow, emerging against the gauzy white curtain like a figure projected onto a screen, the Chosen girl and her little Chosen sister, both of them without coats. They're veering across the not-so-recently plowed street in Rose's direction, dragging what appear to be brand-new shovels, the kind with crooked handles and curved plastic scoops.

"Shovel your walk?" the little one inquires. Her voice is sharp, pushy even, with none of the timidity Rose expects from a girl in a kerchief. "Ten bucks. Twenty and we'll throw in the driveway."

Rose doesn't answer. It's the other one she's looking at, the girl she knows from the bus stop and her daydreams. She's squatting down by the tree, examining an ornament that's fallen into the snow.

"We'll do a good job," the little one promises. She's only eight or nine, too small for her grown-up shovel.

The Chosen girl rises, cupping the ornament—a red, metallic heart—in her outstretched hand, her mouth opening on a question she can't seem to ask.

"They're not coming," Rose declares, her voice breaking with emotion. "She's having an operation. An operation on her thighs."

The Chosen girl says nothing, just stares at Rose with that look of patient suffering that never seems to leave her face.

"She can't hear you," the little one explains.

Of course she can't, Rose realizes. She's suddenly aware of an immense silence in the world, a vast cosmic hush pressing down from the sky, drifting to earth in little pieces, an illusion only shattered when the Chosen girl sniffles and makes a horrible hawking sound in the back of her throat. The poor thing. She looks bedraggled, maybe a bit feverish. Her nose is runny and her kerchief's soaked with melted snow. Her lips have taken on a faint bluish undertone. But still she stands there, holding that heart in the palm of her hand. It seems brighter than it did a moment ago, newly polished.

"Don't go anywhere," Rose tells the little one. "I'll be right back."

SHE ONLY means to run in, grab the coat, and hurry back outside, but it doesn't work out that way. She's barely through the door—the warmth of her house hits her like something solid—when she steps on a glass ball, crunching it underfoot, losing her balance and falling dreamily to the floor. She's lying there, moaning softly to herself, trying to figure out if she's broken anything, when the phone begins to ring. She knows it's Russell even before she hears his voice coming through the answering machine, launching into a complicated, self-pitying apology, reminding her how busy he is and how many responsibilities he has to juggle, and how nice it would be if she could just cut him a little slack instead of trying to make him feel guilty all the time.

"I'm trying, Ma. Can you at least admit that I'm trying?"

Her cheek pressed against the nubby rug, Rose wiggles her fingers, then her toes. Everything seems to be in working order. She picks herself up from the floor, dusts off her pants, and takes a few careful steps toward the closet, where the Sharks jacket is hanging. She slips it off the hanger, pleased by its bulk, only to realize that the price tag is still attached. The scissors should be right on the floor with the tape and the wrapping paper, but they've disappeared. Rose checks the kitchen and hallway before giving up and removing the tag with her teeth. By the time she tiptoes around the broken glass and steps outside, the girls have already gone.

Rose makes her way down to the curb to look for them, but the street is empty in both directions. Even though she's standing right in front of it, she needs a second or two to register the fact that her Christmas tree is no longer lying on the ground like garbage. It just looks so natural the way it is now, standing upright in the snowbank, the remaining ornaments clinging stubbornly to its branches, that it's hard to imagine that it could ever have been otherwise.

THE STORM continues all night, but the tree is still standing on Sunday morning, its branches cupping soft mounds of powder, when Rose sets off in search of the Chosen girl. She's wearing her skirt and sweater again, but this time she cheats a little in deference to the blizzard—galoshes, a fleece jacket under the sweater, a woolen hat instead of the rain bonnet. She's got the Sharks jacket stuffed into a red handlebag from Macy's, along with her best winter gloves and a blue-and-green-plaid scarf.

The walk is longer and more treacherous than she anticipated—almost no one has shoveled yet—and she doesn't reach her destination until a few minutes after nine. She feels weak, a bit disoriented. There's nothing about the Chosen house that marks it as a place of worship. No cross, no sign, no parking lot. Just a shabby gray Colonial with cracked asphalt shingles and a boarded-up attic window tucked between the Quik-Chek and the Army Recruiting Center on a busy stretch of Grand Avenue.

Rose doesn't imagine outsiders are welcome at the service, and her determination falters. *Maybe I should stand here until it's over,* she thinks. *Give the girl the bag on her way out, tell her parents not to let her out of the house without a coat anymore.* But then she notices the freshly cleared and sanded walk leading up to the front steps, the two shovels resting against the porch railing, and it all comes back to her: the girl's blank face, her chattering teeth and chapped hands, her soggy kerchief and snow-crusted sneakers. And deaf on top of that.

You poor thing. It's a sin the way they treat you.

And now she's doing it, not even thinking, just marching up the steps, feeling strong and purposeful, reaching for the doorknob. Pulling it open. Stepping inside. The warmth and the faces. *Oh my.*

Rose has never seen anything quite like this. The floor is bare. No curtains on the windows. The Chosen are seated in folding chairs in a large, otherwise empty room, the men and boys in business suits on one side, the women and girls in kerchiefs and long skirts on the other, each one more drab-looking than the next. There are more of them than Rose realized—the room is packed, the air a bit close—and all their faces are turned in her direction, their expressions welcoming, as if they've been expecting her. A tall, bearded man rises and relieves her of the bag.

"It's for the girl," Rose whispers. "So she won't be cold."

"Thank you." The man is wiry and hungry-looking, his suit jacket a little short in the sleeves.

Rose's errand is done and she knows she should be going, but the bearded man is guiding her with one hand toward an empty chair on the women's side, as though she's an invited guest.

"Sit," he tells her.

Rose obeys. She feels suddenly exhausted, incapable of arguing or facing the cold outside. The woman beside her, whom Rose recognizes from the Stop & Shop, greets her with a quiet nod. The Chosen girl and her sister are sitting two rows ahead, a little to the right. The girl glances at Rose, her eyes crinkling with worry. She looks a lot better than she did yesterday, her hair freshly washed, her kerchief bright and dry. Rose smiles back, clenching and unclenching her hands to speed their thawing.

As if a secret signal's been given, the Chosen all turn to face forward, though there's nothing in front of them but a blank white wall. After a moment or two, a soft murmur rises in the room, a strange melodic mumbling that fills the air like background noise at a party. It doesn't grow louder, and it doesn't die out; it just keeps winding around and around on itself, never resolving, repeating the same uncertain notes of praise and lament. Rose closes her eyes and listens closely. Hard as she tries, she can't quite decide if it's a prayer or a song she's hearing, or just a lot of people muttering to themselves. All she really knows—and it comes to her as something of a surprise—is that her own lips are moving, too, her voice blending in with everyone else's, the words tumbling out of her like she's known them all her life.

THE TEST-TAKER ....➤

THE TEXT ARRIVED LATE ON FRIDAY AFTERNOON, AT the last possible minute.

Tomorrow morning, it said.

I cursed under my breath. I'd been planning on getting drunk that night, but work was work, and Kyle expected us to be available. You'd have to have a pretty good excuse for saying no, an infectious disease or a death in the immediate family. A potential hangover wasn't going to cut it.

I stopped by his house around five to find out who I was and where I was going. Kyle was a junior at MIT, but he ran his business from home, while also doing his laundry.

He was down in his basement lair, playing Call of Duty on a humongous wide-screen with two ridiculously hot sorority girls—spray tans, frosted hair, glittery Greek letters on their tank tops—flanking him on the couch, watching the video-game action like they actually gave a crap what happened. I had no idea where Kyle found these girls—they didn't look like they went to MIT—but there seemed to be a never-ending supply of them at his disposal.

"Yo, bro," he said, glancing away from the screen for a millisecond. "Nice pants."

"Thanks, man." I was rocking my bright red skinny jeans from BR; Kyle owned the exact same pair, but they looked better on him, sleeker and more natural, like they'd been designed specifically for his body.

"Ladies," he said, "this is my boy Josh. Josh, meet Emily and Elise."

The girls said, *Hi, Josh,* in these bored, superior voices. I was just a high school kid to them, a primitive life-form. They probably figured I was there to buy some weed, or maybe score a few Adderall, both of which were among the many products and services offered by Kyle, Incorporated. They had no way of knowing that, far from being a customer, I was actually a valued, highly compensated employee, one of a small group of trusted insiders.

Kyle handed the controller to Emily, the smaller and blonder of the pair.

"I'll be back in a minute," he said. "Don't fucking get me killed."

I followed him into the laundry room at the other end of the basement—it was where we always conducted our business—and waited while he emptied the dryer. It smelled good in there, fabric softener and warm clean clothes. Kyle stood up and dangled a pair of panties in front of my face like a hypnotist trying to make you sleepy. They were pink with little blue hearts.

"Elise," he said, in answer to my unspoken question. "The ladies appreciate it when you do their laundry. It makes them feel loved and respected. Gratitude is an aphrodisiac, dude—remember that when you get to college."

I told him I'd keep it in mind. That was how we rolled—Kyle gave me advice and I took it if I could or filed it away for future reference. It had been like that ever since we'd met at the Pendleton School Summer Day Camp all those years ago, when I was a fifth-grader and he was a Future Leader, the most junior of the junior counselors. On the very first day, he told me that I needed to get myself some acceptable swim trunks, because the ones I had were totally ridiculous, billowing around me like a bright green oil spill when I stepped into the water. In the years that followed, he'd contributed a steady stream of big-brotherly suggestions and helpful hints: *Dude, you need to start working out. . . . Ever think about getting yourself some contact lenses? . . . I hate to say it, bro, but your vocabulary is pitiful. . . . Don't you think it's time to start making some real money?*

"How you doing?" Kyle tossed the panties into his mesh basket and eyeballed me up and down, the way my aunts and uncles sometimes did when they hadn't seen me for a while. "Keeping outta trouble?"

"Pretty much. Just cruising until graduation."

"Senior year." He nodded with nostalgic approval, one eye partially obscured by his floppy hair. He had recently started wearing oversize hipster glasses that made his sharp, handsome features look even more delicate than usual. "I hope you're getting your dick sucked. That's what the sophomore bitches are for, right?"

I felt myself blushing and tried to will the blood away from my face. Despite my upperclassman status, I was not getting my dick sucked; as a matter of fact, I wasn't getting much of anything except a bunch of frustratingly mixed signals from Sarabeth Coen-Brunner, this artsy junior on whom I was nursing a severe unrequited crush that kept me awake at night, not that that was the sort of update I was going to share with Kyle.

"I'm doing all right," I assured him.

"That's my boy." He ruffled my hair like I was still in middle school. "You worked hard. Now it's time to get paid, am I right?"

"Absolutely."

That was it for the small talk. He stood on his tiptoes and retrieved a lumpy manila envelope from a shelf above the washing machine, otherwise occupied by a jug of detergent and a box of dryer sheets.

"Thanks for bailing me out," he said as he pressed the envelope into my hand. "Things got a little complicated this time around. I had to do some big-time juggling to make it work."

"No problem."

"Get a good night's sleep, yo." He held out his fist and I gave it a bump. "And don't forget to sharpen your pencils."

• • •

I WAITED until I got home to open the envelope. It contained a stack of crisp twenties—my usual fee of five hundred dollars—along with an admission ticket for tomorrow's test, a fake photo ID, and directions to the testing center. It was all pretty routine, except for the ID, which I couldn't stop staring at.

I'd taken the SATs seven times so far, twice for myself, and five times for Kyle's clients. Up to now, the kids I'd impersonated had all been strangers from nearby towns. Their names had meant nothing to me, and their bogus school IDs—accurate though they may have been—always struck me as cheap and phony, props in a half-assed game of make-believe.

This time, though, the ID came from my own school, Greenwood High. It looked totally official, a dead ringer for the one I carried in my backpack. It even had the same unflattering picture of me—a pudgy nerd with a pained smile and a touch of bedhead—plastered above the bar code. The only difference was the name beside the photo: *Jacob T. Harlowe*. That was the thing I couldn't stop staring at.

Jake Harlowe was in my AP psych class. He was a junior jock, a football and lacrosse star, one of those popular, good-looking kids everybody knows and likes. The Harlowes were Greenwood royalty; his older brother, Scott, had been an all-county quarterback a couple of years ago—Scott had since gone on to Amherst, where the family had some kind of crazy legacy, five generations or whatever—and Jake had stepped right into his shoes, another square-jawed scholar-athlete, humble and easygoing, varsity starter in his sophomore year.

For a couple of minutes, I thought about calling Kyle and trying to back out, maybe asking him to switch me with someone else, but I knew it was hopeless. He wouldn't have had time to make the new IDs and wouldn't have said yes even if he did. Kyle wasn't that kind of boss. And besides, I wouldn't have known what to tell him, how to articulate my misgivings about this particular assignment.

It wasn't that I was worried about getting caught. The test was being administered at a private school about a half hour away, where I didn't expect to run into anyone I knew. I'd never tested there before—Kyle tried to avoid sending us to the same place twice—and I couldn't imagine that the proctors would know Jake Harlowe or have any reason to suspect that I wasn't him. All they ever did was glance at the ID and make sure it matched the name on the admission ticket.

And it wasn't like I'd come down with a sudden attack of conscience, either. I honestly didn't mind cheating for strangers. If somebody wanted to pay me to help them get into a good college, I didn't see any problem with that. It wasn't all that different from hiring an expensive tutor, or getting a doctor to diagnose a learning disability so you could buy yourself some extra time. That was just the way system worked. If you had the money, you got special treatment.

My only problem was the client. Jake Harlowe didn't seem like the kind of kid who needed to cheat. I always figured that everything came easily to him, the grades as well as the girls and the games, and it troubled me to discover that this wasn't true. I felt like I'd been peering through his bedroom window and seen something I shouldn't have, a shameful secret I wished he'd kept to himself.

NINE INCHES | 199

• • •

WHEN KYLE hired me, I'd agreed to follow a strict code of professional conduct. It made sense: people were paying us good money to provide a service, and we owed it to them to fulfill our mission with the highest level of competence and discretion.

You will be on time, Kyle had instructed me, reading straight from the rule book. *You will have proper documentation on hand, along with an approved calculator and several sharpened Number Two pencils. You will dress appropriately and never behave in such a way as to draw unnecessary attention from the proctors or your fellow test-takers. Misconduct of any sort is punishable by fine and/or dismissal.*

Kyle's code extended beyond the test day into the rest of our lives. We were not to flash our cash or make extravagant purchases or say anything that might lead others to suspect that we had an illicit source of income. And we were never, *ever,* to mention Kyle's name or the services he provided to anyone, under any circumstances. If someone we knew was struggling with the SATs, or thinking about hiring a tutor, our job was to pass this information up the chain to Kyle— nothing more, nothing less. He would investigate the lead, and if he determined that the individual was a potential client, he would reach out on his own terms. I had no idea how he contacted them or how he arranged the payment. There were other mysteries as well: I didn't know how many other test-takers he employed, what he charged for his services, or even if there was a bigger boss above him, and I wouldn't have dreamed of asking, because this sort of information was only dispensed on a need-to-know basis. These operational safe-guards had been put in place for everyone's benefit, employees and clients alike. The less any individual knew, the less risk of exposure there was for everybody else.

You just fill in the bubbles, he told me. *I'll take care of the rest.*

Given the strictness of the code, it went without saying that partying on the eve of a test was totally prohibited, but Kyle said it anyway: *You will not drink alcohol or take illegal drugs on the night before a test. You will be home in bed by eleven P.M.* I'd never violated this rule before and didn't plan on starting now.

After dinner, I put on my sweatpants, turned on my Xbox, and started campaign mode on Bioshock 2, doing my best not to think about the party I was missing, a party I'd been looking forward to all week. I would've gotten through the night just fine if not for the text I received around nine o'clock. It was from Sarabeth Coen-Brunner, the first one I'd ever received from her, and it put me in an awkward position.

Tequila is here!!! it said. *Where the fuck r u???*

I'D BEEN overweight as a kid, academically gifted but terrible at sports, and middle school had been a nightmare. As a result, I tended to be mumbly and apologetic around girls I liked, as if I had no business wasting their valuable time. With Kyle it was the other way around: he always acted like he was doing the girl a favor, honoring her with the blue ribbon of his attention, allowing her to tag along on his amazing adventures.

But I don't want to make myself sound *too* pathetic. Things had definitely gotten better in the past year. I'd been working out pretty regularly and was finally starting to show some definition in my arms and chest. I'd acquired a new wardrobe, closely modeled on Kyle's, and had started driving to school in my mom's Toyota Matrix.

I wasn't even a virgin anymore. I'd had my first girlfriend in the fall, or at least my first semiregular hookup. It was all on the down-low, just a once-or-twice-a-week, after-school sex break with Iris Leggett—my former lab partner in AP bio—who had the biggest breasts in all of Greenwood High. This wasn't as sexy as it sounds: Iris was short and stocky, but her breasts were enormous, way out of proportion to the rest of her, and they caused her a lot of discomfort, both physical and emotional. The first time we took our clothes off, I said, *Holy shit,* and she started to cry.

I look like a cow, she told me. *I used to love playing soccer, but then I got these and had to stop. And forget about the beach. I can't go anywhere near it.*

We only hooked up five or six times before she called it quits, but it was fun and informative while it lasted and definitely boosted my confidence. If it hadn't been for Iris, I would never have dreamed of talking to Sarabeth Coen-Brunner, let alone flirting with her. She was totally out of my league—a freakishly limber, cheerfully bisexual dancer with eyes like Mila Kunis's—definitely one of the Top Five Hottest Girls in the Junior Class. But one day in the Art Room, I just walked over to her easel and told her how much I liked her painting, this nocturnal scene of a girl in a black cocktail dress standing beneath a streetlight in the rain.

"She just looks so vulnerable," I said. "Like there's nothing to protect her from the elements."

"Tell that to him," she muttered, nodding at Mr. Coyle, who was sitting at his desk, reading a graphic novel with his usual expression of scowling concentration. "He hates it."

Mr. Coyle wasn't wrong; the painting definitely had problems. The girl didn't have much of a face, and the raindrops looked like golf balls, but I chose to focus on the positive.

"I like what you did with the streetlight. And the busted umbrella's a great detail."

"Thanks." I could see how pleased she was. "I worked really hard on that."

We got to be pretty good friends over the spring semester. On Monday mornings she liked to tell me all about her wild weekends: *Oh my God, Josh, I've got to stay away from the tequila. I always end up making out with the wrong person.* Sometimes the wrong person was a guy in our school, sometimes another girl, and sometimes a man in his twenties or early thirties she met at a club (she had a fake ID that never failed her; I wondered if it was one of Kyle's). It would have been pretty excruciating for me, listening to these confessions, except that she always stood really close when she made them, so close that her breasts would sometimes brush against my arm. It was hard to feel jealous when all I could think about was the way my arm seemed to glow where she grazed me.

We'd never spent any time together outside of art class, so it had been a pretty big deal when we realized that we were going to Casey Amandola's party. We'd been joking about it all week—I said I wanted to drink tequila with her, to find out if the rumors of her bad behavior were true, and she said she'd trade me shot for shot until I was a puddle on the floor—but I wasn't sure it was for real until she sent me that text.

Where the fuck r u???

I knew I'd never be her boyfriend, never take her to the movies or walk down the hall with my arm around her shoulder, and I was okay with that. I just wanted to be the wrong person she made out with at a party, a mistake she could confess to her friends on Monday morning, and I had a feeling this was the best chance I'd ever get.

I'll be right there, I texted back. *Don't start without me.*

WHEN I'D imagined getting drunk with Sarabeth, I pictured an intimate, romantic scene, just the two of us off by ourselves, someplace dark and quiet. In front of a roaring fireplace, say, with a big bed nearby and a door that locked from the inside. I certainly hadn't pictured us crowded into a bright kitchen, surrounded by a pack of drunken jocks, with hip-hop blasting in from the living room. In my fantasy, Sarabeth was giving me her undivided attention, laughing at my tragic tequila faces, closely monitoring my slide toward intoxication. In real life, though, she was all the way across the room, standing by the sink, too busy checking her phone and talking to Casey to notice the faces I made when the shots went down.

She looked great, though—at least that part of my fantasy remained intact—casual but festive in a tight white camisole and short black skirt, ruffled at the bottom, that showed off her impressively muscled legs. Her arms were slender and toned, her hair gathered in a sleek ponytail that swayed when she moved, providing periodic glimpses of the tiny, green-tufted carrot tattooed on the back of her neck (when I'd asked her about it in art class, she just shrugged and said she liked carrots). As far as I could tell, she wasn't wearing a bra, and you could see the outline of her nipples pressing through the stretchy fabric of her top, two emphatic dots that commanded the attention of every guy in the room. Brendan Moroney, this ginger-haired lummox who'd been the bane of my middle school existence, nudged me with his elbow.

"Yo, dude, is it just me, or is it getting a little nippy in here?"

I smiled politely, not wanting to offend him, but not wanting to encourage him, either. Brendan was a total jackass, one of my least favorite people in the world. Back in fifth grade, he and his Pop Warner buddies had decided it would be amusing to call me Fosh, a ridiculous nickname I found deeply humiliating (I was pretty sure it stood for Fat Josh or Fag Josh, or maybe a combination of the two). They kept it up for a full year before moving on to the next target. I still hated him for that, though I got the feeling that he barely remembered my real name, let alone the insulting substitute that had made me so miserable.

"Last week she made out with Emma Singer," he informed me. "Capaldo got it on his cell phone. So hot. Like a fucking porno movie."

"I heard about that." Emma Singer was a sophomore who'd gotten kicked out of private school for some kind of scandalous offense—arson, drugs, or sexting, depending on whom you asked. Last Monday, Sarabeth had told me she was a lousy kisser.

"I think Emma's here tonight," he said. "If we're lucky, we'll get an encore."

I didn't answer because Sarabeth was heading our way, passing out lime wedges for the next round. When she got to me, I smiled and asked how she was doing, but she didn't seem to hear the question. She was looking up at Brendan, shaking her head in mock exasperation.

"You're such a pig," she told him, but her voice was sweet and friendly, as if *pig* were a compliment.

"What?" Brendan raised both hands in self-defense. "What did I do?"

"You know," she teased him. "Don't even try to deny it."

Casey Amandola followed close behind Sarabeth, pouring tequila into our plastic cups. When everybody was ready, Sarabeth counted to three, and we all drank at once, tossing back the shots and sucking on our limes.

"Goddam!" Brendan said, punching himself hard in the chest. "That shit is poison!"

AFTER A while, Brendan got bored and drifted off, to my great relief. I probably should have left, too—three shots of tequila are enough for anyone—but I didn't want to let Sarabeth out of my sight. I figured that sooner or later we'd get a chance to talk, and I was planning on coming right out and telling her how pretty she was, just state it like an obvious fact and see how she reacted.

In any case, the kitchen wasn't the worst place to be. All sorts of people drifted in and out—there was a keg on the back patio—and I found myself hugging a whole bunch of them, including some I barely knew, and one or two I didn't especially like. Most of us were seniors who'd already gotten our college acceptances—I was heading across the country to Pomona—and a generalized cloud of goodwill was in the air, that sense of connection that comes from having a shared past and one foot out the door.

One of the few people who didn't hug me was Iris Leggett. She just sort of materialized by my side while I was recovering from shot number four, which had gone down easier than its predecessors and then detonated like a fireball in my stomach. I had to close my eyes and wait for the uproar to subside.

"You okay?" she said, tugging gently on my shirtsleeve.

"I think so." I blinked a few times, getting the world back in focus. "Just a little wobbly."

After that there was an awkward pause. Despite our promise to remain friends after the break-up, Iris and I had been avoiding each other for months, and now here she was, squinting up at me with an expression that seemed to hover somewhere between amusement and concern. I was also a bit distracted by her shirt, so tight and low-cut that it could barely contain her breasts. In school she always covered up, usually with an extra-large hoodie that hung down to her knees.

"I know." She nodded ruefully, following my gaze down to her impressive cleavage. "*Holy shit,* right?"

I winced and mumbled an apology. I still felt bad about blurting that out, making her cry the first time we had sex—the first time for both of us.

"It's okay," she told me. "I'm trying to own it, you know? I'm sick of hating my body."

"That's good," I said. "That's a really healthy attitude."

"Fuck it, right?" There was something a little off about her smile, or maybe the tone of her voice. "If guys want to stare at my tits, who am I to stop them? I'm like, *Here they are, dudes. Knock yourselves out.*"

"Are you drunk?"

She raised her red plastic cup, tilting it to show me the contents. It was pretty big, at least twenty-four ounces, and more than halfway full. "Turns out I like beer," she said, shrugging in a who-woulda-thunk-it sort of way.

"You should try some tequila. That's pretty good, too."

"Maybe," she said, but her attention had shifted from me to Sarabeth, who was taking a selfie by the sink, making a supermodel face for the camera. It seemed like everybody in the room was watching her.

"She's pretty," Iris observed. "But she's such an exhibitionist."

"She's nice," I said. "She's in my art class."

Casey joined Sarabeth for the next picture, the two of them posing with the tequila bottle. On the one after that, they gave each other a playful kiss. Some guys started cheering for more, but Casey pulled away and gave them the finger, telling them to dream on.

"I should've gone to more parties," Iris said. "I used to act like they were stupid, but that was bullshit. I pretty much wasted the past four years pretending I was above it all. But the joke was on me, you know?"

"You didn't waste it," I told her. "You worked your ass off and got into a great college. I bet you're gonna love it at North-western."

"I'm gonna go to more parties, that's for sure." She swirled the beer in her cup as if it were fine wine. "I just wanna have some fun for once."

There was a disturbance just then, a bunch of football players scuffling in the hallway. From the sound of it, I thought it might be a real fight, but they were just goofing around, Brendan and Chad Capaldo and Dontay Williamson tugging on one of their buddies, dragging him forcibly into the kitchen.

"Get this man a shot!" Brendan shouted as they spilled through the doorway. "It's his birthday next week!"

Dontay was blocking my view of the birthday boy, but then he moved and I saw that it was Jake Harlowe. He looked sweaty and a little flustered, his blue oxford shirt rumpled and askew.

"I can't drink tonight," he said, realigning the buttons on shirt. "I have to take the SATs tomorrow."

I was impressed by the smoothness of the lie, the note of regretful sincerity in his voice. And that look on his face, so anxious and innocent, like he didn't want to be a party pooper, but couldn't help it.

"Fuck the SATs!" Capaldo hauled off and punched him in the arm, pretty hard. "You only turn seventeen once!"

Jake frowned and rubbed his shoulder. Some guys started chanting, *Birthday shot! Birthday shot! Birthday shot!*

"Really," he said. "I can't."

"Come on," Dontay taunted. "Don't be a pussy."

I turned back to Iris, shaking my head like I couldn't believe what a bunch of immature assholes they were, but she wasn't even looking at them.

"Just so you know," she said in this melancholy, thoughtful voice. "I don't hate you anymore."

I laughed, though it didn't sound like she was joking.

"Why would you hate me?"

"Why wouldn't I? You came to my house, you fucked me, and then you left. You never said anything nice, never took me out, never called to ask how I was doing. You acted like it was your *job* or something."

"That's not fair," I said. "That was your idea. You wanted to keep it casual."

"I know." She nodded for a long time, accepting her responsibility. "But you weren't even grateful."

Drunk as I was, I knew she was right, knew that I owed her an apology. But for some reason I was looking at Jake again, watching as he accepted his birthday shot from Casey with an attitude of reluctant surrender, a good guy defeated by peer pressure. Smiling sheepishly, he toasted the onlookers and tossed it back to widespread applause.

"He really shouldn't be doing that," I said, but Iris was already slipping past me, shaking her head in disgust as she veered toward the hallway.

I WAS a conscientious employee, you have to give me that much. Even with a splitting headache and a broken heart, I managed to drag myself out of bed at six-fifteen the next morning, force down two Advil and a cup of black coffee, and drive out to the Brackett Academy, an exclusive prep school that had a nicer campus than some of the colleges I'd visited. I trudged into Winthrop Hall and joined a long line of nervous-looking kids waiting to take the most important test of their lives.

Getting through security wasn't a problem. The proctor just made the usual cursory inspection of my ticket and ID before waving me inside. When the room was full, he passed out the test booklets, recited the rules and regulations, and told us to get started. My forehead was clammy and there was an ominous sloshing sensation in my stomach; I wasn't sure I'd be able to make it through the next three hours without passing out or throwing up.

I'd known that fifth shot was a mistake even as I was bringing it to my lips, but by then I didn't care. I'd already realized what was happening between Jake and Sarabeth, seen the way she'd chosen him, the way she pressed her body against his arm and whispered in his ear, the way he laughed at whatever it was she told him. All I could do was watch from across the room, my face burning with a rage that felt like shame, or a shame that felt like rage.

Fuck my life, I thought, and I swallowed that last gulp of poison.

At least it got me out of the kitchen. They had just started kissing when I rushed for the door and staggered out into the fresh night air. I wanted to make it to the grass, but it was too far away, so I barfed on the slate patio, right in front of a group of weed-smoking juniors who thought it was hilarious and couldn't stop marveling at the amount of awfulness that was spewing out of me.

SICK AS I was, my mouth still sour from last night's vomit, I could still manage the test without too much trouble. Most of the questions were ridiculously easy, as if they'd been designed for idiots. For example, Question #1 in the Critical Reading section was a sentence—*A man of _____, he never went back on his word*—that we were supposed to complete with one of the following options:

(A) hypocrisy
(B) integrity
(C) flexibility
(D) inconsistency
(E) solidarity

The correct answer was obviously B, but Jake Harlowe, fool that he was, chose D. And he kept doing that, question after question, always picking the wrong answer, often the wrongest one possible. But it served him right, I thought, going to a party the night before a big test, getting drunk and hooking up with a girl he didn't even deserve.

I knew Kyle would be furious, but I didn't care about him. I was just sorry we'd ever met, sorry I'd accepted his job offer, sorry I'd let him turn me into the kind of person I'd become.

I wasn't all that worried about Jake, either. He'd get another shot at the SATs in September, and I was sure he'd do better the next time around. Maybe not good enough to get into Amherst like his brother, but so what? There were a lot of schools out there. In the meantime, he was going to have to suffer through that humiliating moment when his scores arrived; they were going to be a *big* disappointment. I could imagine the sense of helpless failure that would overwhelm him, the knowledge that something terrible and unfair had happened that he couldn't even complain about. I thought it might do him some good, just this once, to feel the way I'd felt the night before, the way I was feeling at that very moment, darkening those bubbles with my Number Two pencil, making one stupid mistake after another.

THE ALL-NIGHT PARTY ·······➤

LIZ GOT SUCKERED INTO TAKING THE GRAVEYARD SHIFT at the All-Night Party the same way she'd gotten suckered into every other thankless task in her long parental career—organizing soccer banquets, soliciting donations for the Dahlkamper Elementary School Auction, canvassing against the perennial threat of budget cuts and teacher layoffs, feeding her friends' cats and turtles and babysitting their kids while they went off on business trips to Vegas or second honeymoons to St. Bart's. She could've just said no, of course—she was a working mother with way too much on her plate—but she could never escape the feeling that everything depended on her, that if she didn't do it, it simply wouldn't get done. There would be no money for championship jackets, class size would skyrocket, marriages would crumble, beloved pets would starve. And maybe somebody somewhere would think it was her fault and decide that she was a bad mother, a bad neighbor, a bad citizen. Liz didn't know why that possibility bothered her so much, but it did.

The All-Night Party Committee knew exactly how to push her buttons. First, they'd softened her up with a never-ending barrage of e-mails, the tone friendly and inspirational in March (*Let's Uphold a Great Tradition; Please Help Keep Our Seniors Safe on Graduation Night*), turning mildly reproachful in April (*Don't Leave Us in the Lurch!; Junior Parents, It's Time to Step Up and Do Your Part!*), before reaching a fever pitch of hectoring intensity as May edged into June (***ALL-NIGHT PARTY IN DESPERATE NEED OF VOLUNTEERS! NO MORE EXCUSES!! THIS MEANS YOU!!!***).

Liz had felt her resolve weakening throughout the spring, but she was determined not to give in. She was swamped at work, she was feeling down (the reality of the divorce finally beginning to sink in), and still nurturing resentment from the soccer season, during which she'd done more than her fair share of the heavy lifting, hosting two team dinners, supervising the sale and distribution of eight hundred boxes of frozen cookie dough for the Booster Club fund-raiser, even manning the ticket booth in a couple of emergencies. And now that Dana had been elected captain for next year, Liz's responsibilities on that front would only increase. So just this once, couldn't they leave her alone and throw the goddam party without her? Was that too much to ask?

She knew from experience that the Committee would escalate its recruiting efforts in the home stretch, cranking up the peer pressure, twisting the arms of reluctant volunteers. Liz opted for the time-honored strategy of cowardly avoidance—keep your head down, let the calls go to voice mail, and then, if pressed, claim you'd never gotten the messages. *My machine's been acting up; I really have to get a new one.* No one would believe her, but so what? Summer vacation—that blissful season of amnesia and forgiveness—was just around the corner, everyone's slate wiped clean until September.

Her plan might have worked if the call had come from Marilyn Tresca, the sanctimonious Volunteer Coordinator, or Ken Lorimer, the red-bearded blowhard who headed the Clean-Up Brigade. But the Committee was too smart to lob her a softball like that.

"Liz?" said the wryly apologetic voice issuing from the speaker of her answering machine. "Are you there? It's me, Sally . . ."

Oh, shit, Liz thought. *That's not fair.* Sally Cleaves was the one member of the Committee she actually liked. Their daughters had been playing soccer together for the past ten years, attending the same skills clinics and summer camps, carpooling to club practices and indoor matches. Liz and Sally weren't friends, exactly, but they were better-than-average bleacher buddies, thrown together on countless autumn evenings, cheering for their girls, sharing umbrellas and blankets in nasty weather.

"I guess you're not home," Sally continued. "I'll try you ag—"

Liz had no choice but to pick up the phone.

"I'm here," she said, panting a little for effect. "I was just in the laundry room."

"Laundry," Sally commiserated. "It never ends, does it?"

"No, it doesn't," Liz agreed, though she was thinking that

it actually would, that in a little over a year Dana would leave for college, and Liz would have no one's clothes to wash but her own, no one to cook for, no one to talk to at the breakfast table. It would just be herself, brooding in the empty nest, bored out of her skull. "How are you, Sally?"

"Good, pretty good. How about you?"

"Okay, I guess. Better than I was a few months ago."

"I'm glad. I know it's been a tough year." Sally let a few seconds go by, marking the transition between small talk and business. "Listen, Liz, I really hate to bother you about the All-Night Party. I know how busy you are."

"Not half as busy as you," Liz countered. Sally was a patent lawyer who somehow managed to work full-time, raise three kids, serve on the School Board and Friends of Gifford Soccer, and run at least two marathons a year. Of course, she had a husband who loved her, so that made things a little easier. Or maybe a lot easier. Liz had no way of knowing how much of a difference something like that might make.

"Oh, I doubt it," Sally said, her voice full of the warmth Liz had been so grateful for during the soccer season, the first one she'd had to navigate as half of a divorced couple. It was horrible, suffering through game after game with Tony sitting just a few rows away, his shoulders rigid with anger, acting like he didn't even know her, like the mother of his child didn't merit the common courtesy of a hello.

God, Sally had remarked one night, totally out of the blue. *He's a cold-hearted bastard, isn't he?*

Always was, Liz replied. *From the day that we met.*

"Anyway," Sally went on, "we're in a really tight spot, or I wouldn't even bother you. You do so much already."

Liz released a martyr's sigh. She felt the all-too-familiar, almost-pleasurable sensation of buckling under pressure, surrendering to the inevitable.

"It's okay," she said. "What do you want me to do?"

SHE ARRIVED at the high school a few minutes before midnight, making her way down the rumpled, confetti-sprinkled red carpet leading to the side entrance. It must have been quite a scene a few hours earlier—a swarm of well-wishers cheering and blowing kisses at the graduates as they paraded in, a fireworks display of flashing cameras—but right now it was desolate, just Liz and a bored-looking cop sitting in a folding chair by the metal doors, beneath a hand-painted sign that said CLASS OF 2011 YOU ROCK!

The cop had his head down—he was watching something on his iPhone—but Liz recognized him right away as the meathead who'd written her a ticket a few years ago for rolling through a stop sign on Whitetail Way. Just a glimpse of his *Jersey Shore* physique brought it all back to her: the way he'd ignored her when she tried to explain that her daughter was late for practice, and then his crazy overreaction when Dana attempted to get out and walk the rest of the way to the field, which was only a couple of blocks away.

Remain in the vehicle! he'd barked, placing his hand on the butt of his holstered gun. Dana was only thirteen at the time and barely weighed a hundred pounds. *If you exit the vehicle, you will be placed under arrest!*

And then, out of spite, knowing they were in a hurry, he'd made them wait in the car for what felt like an eternity while he checked Liz's license and registration, a routine task that should have taken a minute or two at most. By the time he finally strutted over to deliver the ticket—along with a condescending lecture about driving more carefully in the future—Liz had had enough.

Just so you know, she told him, *I'm going to be writing a formal letter of complaint to the police department about your rude and unprofessional behavior. And I'll make sure the mayor gets a copy.*

Go right ahead, he shot back, his face flushing pink beneath the bronze of his permanent tan. *My name's Brian Yanuzzi. With two z's.*

Liz never wrote the letter—Tony convinced her it was a bad idea, feuding with the cops in a town as small as Gifford— but she had cultivated a lively private grudge against Officer Yanuzzi in the intervening years, cursing under her breath whenever she caught a glimpse of him directing traffic around a construction site, or sitting in his cruiser in the center of town, monitoring the pedestrian crossings. He was such a vivid figure in her mental universe that she was surprised, and even a bit disappointed, by the bland friendliness on his face when he looked up from the phone, as if she were any other well-meaning taxpayer.

"Evening," he said.

"Hi." She made a point of not returning his smile. "I'm a volunteer?"

"Too bad," he said with a chuckle. "Looks like you got the short straw."

"Looks like we both did."

"Least I'm getting paid."

Liz nodded, conceding the point. She could hear music leaking through the closed double doors, the muffled *whump, wah-whump* of the beat, a girlish voice floating on top. She wondered if she might be able to get in a little dancing later on, if adults were allowed to join the fun. She hadn't danced in a long time.

"So how's it going?" she asked, not quite sure why she was prolonging this encounter with a man she actively disliked. It was almost as if she were giving him a second chance, holding out for a sign of belated recognition—*Hey, wait a minute, aren't you that lady . . . ?*—some scrap of proof that she wasn't as completely forgettable as she seemed to be. "Everyone behaving themselves?"

"They're good kids." Yanuzzi's face seemed softer than she remembered, a little more boyish. "Not like when I was in high school."

"Tell me about it. My graduation night was insane. The little of it I can remember."

"Oh, yeah?" The cop looked intrigued, as if he were seeing her in a new light. "You were a party girl, huh?"

"Not quite," Liz told him, making a conscious decision to leave it at that, to spare him the details of that disastrous evening, the Southern Comfort and the tears, the fact that she'd made out with three different guys, none of whom she'd even liked, and then thrown up in Sandy Deaver's kidney-shaped pool, thereby ensuring that her classmates would have at least one thing to remember her by at their upcoming twenty-fifth reunion. "I was just young and stupid."

Yanuzzi nodded slowly, as though she'd said something profound.

"So were those kids who died," he observed. "They were just young and stupid, too."

THOSE KIDS *who died.*

Liz had been hearing about those kids for the past twelve years, ever since she'd moved to Gifford. The accident was fresh in everyone's mind back then, five friends speeding in a Jeep on graduation night, open containers, no seatbelts. Good-looking, popular, three boys and two girls, never in any kind of trouble, just a terrible mistake, the kind kids make when they're drunk and happy.

The memory of those kids was a dark cloud hanging over the town. You'd see people having a hushed conversation on a street corner, or a woman touching another woman's arm in the Stop & Shop, or a man wiping away a tear while he pumped his gas, and you'd think, *Those kids who died.*

There were memorial services in the fall, the football season dedicated to the memory of the victims. Everywhere you went you saw their names soaped on the rear windows of cars, usually listed in alphabetical order, along with the date of their deaths, and the phrase IN LOVING MEMORY. The school district increased funding for drug and alcohol education; the cops cracked down hard on underage drinking. And on graduation night the following June, Gifford High held the first annual All-Night Party, a heavily supervised affair at which the graduates could celebrate in a safe, substance-free, vehicle-free environment. Parents loved the idea, and it turned out the kids liked it, too.

Over the past decade the All-Night Party had outgrown

its sad origins, maturing into a beloved institution that was the source of genuine local pride. Each year's cohort of junior parents vied to outdo their predecessors in the lavishness of the decorations and the novelty of the offerings—a Nerf-gun war, a circus trapeze, a climbing wall, sumo-wrestling suits, and, memorably, an enormous Moonwalk castle that had to be deflated well before dawn, due to highly credible reports of sexual shenanigans unfolding within remote inner chambers. More recently, the party had gone thematic—last year was *Twilight* and vampires, and the year before *Harry Potter,* complete with lightning-bolt face tattoos, a Sorting Hat, and a Quidditch tournament in the gym. For this year's theme, the Committee had given serious thought to *The Hunger Games*—too depressing, they'd decided—before settling on Gifford Goes Hollywood, a more open-ended concept that accounted for both the red carpet outside and the lifelike Oscar statue that greeted Liz when she entered the building, an eight-foot, three-dimensional replica of the trophy with a sign taped to its base: FOR BEST PERFORMANCE BY A GRADUATING CLASS.

SALLY WAS manning the Volunteer Sign-In table along with Jeff Hammer, the presidente-for-life of the Gifford Youth Hockey Association, and a ubiquitous figure at local athletic and charitable events. Hammer didn't bother to acknowledge Liz's arrival—he'd been cold to her for the past several years, ever since Dana had quit a promising hockey career to focus on indoor soccer during the winter season—but Sally's greeting was so warm Liz barely registered his snub.

222 | TOM PERROTTA

"Thank you so much for coming," she said, rising from her chair with a wan but sincere smile. She looked washed-out, as if she hadn't slept for days. "You're my hero."

"Not a problem." Liz leaned across the table for a quick hug and kiss. "How's it going?"

"Great."

Sally glanced at Hammer for confirmation, and he responded with a grudging nod. He was an unpleasantly handsome man with a mustache he couldn't keep his fingers off.

"Kids are having a blast," he admitted.

With the indifference of a clerk at the DMV, Hammer slid a blank name tag and a Sharpie in Liz's direction. After a moment's hesitation, she scrawled her married name—LIZ MERCATTO—and affixed the white rectangle to her shirt. At least this way everyone would know she was Dana's mom, instead of some random adult who'd wandered in off the street.

"Ready?" Sally circled the table and took Liz by the arm. "They're waiting for you at the Chilling Station."

"The what?"

"It's a place to relax and hang out, kind of away from it all. You know, if the kids need a little downtime. I think you'll like it."

They set off toward the distant clamor of the party, turning right at the library, heading down a long hallway paved with a galaxy of construction-paper stars, each one bearing the name of a graduate.

"This is our Walk of Fame," Sally explained. "We stayed up until two-thirty cutting out the stars and writing the names. And then it took us all afternoon to arrange them on the floor."

"How many are there?"

"Two hundred forty-three." Liz could hear the pride in Sally's voice. "But who's counting, right?"

They veered apart, making way for a pack of pretty girls charging by in short skirts and high heels, each one taller and skinnier than the next, glammed up as if they were heading to a nightclub. Not a single member of the posse bothered to glance at Liz or Sally as they passed, let alone say, *Hi* or *Excuse me*.

"Aren't they beautiful?" Sally watched with a wistful expression as the girls clattered down the hallway, talking in loud, theatrical voices. "They have no idea how beautiful they are."

Oh, they know, Liz thought. *The world only reminds them every day.*

"They probably think their butts are too big or their boobs are too small," Sally continued. "That's how I felt when I was their age. Like I could never measure up."

"Me, too." Liz decided not to mention that the feeling had never gone away. "All through high school I tried to be the last person out of the classroom after the bell rang. I didn't want any boys walking behind me, snickering at my ass."

The girls stopped midway down the hall to take cell-phone pictures of a star that must have belonged to one of them, or maybe to a boy they liked.

"They're probably on some ridiculous carrot-stick diet," Sally said. "But they're perfect just the way they are, you know? That's what I keep telling Jamie, but I can't seem to get through to her."

Liz nodded, not quite sure how they'd segued from the high-heeled hotties to the entirely different subject of Jamie, an Amazonian three-sport athlete who only ever seemed at home in sweats or a team uniform. Tony always referred to her as a "bruiser," insisting that he meant it as a compliment.

"It's hard being a girl," Liz observed. "Doesn't matter what you look like."

"What about Dana? She have any issues like that? You know, body image or whatever?"

"Not really." Liz flinched as two boys barreled past, one of them trying to bash the other in the head with a pink flotation noodle. They looked sweaty and slightly crazed. "She's been lucky like that. Never had to worry about her weight or her complexion, none of it."

Sally nodded, as if she'd figured as much. "She's always been such a pretty girl. Ever since she was little."

"It's a fluke." Liz added the obligatory disclaimer: "God knows she didn't get it from her mother."

They stopped to peek into the cafeteria, half of which had been cleared to make a dance floor. A mob of kids were out there, most of them moving with a confidence Liz could only have dreamed about at their age. A few looked like trained professionals, or at least like they'd spent a lot of time practicing in front of their bedroom mirror.

"I'm glad it's finally picking up," Sally said. "When the DJ started, the boys were hiding out in the gym, shooting hoops and beating up on one another. The girls had to drag them over here."

"Well, it looks like they're having fun."

Liz would have liked to stick around, but Sally was in no mood to linger. Her shift was over; she just wanted to get Liz settled, then go home and get some sleep.

"I saw Dana's prom pictures on Facebook," Sally said, as they rounded the corner onto a corridor lined with cardboard cutouts of Hollywood stars, Meryl Streep sandwiched by Dirty Harry and Homer Simpson, Jeff Bridges with an eye-patch. "She and Chris looked really happy together. Such a perfect couple."

"I guess," Liz agreed without enthusiasm. "I just wish they weren't so serious."

"They've been together for a while, right?"

"Ever since freshman year."

Sally hesitated, shooting Liz an apologetic sidelong glance before venturing the inevitable question.

"I know it's none of my business, but are they . . . ?"

Liz shrugged, trying to hide her discomfort. It was weird how many other parents felt that it was okay to inquire about her daughter's sex life just because she'd been dating the same boy for the past couple of years.

"I don't know," she said. "We don't really talk about it."

TECHNICALLY SPEAKING, this wasn't a lie. The one time Liz had asked her daughter straight out if she and Chris had *gone all the way,* Dana just rolled her eyes and said, *Mom, I'm really not comfortable with this conversation,* and that was where they'd left it.

Of course, this exchange had taken place over a year ago, and a lot had happened since then. But what was Liz supposed to do? Tell Sally the truth, which was that Chris sometimes spent the night in Dana's bedroom and, in fact, was doing so that very night? Because Liz knew exactly how that would go.

Sally would pretend not to be shocked and then say, *Really? And you're all right with that?* And then Liz would either have to lie and say yes or admit that she hated the situation, but felt powerless to change it.

It was a fait accompli, she would have had to explain. *Nobody asked my permission.*

Ever since freshman year, Dana had been spending the occasional weekend with Chris's family at their vacation house in Vermont. It was a lovely second home, by all accounts, just twenty minutes from Killington, and Chris's parents were lovely people. The dad, Warren, was a financial guy, and the mom, Jodie, a working artist with her own studio and a gallery in Boston, the kind of limber, fresh-faced woman who could let herself go gray and seem all the more youthful and attractive as a result. Both parents thought the world of Dana, repeatedly telling Liz what a pleasure it was to have her as a houseguest, such a polite girl, always helping with the dishes—something she rarely did at home, Liz always wanted to interject, though she never did—and so beautiful, too, such a graceful, fearless skier.

This past winter, Jodie had phoned Liz after Presidents' Day weekend. She started by reciting the usual compliments, but then her tone changed, turned solemn and careful.

"I thought you should know," she said. "The kids have been sharing a bedroom. At the ski house."

"What?"

"Dana said you were okay with it, but I wanted to double-check."

"She said I was okay with it?"

"More or less. She said you wouldn't care."

"Of course, I care." Liz was glad Jodie couldn't see the color spreading across her cheeks. "They're just so young to be—"

"I know." Jodie's voice was dreamy and forgiving. "But they love each other. And they seem really responsible. To tell you the truth, Liz, I think they've been sneaking around for a while now, playing musical beds in the middle of the night. At least this way it's out in the open. I just don't want them to think there's anything to be ashamed of. As long as you're all right with it."

Liz knew the moment had arrived to state her objections. The problem was, she wasn't quite sure what she was objecting to. She'd slept with college boyfriends when she was just a little older than Dana, guys she'd known for a lot less time than Dana had known Chris, guys who didn't even pretend to be nice to her, let alone love her. And besides, she knew it wasn't Dana's age or the sex itself that bothered her. It was more that she resented her daughter for getting everything all at once, for being so pretty and happy and lucky, skiing all day and then slipping under the warm covers with her ridiculously cute, totally adoring boyfriend. But how could you even begin to talk about that?

"Liz? Are you there?"

"No, you're right, Jodie. There's nothing to be ashamed of. Just as long as they're being careful."

"That's exactly what I told them."

At the time, Liz had consoled herself with the knowledge that winter was almost over, that there wouldn't be many more Vermont getaways before the snow melted and club soccer started up. Pretty soon everything would be back to normal.

The trouble was, Dana and Chris liked sleeping together,

and it didn't make sense to them that they could share a bed in Vermont, but not in Gifford. Before long, Dana was heading out on Friday night and not coming home until Sunday afternoon. Liz made a belated effort to put a stop to the sleepovers, telling her daughter that she missed her and needed to spend time with her on the weekends, but the only result of this intervention was that the lovebirds started switching off, spending one night with Chris's parents, and the next with Liz, like newlyweds trying to keep both sets of in-laws happy.

It was actually kind of fun to have them around. Sometimes the three of them would watch a movie together or play Scrabble or go out for ice cream; Dana and Chris were less self-centered, a lot more available to Liz, now that they knew they'd have all the alone time they wanted once they went to bed. The only real awkwardness came after lights out, when Liz had nothing to do but lie awake and listen for the telltale sounds of passion coming from down the hall, wondering how two teenagers managed to be so utterly silent, making it seem like the only sex in the house was taking place inside her own muddled, dirty-minded head.

THE CHILLING Station was a smart concept, a makeshift living-room/rest area that glowed like a mirage at the end of a deserted corridor, a cozy, lamplit oasis. It was equipped with a motley array of furniture—couches and chairs, two army cots, even a freestanding hammock—along with a stack of board games and some rickety card tables to play them on. The only thing missing was the kids.

"It's been dead," grumbled Craig Waters, the volunteer on

the eight-to-midnight shift. He'd been napping on the re-cliner when Liz and Sally arrived and still looked a little out of it. "There were a couple of chess nerds early on, but nothing for the past two hours."

"It'll pick up," Sally said. "The kids get pretty tired around four in the morning."

Craig pondered Liz with groggy curiosity. "How late are you staying?"

"Till the bitter end," she told him. "Six A.M."

"Wow." He yawned. "Good for you."

And then they were gone, leaving Liz alone among the mismatched furniture, with nothing to do except kick herself for not having brought something to read. It was a ridiculous oversight, considering that it was her policy never to leave home without a book, a soccer mom's best friend when prac-tice ran late. But she happened to be reading *The Girl Who Kicked the Hornet's Nest,* and the library hardcover was mas-sive, not the sort of volume you could easily slip into your purse on the way to a graduation party. So she'd left it on her bedside table, where it was doing no one any good.

She could hear music and voices from the other end of the building, the sound of young people having fun, and it struck her almost like a taunt, a reminder of everything she was miss-ing, not just tonight but every night, the void that had become her life. She felt a minor panic attack coming on—or maybe just an urgent need for fresh air and human contact—and won-dered what would happen if she marched back to the sign-in ta-ble and demanded a better assignment, something that would at least allow her to join the party, to interact with the kids and the other volunteers. The worst they could do was tell her no.

Oh, come on, she scolded herself. *Don't be such a baby. It's not even twelve-thirty.*

But that was the problem, wasn't it? She still had five and a half hours to go. *Five and a half hours.* A whole endless night. Just the thought of it was exhausting. She found herself sneaking glances at the beige velour recliner that had been Craig's undoing, imagining how sweet it would feel to crank back the handle and put her feet up. But there was no way she was going to allow herself to fall asleep in public, to be that vulnerable in front of people she didn't know, especially teenagers.

Hoping to clear her head, she slipped into the narrow space between the hammock and the fire doors and did a few yoga stretches. She'd been trying to find a regular class for a while now, but somehow the timing was never convenient, or she didn't like the teacher, or the other students were show-offs. It was too bad, because yoga never failed to cheer her up. She could feel the magic working right away—her muscles warming and loosening, the tension dissolving in waves, her mind emptying itself of negative thoughts—despite the cramped space, the lack of a mat, and jeans that hadn't been designed for sun salutations.

It's just one night, she reminded herself. *It's going to be fine.*

Arching into upward dog, she was startled by the sound of soft voices and muffled laughter. It was coming from right in front of her.

"Hello?" she called out as the fire door creaked open. "Excuse me?"

The intruders froze in the doorway as Liz scrambled to her feet. They were a couple, a tall boy in a WESLEYAN LACROSSE shirt and a short, plump girl with multiple piercings and too much makeup.

"Where did you come from?" Liz demanded. She'd been told that the fire doors were off-limits, except in case of emergency. "You're not supposed to be here."

The boy let go of his girlfriend's hand. He was clean-cut and preppy, with the bland good looks that were his Gifford birthright. She was more of a townie, in skimpy denim shorts that did her thighs no favors, and an orange V-neck tee that was two sizes too small.

"Mr. Waters told us it was okay," the boy explained after a moment. He looked Liz straight in the eye, his voice calm and confident. "Jenna needed her medication."

The girl giggled a little too loudly. She had dirt on her knees and a big pink blotch spreading across her chest.

"I have asthma," she said. Something about the way she pronounced her ailment made Liz realize she'd been drinking. "Hadda go home for my inhaler."

Liz knew they were lying. She figured that they'd slipped out while Craig was sleeping and had hoped to slip back in undetected, but what was she supposed to do? Report them to the authorities? It was their graduation night, and they weren't hurting anyone. And besides, how could she object to a teenaged tryst when her own daughter was home in bed with her boyfriend? She was a lot of things, but she tried not to be a hypocrite.

"Just get outta here," she said, waving them in the direction of the cafeteria. "Go enjoy your party."

• • •

A FLOCK of artsy girls descended upon the Chilling Station around one o'clock, packing themselves into the couches and chairs, talking in low, animated voices, as if hatching a conspiracy. They were a strikingly multicultural bunch, at least by Gifford standards—there were two Asians in the mix, a tall black girl who looked like a ballerina, and a round-faced, red-lipped Muslim girl in a headscarf. One member of the group was in a wheelchair; another wore a bandanna to conceal what Liz assumed was chemo-induced hair loss. The smaller of the Asian girls—she had an adorable teardrop face, and a streak of purple in her hair—sat on the lap of a butch white girl in a baseball cap.

Liz didn't recognize any of them from the soccer field; she figured they were denizens of the art room and the dance studio, editors of the literary magazine, officers of the Gay/ Straight Alliance, members of the Performing Arts Club. Some of them were cute, but mostly not in a way that a high school boy would appreciate—not that all of them would be equally interested in eliciting the approval of high school boys—and they seemed collectively resigned to their wallflower status at the All-Night Party. Liz's heart went out to them; she wanted to hug each and every one, to let them know they'd be happier in college, that the world was about to become much larger and more forgiving, at least for a little while.

After they moved on, a handful of other visitors trickled in and out. A pair of identical-twin boys played a cutthroat game of Yahtzee, insulting each other with language so vile Liz had to ask them to tone it down. A scruffy-bearded troubadour—he looked a little too old for high school—strummed

NINE INCHES | 233

an acoustic guitar, serenading his hippie friends with ever-green songs by Cat Stevens and Neil Young. Four football players held a round-robin arm-wrestling tournament, grunt-ing and grimacing like constipated old men while their girl-friends cheered them on from the sidelines.

By two-thirty it was dead again, but at least Liz had a year-book to keep her occupied, a copy left behind by someone named Corinne. She leafed through the glossy pages, reading the inscriptions, searching for familiar faces. There was a photo of Dana in the section devoted to Girls' Soccer, an ac-tion shot in which she leapt for a header, her ponytail a golden blur: *Striker Dana Mercatto rises to the occasion against Rose-dale.* Liz flipped ahead to the junior-class pictures, locating her daughter's face among the rows of black-and-white thumb-nails. It was a photo she knew well—a color version of it was framed on her dresser—Dana gazing coolly into the camera, so lovely and self-possessed, utterly at peace with herself. Liz couldn't help remembering her own senior picture, the too-big smile, the desperation in her eyes, as if she were begging the world not to hate her.

Ugh! she used to say. *I can't stand that picture. It doesn't even look like me.* But that wasn't really the problem.

She heard footsteps and closed the book. Setting it down on the coffee table, she turned and saw Officer Yanuzzi head-ing in her direction, his uniformed figure squat and ominous in the murky light, as if he were coming to arrest her. But when his face finally came into view, he just looked amused.

"Party Girl," he called out in a friendly voice. "I was won-dering where you were hiding."

"Right here in Siberia," she told him. "Taking one for the team."

"Could be worse." He took a sip of coffee from a paper cup, surveying the furniture with what appeared to be sincere interest. "You could be stuck outside all night on a folding chair."

"Least you're getting paid."

"Good one." He chalked up a point for Liz on an imaginary scoreboard. "Guess I can't complain."

"Not to mention that you seem to be inside at the moment."

"Just making my rounds," he said, threading his way between the couch and the hammock. He opened one of the fire doors and peered into the vestibule, checking for suspicious activity. "Though I gotta say, it is getting a little chilly out. I shoulda brought a jacket. But it's June, you know? I'm not really thinking jacket."

He took a seat on the couch, directly across from Liz, as if she'd invited him to join her. He set his coffee on the table and held out his hand.

"I'm Brian."

"Liz."

"Mercatto, huh?" He studied her name tag with a quizzical expression. "Why do I know that name?"

She was tempted to remind him of their unfortunate encounter on Whitetail Way—*You were rude and you scared my daughter*—but couldn't see the point of dredging it up at this late date. Besides, it was three in the morning, and she was grateful for the company.

"Mercatto's my ex-husband's name. I usually go by Casey."

"I'm not too good with names," he said, reaching for his cup. He paused before drinking. "If I'd known you were here, I woulda brought you some."

"No worries."

"They got those little one-cup things. K-Cups or whatever." He extended the cup in her direction. "You want a sip? It's nice and hot."

"No, thanks. I'm fine."

"You sure? I could take the lid off. That's where all the germs are."

"I'm more of a tea drinker anyway."

"Well, don't say I didn't offer."

He kept his eyes on her as he brought the cup to his lips. She got the feeling he was searching his memory, trying to locate a file marked *Mercatto*. She averted her gaze, found herself staring at the gun in his holster, remembering the way he'd touched it when he yelled at Dana.

"I'm glad I found you," he said, just as the silence was getting awkward. "I was feeling bad about what I said before."

"What did you say?"

"You know, about those kids who died. That they were young and stupid." He shook his head, as if pained by the memory. "I don't know why I said that."

"It's okay. No big deal."

"They were my friends," he said. "We went to school together."

She studied his face, performing some quick mental calculations. He was probably about thirty, so the math worked out.

"Oh, God. I'm sorry."

Yanuzzi shrugged. He took off his hat, ran a hand over his gelled buzz cut.

"The driver was a kid named Jimmy Polito. He was my best friend. We were gonna start a landscaping business." Yanuzzi closed his eyes for a moment. "Anyway, we were all at the party together, playing quarters, getting drunk off our asses, when everybody suddenly decided to drive to the beach. The only reason I didn't go is that I was trying to hook up with this girl. She was somebody's cousin. Didn't even go to our school." Yanuzzi laughed softly. His face looked young and defenseless. "They got killed and I got laid. That's the whole story."

"I'm sorry," Liz said again.

"Not your fault."

A few seconds went by. Yanuzzi rubbed his jaw, as if checking the closeness of his shave. "I didn't even really get laid," he said. "We were both too wasted to make it across the finish line."

IT MUST have been close to four in the morning when she set off for the restroom. Officer Yanuzzi kindly agreed to hold down the fort until she returned.

"No problem," he said. "I'd stay here the rest of the night if I could. This is a really comfortable couch."

"Just don't fall asleep on me, okay?"

"Don't worry about that." He had his hands behind his head, his bulky cop shoes resting on the coffee table. "I've had at least ten cups of coffee since I started my shift. I'll be wide awake until noon."

They'd been talking for almost an hour at that point, not just about the tragedy of his graduation night, but about her divorce, and the engagement he'd broken off the previous summer, the suffocating sense he'd had that he was drifting into marriage because other people expected it, not because he'd made a choice to spend his life with Katie. He'd bailed out two months before the wedding, alienating lots of friends and even a few relatives, but he knew he'd done the right thing.

"Every morning I wake up and thank God I dodged that bullet."

It was almost embarrassing how badly she'd misjudged him. Brian was a sweet guy, way more thoughtful and self-aware than Tony or any of the jerks she'd corresponded with on Match.com, the handful that would stoop to consider a woman on the wrong side of forty. He was kinda cute, too, if you could get past the gym-rat muscles and the look of squinty irritation that seemed to be his default expression, not that she was suffering from any romantic delusions. What was the point? She was twelve years his senior, a divorcée with a teenaged daughter, and no cougar by any stretch of the imagination. Even so, it was encouraging just to know that she was still in the game, that a guy like Brian would take the trouble to seek her out for a conversation, even if he was just trying to kill some time on the night shift.

She walked quickly past the phalanx of cardboard movie stars—they gave her the willies, all those famous people frozen in mid-gesture, grinning with manic intensity—and then turned left, onto an even more desolate hallway, in search of the faculty women's room Sally had told her about.

Trust me, she'd said. *It's a lot cleaner than the other one.*

She found it on the right, beyond two science labs and a bulletin board dedicated to the subject of "Careers in Health Care: A Growing Sector of Our Economy!" Liz stepped inside. She'd thought the restroom might be single occupancy, but it turned out to be large and well lit, four stalls facing a row of sinks and mirrors.

It took her a moment or two to realize that something was wrong—a sour smell in the air, a barely audible whimper—and by then she was already peering into the first stall, the door of which was slightly ajar.

"Oh, you poor thing."

The girl was splayed awkwardly on the floor, her forehead resting on the lip of the bowl. Liz couldn't see her face—too much dark hair was hanging in the way—but she recognized the orange T-shirt and these awful denim shorts.

"Sweetie," Liz murmured, kneeling down, carefully extracting a strand of hair from inside the bowl. "I'm right here."

LIZ WIPED the girl's face and neck with a moist paper towel, as if she were a baby who'd just eaten a messy dinner. Her hair was harder to deal with, the sour smell lingering even after all the visible residue had been removed. A few stray clumps remained on her shirt, but she'd have to deal with those on her own.

"Your name's Jenna, right?"

"Yeah," she said, after a long hesitation.

"What were you drinking, Jenna?"

The girl's eyes were cloudy, her expression somehow pathetic and defiant at the same time.

"Vodka," she muttered in a feeble voice. "I fucking hate that shit."

"How much?"

Jenna glanced at the toilet, which was going to spoil some poor janitor's morning.

"Too much. Obviously."

"Am I gonna have to call an ambulance?"

The girl bristled at the question.

"I just puked. I'm hardly even drunk anymore."

Liz remembered the phenomenon from her own drinking days, the sudden bleak sobriety that follows the purge. She knew girls in college who carried little bottles of mouthwash in their purse so they could return to the party and get wasted all over again. She'd done it herself, once or twice.

"Can you stand up?"

Jenna gave a tentative nod and took hold of Liz's proffered hand. It wasn't easy to get her on her feet; she was either denser than she looked or drunker than she claimed.

"What about your boyfriend?" Liz asked. "Was he drinking, too?"

Jenna wobbled a bit, using the wall for balance.

"I don't have a boyfriend."

"Come on," Liz said. "I saw you with him. When you snuck in?"

"Who, Quinn?" Jenna made a hocking sound in her throat, then swirled her studded tongue around her lips. She didn't look too happy about the taste in her mouth. "He's not my boyfriend."

"All right, whatever. I'm just trying to—"

Jenna leaned closer to Liz, as if sharing a secret.

"You know who his girlfriend is?" There was an odd sort of pride in her voice. "Mandy Gleason. Can you believe that? Quinn's fucking Mandy Gleason. They're dancing together right now."

Liz had never seen Mandy Gleason, but she'd heard of her. Her beauty was common knowledge, the gold standard for Gifford girls. She was smart and athletic, too, captain of the tennis team, headed for Dartmouth in the fall. Lots of people said Dana reminded them of Mandy.

"Oh," Liz said. "So you and Quinn aren't . . ."

"She's his girlfriend," Jenna explained matter-of-factly. "I just suck his dick."

She made a brave attempt at a smile, as if to say, *That's how it is and I'm cool with it,* but it didn't work, and she burst into tears. Liz held her while she sobbed, wishing there were something she could say to salvage the girl's graduation night, a little adult wisdom that would take the edge off her pain, maybe put things in perspective. But when she did finally manage to speak, she found that she was crying, too.

"It hurts," she heard herself whisper. "It just hurts so much."

A SUBTLE odor of vomit clung to Liz for the rest of the night, like a badly chosen perfume. It was unfortunate, because the Chilling Station grew increasingly popular as the party wound down. Exhausted kids began trickling in around four-thirty, occupying the couches and chairs, the army cots and the hammock, and then, when all the furniture was spoken for, just giving up and stretching out on the floor like travelers stranded in an airport. There was something sweet about the way they curled up together, bodies innocently touching, heads resting on laps or shoulders. Even the ones who kept their eyes open didn't have much to say. They seemed content to just pass the time, surrounded by classmates, silently marking the end of an era.

By then Liz was pretty tired herself—light-headed and achy in her joints—but she did what she could, offering bottled water and energy bars to the new arrivals, making small talk with the handful of kids she recognized, mostly from Dana's soccer team. It was the busiest she'd been all night.

She might have enjoyed herself more if she hadn't been so worried about Jenna. Liz wasn't sure if she'd done the right thing, letting her sneak out of the party and walk home half-drunk in the predawn darkness, but that was the girl's choice. She just wanted to get the hell out of the building, to put high school behind her once and for all, to not have to look at Quinn and Mandy or put on a happy face for a bunch of people who didn't like her and wouldn't even remember her name in a couple of months.

Liz felt guilty about lying to Officer Yanuzzi as well, telling him that Jenna was having severe menstrual cramps and needed to lie down for a while. He was suspicious—asked Liz twice if the girl needed medical attention—but Liz had kept her arm tight around Jenna's shoulder, insisting that everything was under control, that she would take care of it.

It's been really nice talking to you, she told him, trying to dismiss him and apologize at the same time.

Same here, he said, a bit grudgingly. *Guess I better head back.*

As soon as he was gone, Liz opened the fire doors and led Jenna through the vestibule to the emergency exit.

You take care of yourself. Liz touched her lightly on the shoulder. *Go straight home, okay?*

Jenna nodded and stepped outside, into the chilly night. Liz remained in the doorway, following the girl's slow, unsteady progress across the athletic fields until she was lost to the darkness.

THE SCHOOL bell rang like an alarm clock at six A.M., bringing the All-Night Party to its official close. The kids in the Chilling Station stirred slowly, stretching and rubbing their eyes, then rose and shuffled off toward the main exit. Liz took a moment to straighten the furniture and check the area for lost objects before joining the zombie procession through the hallways.

It was a shock to step into daylight, birds chattering away, the nighttime chill already receding. Even now, the kids didn't want to leave. They lingered en masse outside the building, engaging in a round-robin of high fives, friend hugs, and weepy farewells. Feeling lost and invisible among the teenagers, Liz searched the crowd for adult faces, but none were in sight. She wondered if the other volunteers had used a different exit or were maybe still inside, toasting each other with cups of fresh coffee. Either way, they hadn't bothered to include her in their plans.

Smiling and apologizing, she wove through the thicket of young bodies, making her way toward the parking lot. She had almost completed her escape when a glimpse of a shirt—two overlapping lacrosse sticks against a field of gray—made her stop and turn her head. It was Quinn, his arm draped around the shoulders of a girl who could only have been Mandy Gleason. He looked sleepy and happy, utterly pleased with himself, a golden boy on a summer morning.

You little shit, she thought.

Some part of her brain was telling her to be sensible, reminding her that a high school kid's love life was none of her business, but she was already moving toward him, pushing her way through the bystanders, not bothering to excuse herself. Quinn noticed the commotion and seemed to realize she was coming for him. He let go of Mandy and turned toward Liz, scowling like he'd already been accused of something.

"What?" he demanded, at almost the same moment she slapped him across the face. The blow was harder than she'd intended, and much louder. It cracked in the air like a handclap, a teacher's demand for silence.

"What the fuck?" cried Quinn.

"That's for Jenna."

Mandy stared at Quinn with a look of almost comical bewilderment. "Who's Jenna?"

"Nobody," he said, like a sullen little boy. "This bitch is crazy."

"Jenna's his other girlfriend," Liz explained. "The one he treats like shit."

"She's not my girlfriend," Quinn scoffed. The imprint of

Liz's hand was already blooming on his face. "She's just a slut."

Liz looked at Mandy. She was as beautiful as everyone claimed, perfect skin and clear blue eyes, long legs, and a tiny waist.

"Trust me," Liz told her. "He doesn't deserve either one of you."

SHE HUSTLED across the parking lot, her cheeks burning with shame and regret. As satisfying as it had been to wipe the smugness off Quinn's face, she knew she'd made a mistake. An adult couldn't hit a kid, even if it was just a slap and the "kid" was more or less a grown man, a high school graduate who outweighed her by forty pounds. She'd heard of teachers getting fired for lesser offenses, coaches getting arrested or sued or publicly humiliated. At the very least, she'd have to apologize to Quinn and his parents, to take responsibility for her actions, to pretend he was nothing but an innocent victim.

I was exhausted, she imagined herself telling them. *My blood sugar was low, and I wasn't thinking straight. I promise I'll get counseling . . .*

Her hands were shaking as she turned the key in the ignition, her nerves buzzing with adrenaline. She just wanted to get out of there, to go home and pretend she'd never heard of Quinn or Jenna or the All-Night Party. Maybe the whole incident would just disappear like a bad dream.

Oh, fuck, she thought, as the police car appeared in her rearview mirror. It pulled up right behind her, blocking her getaway. *This isn't happening.*

The cop who got out was Brian Yanuzzi—who else could it be?—but that didn't make her feel any better. He circled the hood of his cruiser and swaggered up to her door, all-business, just like the last time. She brought down her window.

"Something wrong?" she asked, trying to play it cool.

"What?" He seemed puzzled by the question, or maybe just her tone. "No, I just . . . I just wanted to tell you how much I enjoyed talking to you last night."

Liz was so relieved she almost laughed.

"Me, too," she said, after a brief hesitation. "It was really nice."

He bent down, tilting his head so he could see her better.

"So how's that girl? The one with the cramps?"

"She's okay. She just needed some rest."

"That's good." He crouched lower, his hands resting on his thighs. "So, uh . . . you going home?"

She was about to say yes when she realized that home was the last place she wanted to be. She hated the mornings after Chris stayed over, the young lovers sleeping in, then lazing around in their pajamas, trading secret smiles while Liz swept the floor and emptied the dishwasher and folded the laundry.

"Not necessarily," she said.

"I was thinking about maybe getting some breakfast." He straightened up, rolling his neck in a slow semicircle, first one way, then the other. "You hungry?"

Later, in the diner, they had a laugh about how long it took her to respond to his invitation. She just kept staring at him, and he started to worry that maybe he'd made a mistake, that she was trying to come up with an excuse, a gentle way to let him down. She had to explain that it was just a brain freeze, the kind of thing that happens when you've been up all night. You're in the middle of a conversation, and you check out for a few seconds, like somebody flipped a switch. For a little while, it's like the world just stops, and there's nothing you can do but sit tight and wait for it to start moving again.